LETTERS

A Twelve Step Journey

LETTERS

A Twelve Step Journey

By Ken Davies and April McKernan

Bush League Studios Press

For those who know our story.

Thank you for convincing us to tell it.

LETTERS

A Twelve Step Journey

Chapter One
Admission Is Free

January 2018

My name is Summer Anne D. and I'm an alcoholic. I've been sober for thirty one years. The following is Steve's story. A story told through the many letters he wrote and mailed to the AA Central Office in New York over a period of thirty nine years.

Some of my story is told as well; I can't tell you Steve's story without letting you know who I am and how I came to know of Steve. Along with that is a mention or two of a few other struggling alcoholics Steve has sponsored in recovery.

For those who don't know, being *sponsored in recovery* is simply a state of one having a *sponsor*. Great explanation, right? I'm not done yet so stay tuned. First a little on what Alcoholics Anonymous is and what it's all about.

***

The AA Program contains Twelve Steps. An alcoholic does, takes, and/or works the Twelve Steps to the best of their ability and this results in recovery from alcoholism.

Does this mean a recovered alcoholic will then be fine and dandy, sugar sweet, able to drink the occasional glass of chardonnay while chit-chatting with a girlfriend or down a couple of tequila shots with a beer or two on a fun night out with the girls from the office?

My answer to that is it's the wrong question to ask. And for me, that is the Zen Heart of AA. More on that later. Right now, let's move on to sponsors and sponsees.

A sponsor is a person who is like a guide, a mentor, a sensei, one who came before. A sponsor has been sober for a while - or at least most often longer than her or his sponsee(s). A sponsor has worked through the Twelve Steps herself or himself and experienced some of the challenges of living life in a new way, a sober way. This allows for a sponsor to help her or his sponsees work the Steps themselves and navigate through life as sober alcoholics.

Okay, enough of all that for now. I want to get back to Steve. But first I have to tell you a little bit about myself and how I came across Steve's letters. And to do that I have to qualify or what am I writing about, right?

Yes, I said, *qualify*. Hang in there. If you don't know what that means, you soon will.

***

Steve's letters...it was 1988 when I read the first few of them. I was volunteering back then for a few hours a week at the Central Office in Midtown - that's Manhattan, New York City. I was in charge of sorting and filing all the correspondence and general mailing items needing a home but which weren't critical like current billings or that sort of thing. Most often these were invoices already paid, completed actions for requests for literature and items of that nature.

Two days a week I'd go into the office and Beryl B. - she ran the Correspondence and Archives Department - would have piles of papers and letters stacked atop a sorting desk. It all would get filed. Filed in a folder somewhere in the row of twelve cabinets along the wall opposite the sorting desk. Yes, there really were Twelve Cabinets just like there are Twelve Steps.

Beryl had a system. A system for filing all the papers I was there to file. She explained it to me many times.

"Honey, the filing system is set up like the Steps. If it's a paid plumbing invoice it goes in Cabinet Eleven in the paid plumbing invoices file. Improvements, some might call it maintenance, but I say improvement, because it's better than it was before. Step Eleven. And if it's a request for pamphlet literature from a meeting hall in Noblesville, Indiana it goes in Cabinet Twelve with the requests for pamphlet literature from meeting halls in Noblesville, Indiana file. Carrying the message. Step Twelve. If it's a first-time request from a new meeting hall in Tulsa, it goes in Cabinet Two. They came to believe. Step Two. See?"

I shook my head with what I'm sure was a very confused look on my face. "Don't worry Honey," she said, "You'll get it."

It took me a few years to get it. It took me working through the Steps in my life to get it. Beryl of course knew that would be the case. I saw her as a somewhat guarded no-nonsense woman in those early days. But I saw everyone who knew of the unguarded nonsense which defined my behavior as being that way. In any event I quickly found I was wrong about Beryl. She was fun loving with an open heart and mind. She also had a soft spot for me because of that she'd long had for her husband, my Uncle Rick. They weren't yet married at this point and were living together in an apartment in Tribeca. I'm sensing a veering off topic as I am prone to do so without further ado...now to my qualifying.

***

My Uncle Rick had saved my life just a year and a half before, literally picking me up out of the gutter - a gutter in a bad part of Midtown - carrying me back to his place in the middle of the night and the next day taking me to my first AA meeting.

I say he saved me. He'd say I saved myself with the help of AA. I'd tell him I agreed and then hug him and thank him again for saving me. He'd shake his head and tell me I was as nutty as my mother, his hippie sister, as he referred to her.

My mother wasn't my only hippie parent. My father was too. Which explains why I was born in Golden Gate Park, San Francisco at the Human Be-In in early 1967. The Be-In was a gathering of people and rock bands who played a free concert at the Polo Fields in the park. My mother had started labor when the Grateful Dead came out to play. She was sure she could hold out for a couple hours though I was in a hurry apparently, as she often would say to me growing up.

"You need to learn how to slow down Summer Anne. You've always been in a hurry. As soon as you heard Jerry Garcia starting up on *Morning Dew* you were in a hurry to get on out and enter the world. By *Viola Lee Blues* your father had run off to ask the police to radio for an ambulance but before they could get me on the gurney, out you came as Ronnie belted out *Good Morning Little Schoolgirl* – which while inappropriate was also appropriate. And that was his terribly tragic life story. We knew each other well while I was at college. He worked at a record store not far from the Stanford campus. Some of us girls would go there after study group to listen to Blues records. I loved those old songs. And so did Ronnie. He just loved the Blues. And like the rest of us he drank too much. But you know, Summer Anne, Ronnie was the Zen Heart of the Grateful Dead..."

And off she'd go for the zillionth time with recollections of meeting my father at the record store and upon her graduation from Stanford the two of them hitchhiking to New York and showing up at my grandparents' house in Schenectady. These were my mom's parents, Grandma May and Grandpa Rudi. The two were not excited by their daughter and new husband's surprise arrival. My mom and dad decided a quick return to San Francisco would be best. On their way back they filled roles as Pranksters when they found themselves on Ken Kesey's bus and...sorry. There I go again. Carrying on. I guess I know who I get it from. Back to Beryl and AA.

***

Beryl was a paid employee of AA. Being a non-profit AA didn't have many employees per its Eighth Tradition, "Alcoholics Anonymous should remain forever nonprofessional, but our service centers may employ special workers." AA's Central Office didn't need many employees because there was no shortage of volunteers. There was an actual waiting list to volunteer back then.

Beryl had run the Correspondence Office for years. She was employed as a "special worker," meaning she was a necessary paid employee. Three years later I too became a paid employee at the Central Office. This began for me an incredibly rewarding career working for the organization which, along with Uncle Rick, had saved my life. It was a career I could have never imagined having, nor been remotely interested in having when I was a 19-year-old college drop-out with a severe drinking problem.

When I first came into AA it was important, like I said before, to tell your story early on or *qualify* as we termed it back then. We do that, we *qualify*, by telling our story of alcoholism in an AA meeting.

Now technically, an AA meeting can take place anywhere, anytime because a meeting is simply two or more alcoholics getting together to discuss their common problem. It can take place at a back booth in a diner, on a park bench, or in somebody's living room. On the subway, in the back of a cab in downtown traffic or on a road trip upstate. Those are impromptu meetings for the most part and you can't plan on that. This is why there are regular daily and weekly scheduled meetings of AA all over the city, the country, and the world. And by far most of them take place in churches.

Churches of most denominations are typically open to providing space for AA folks to gather and meet for an hour or two, once or twice a week. In many locations meetings are held every day of the week. The meetings are usually held in their basements or back rooms. They don't really want us upstairs in the ballroom with all the expensive decorations, you know.

We understand, many of us are colorful characters to say the least. We don't care about being relegated to basements and backrooms. We're simply happy to be off the streets, sober and working toward a better life with others of our kind. And we don't want a free ride.

We pay rent. It's nominal but it's cash we raise at every meeting through those who can afford it putting a dollar or two in a basket. That is our Seventh Tradition – AA is Self-Supporting. Yes, AA has Twelve Traditions along with its Twelve Steps.

We provide our own coffee, tea and sometimes cookies. We clean up after ourselves. An old AA friend once described it to me saying, "It's a win-win scenario. We AA's get a safe place out of the weather to meet year-round and the churches make a few bucks while getting some street cred with God."

When qualifying in an AA meeting it was best for me, as with most others, to do it at a meeting I regularly attended, a meeting I went to without fail every week; my homegroup meeting.

The theory of an AA meeting is it's a gathering of alcoholics seeking recovery from alcoholism. These people are exceedingly well behaved considering who they are and where they've come from. During the gathering, the meeting, when someone speaks - *shares* as we call it - the others listen respectfully and then time and format permitting, get their chance to share. Or to stay quiet and listen if they so choose.

It's a place where nobody interrupts another person when they are sharing. And after a person is done sharing nobody attempts to shame, guilt, or belittle them. It's a place safe from recriminations and gossip. A place free of disruptive ego eccentricities with all participants speaking only in the first person. It's a place where what you say there, stays there. It's called Alcoholics Anonymous for a reason.

Sounds pretty idyllic, right?

In reality Alcoholics Anonymous meetings live up to all of that theory to the best of their collective ability. Remember, AA meetings are populated by alcoholics. Many of them are newly sober and some who have been around for a while. And behind each and every alcoholic is a reason for their destructive drinking. The AA Big Book states referring to alcoholics, "Our liquor was but a symptom. We had to get down to causes and conditions." And referring to the AA Program, "It's main object is to enable you to find a Power greater than yourself which will solve your problem."

We are alcoholics. Alcoholics of every type, ethnicity, social background, status, and creed. All of us crazy drunks. From the 80-year-old blueblood heiress of an old money fortune living in a Central Park penthouse to a 21-year-old out of work drywaller couch surfing in the Bowery. And everything in-between.

All of us get together and meet to discuss our common problem, the Twelve Steps and our journey in recovery. In doing that we form a Fellowship. This isn't like the Fellowship of the Ring. It's the Fellowship of AA. This is much better. Much more inclusive. You don't have to be an elf, a dwarf, a king in disguise or a hobbit. You only need to be a drunk to belong. And you belong if you say you belong. Nobody else says it for you.

And while it's safe to say the AA Program promotes a way of living which allows its members to aspire to a nirvana-like place of human awareness and healthy peaceful interactions, it is at best, a work in progress.

And at worse, it's a work in progress. There aren't too many things I know of in this life which can be described quite like that. This is why I consider AA to be as close to perfect as perfect can be.

To quote the AA Big Book again, "We claim spiritual progress rather than spiritual perfection." In my experience this occurs individually and collectively. This is the Zen Mind of AA. That's the way I think about it. A Zen Heart and a Zen Mind. I like that. I like seeing the AA Program this way. It works for me.

***

OK...Steve, it's his story, so I keep saying. And remember, I'm not writing it. He did that himself. He did it in the sixty four letters he mailed to the Central Office in New York City over a period of nearly forty years. All I did was read the letters. For twenty-years. Then I began to reply to the letters.

I don't want to get ahead of myself here. I still haven't qualified. Uncle Rick and AA saved my life. I told you that.

When my uncle found me that night, I was kneeling on the sidewalk at the corner of 6th and West 42nd. I was drunk. I was sick. Vomiting, throwing up. Right into the street. Right out in front of a very seedy peep show joint.

Uncle Rick had seen me by chance, or like he said, "I was guided, Summer Anne, guided by God." He occasionally roved the mean streets - as he referred to the area around Times Square - looking to help practicing alcoholics who might want to go to a meeting, get to a meeting. And when there he'd also keep an eye out to ward off the predators who also regularly roved looking for unsuspecting and vulnerable people to hustle, rob and worse.

Unlike him I did not occasionally, nor did I ever go there, instead preferring the bars in the Village which were walking distance from the apartment I shared with friends from college.

8

Where Uncle Rick found me was a bad part of Midtown in 1986. The dark, dark edges of Times Square. Yes, it may have been all lit up but there was a darkness like black ink which spilled from the alleys, crumbling tenements, porn theatres and dive bars out onto the streets. The mean streets.

To this day I still don't know how I ended up there. It was just another drunken night at work with more drinking after work. I worked in a bar in the Village and guys loved buying me the drinks I loved drinking while serving them. But for the sake of this story that doesn't matter.

What matters is a power greater than myself intervened that night and whether that power was Uncle Rick on his own or if he was divinely directed doesn't matter either. What matters is someone found me, someone who cared far more about me than I cared about myself at the time. And that someone was Uncle Rick.

He later told me he'd almost walked right by thinking I was just another whore on the mean streets, "Blowing out what she'd just blown in." Uncle Rick had a real way with words.

I was no working girl on those streets though I guess I looked the part. I had a thing for short skirts and tall boots back then.

Apparently after throwing up I had fallen over and rolled off the sidewalk and into the gutter of the street. When Uncle Rick glanced over as he was walking by he saw not another runaway teenager from Columbus, Ohio or Athens, Georgia. He saw a New York girl running away from her own life who happened to be his niece.

"Fuck a duck!" he'd said. It was his standard exclamation in good times and bad. "Fuck a duck, Summer Anne, is that you?"

"Ugh...." I'd answered in my drunken haze. "Ughha Righaik?"

And then there were a few more "Fuck a ducks" as he lifted me out of the street and began carrying me right down the center of a Saturday night crowd on West 42nd yelling at everyone to "get the fuck" out of his way. And they did with no delay because he was a big man and very fit for his age. And he was a known entity in the area. He'd played football for the Jets in the early 1960's.

9

After leaving football upon the death of his wife, my Aunt Bonnie, he developed problems with his drinking and especially his bent toward being violent when drinking.

"It took three years in fuck a duck Attica to get me to see the light, the error of my ways," he'd say often. Uncle Rick had come to AA while serving time in prison for manslaughter committed during a terrible barfight. He'd been stabbed and his lawyer worked hard to convince the jury Uncle Rick was only defending himself. Eyewitness accounts corroborated the stabbing but they were also in agreement with what had happened next. With a knife stuck in his side Uncle Rick had picked up his attacker and while holding him over his head he'd walked out of the bar and thrown him into the street. Unfortunately for his attacker a cab had been speeding by at that very moment.

I have a hazy memory of Uncle Rick carrying me in a run all the way back to the apartment he shared with Beryl. I think he was crying though I never asked him about it.

The next morning when I woke up on his couch I knew I'd hit my bottom. I knew I didn't want to drink anymore. I knew I'd do whatever it took to not drink anymore. Beryl, who would later help me get the volunteer position and my eventual job at the Central Office was with him in the kitchen cooking breakfast.

Seeing the two of them together, so much in love and the smell of coffee brewing, bacon frying, Uncle Rick flipping pancakes high in the air as Beryl laughed...it gave me an appetite for much more than the hearty breakfast my emaciated body craved. For the first time in my life I was hungry for not just life but the life I knew I could have, a good life. A life of value, purpose, and happiness. I felt that hunger just wash over me like the shower I desperately needed. I got up from the couch and thanked my uncle for saving my life.

He had said picking me up and carrying me back to his place was no more trouble than carrying a fumbled football down the field. Except the football weighed more. "Summer Anne," he'd said.

"You've always been a dainty little flower of a thing, all clean and girly but right now you smell worse than a locker room shitter on a hot summer night at training camp."

Beryl laughing at him said, "Rick, good gracious." And then to me, "Honey, let me get you a towel and some things to wear. You jump in the shower and take your time and we'll have breakfast ready for you when you get out."

I looked Beryl in the eye saying thank you. She looked right back at me and I saw something I'd never seen before. It's hard to describe. I'll never forget what happened next. It was my moment of clarity – we say that in AA, that we have a moment of clarity. That's when an alcoholic sees through the pain, the torment, the destructiveness of their behavior, the wreckage of their life. They see through all that.

When Beryl looked back at me I saw through all my pain and all my torment, all my destructiveness. I saw through the wreckage I had created of my life. I saw past it and envisioned the beauty and promise of life on life's terms. Life without running away from myself but instead a life dealt with straight on. Life. A real life. My life.

In the space of a moment, a timeless moment I saw in her eyes not only caring and concern but purity, sincerity, a genuineness of belief. Belief in me. Beryl believed in me and I would not disappoint her. I would honor her belief. I would not disappoint myself.

Okay, like my mother, I can really go on. And on and on. But that's enough of my qualifying for now except to say I later clocked the distance of how far Uncle Rick had carried me that night. It was over three and a half miles.

Flip forward, it's a year and a half later and I was a year and a half sober doing my sorting and filing in the office with Beryl.

A paid electrical bill. I asked Beryl where to file it. "Honey, in Cabinet Two of course, Came To Believe."

I laughed and she laughed with me. I picked up the next item and it looked like a personal letter. The Central Office address and return address handwritten. In lefty cursive. It caught my eye because I'm a lefty. The return address was in Washington. I immediately thought D. C. But it had a zip code starting with a 9. I looked closer and read, Bellevue, Washington. Hmmm...of course they would have AA there, but it was so far away I had never thought about it.

I opened the letter expecting to find a request from a meeting for literature. What I found was this:

*****

May 1988

Dear AA,

I'm trying to learn this meditation deal. When the Eleventh Step comes up as the topic in meetings, I'm at a loss for words. Most of my attempts at meditation are fruitless. The failure of my attempts to meditate are due mainly to my overactive mind. I tend to daydream, and I have a hard time focusing on getting my mind to quiet down.

People in the meetings share amazing stories about meditating with gurus in Nepal and Bhutan. These marvelous meditation stories make me feel inferior to the other members. I feel like I'm under pressure to have a more coherent meditation message at my ready. So, I decided to get serious about learning this meditation stuff.

I went to Seattle and bought a meditation rug, a box of patchouli incense, and a CD of Ravi Shankar's greatest hits. I purchased everything at a cool store in the Fremont neighborhood, which by the way is known as the Center of the Universe. The store had a black light room with bean bag chairs. The black light room had black light posters, including the Jimi Hendrix one everyone had in their bedroom. But I digress.

12

I took my meditation gear home and set it up. I tried to sit in that upright position like all the gurus in the movies and tv shows. I realized I was going to need some intense Pilates or chiropractic care in order to be able to sit like that. The meditation book said to get comfortable, clearing your mind of thoughts. I sat there on my rug, listening to the sitar music, the patchouli incense smoke wafting through my house.

My mind immediately wandered into thoughts about the sitar. I had a million questions about this mysterious instrument. I wondered if it would be hard to learn how to play the sitar. I also pondered whether I could ever figure out how to tune a sitar properly. The sitar already sounds out of tune. It has those kooky looking pegs and weird strings. I'm always up to a new challenge so I considered trying to tackle the project.

I continued wondering. How much do sitars cost? Can you take lessons? Can you rent a sitar and then turn it in if you can't figure it out? Will the teacher be some Mr. Miyagi mystic who would expect me to wax a car for two weeks before we could start jamming?

I then remembered I was trying to meditate, and the goal was to clear my mind of thoughts, or so I thought. I took a deep breath and tried hard not to think. After about two seconds of silence my mind took off on another tangent. I started to think about the incense.

Why is it all imported from overseas? How come there's no domestic production? Incense is light so they must be getting killed on the freight rate. I wondered if I could start making it here, right in the good old U.S. of A. I recognized I would have to set up regional production facilities as the LTL trucking rates would be a killer for such a light commodity.

I came up with an answer to the trucking problem. I would lease a fleet of my own trucks to deliver the product. The incense trucks would have pictures of the Himalayas painted on their trailers. I could have an artist come up with an Eastern looking spiritualist as my company mascot. We could pattern him after the Dali Lama or Ram Dass or one of those Yogi guys. I didn't think any of them would sue me. I snapped back to reality once again and realized I was day-dreaming and not meditating.

I resolved to take a new approach to meditation. I decided to go out in nature with the goal being to achieve a quiet mind. I had visions of going full blown John Denver. I could see Colorado, a clear mountain stream, and the Rocky Mountain high.

I went to REI in Seattle and bought a bunch of hiking equipment. I picked up a book about the trails of the Cascade Mountains. The next weekend I put on all my hiking gear and went for a trek in the wilderness thinking I could achieve Zen through meditation if I became one with nature.

I hiked up a long steep trail which led to a lake I'd camped at a few years before with the local One Trudge At A Time AA hiking group. I sat on a big rock and tried to shut off my mind. My first thought was I had worn the wrong boots because my feet were developing blisters. I took off my boots and socks and rubbed my feet and looked at the beautiful alpine lake. The surrounding peaks formed a perfectly reflected image in the glass calm water. I took deep breaths and tried to shut off my mind.

Then I wondered if I could start a hiking guide service. I could lead inexperienced hikers on treks through the Cascades. I could imagine the business starting out small with me leading a few brave souls on their first journey to this beautiful alpine lake.

These people would have such a life changing experience they would go home and tell others. My business would take off like a rocket. I'd have to hire a few assistants to help lead the hikes. Soon my enterprise would gain worldwide fame. I'd have celebrities go on hikes with me.

I thought about what a boom to business it would be if I could get Oprah to go with me on a hike. She and I would venture into the Cascades with a camera crew. She too would have a life changing experience in the mountains. She would go back and tell *all her fans about it. I might even sell her a portion of the business. Our headquarters would occupy three floors of a downtown Seattle skyscraper.*

I knew Oprah was a good businesswoman and I'd have to get a top-notch attorney to help me draw up all the paperwork. I'd have to pay the attorney a lot of money, but it would be cash well spent.

I started thinking about how difficult it might be to manage a business with Oprah. She might try to oversee it through a proxy or representative. Problems might develop if I didn't get along with Oprah's hand appointed manager.

I foresaw a giant struggle for control of the business. I decided I would have to buy Oprah's share of the stock if our relationship soured. I felt sad because in this fantasy I had created, Oprah Winfrey had had a life changing experience. I shared that miracle with her. Now we were embroiled in a struggle for the business we created together.

Things were looking bleak for this venture. My partnership with Oprah had unraveled. She was gone and I would have to go it alone.

I then started thinking about the liability issues for the business. I'd have to obtain a multimillion-dollar policy as we would be hiking some very treacherous and difficult terrain. With the payroll and the associated taxes, half of the social security, FICA, Washington State Labor and Industries fees and the health insurance on my employees I started to see this enterprise was doomed.

I would lose money. I would have to lay people off. I would have to cut back to the basics and just lead the hikers by myself. I shifted on the rock and rubbed my sore feet.

Once again, I had fantasized a doomsday scenario. It was like I was back at the AA dance, saw the beautiful girl, and had gone down the mental rabbit hole again. I was upset with myself, with my mind, for the way it acted.

I had hiked up into the Cascades and discovered a serene alpine lake. I had sat quietly and tried to meditate. By the time I snapped back to reality I had been involved in a nasty legal battle with Oprah Winfrey over control of a multimillion-dollar business. By the time this fantasy ended I was reduced to driving people to the trailhead in my 1979 Dodge Tradesman van; a dented, scratched, oil burning rolling hunk of rusting steel I had purchased for two hundred and fifty dollars at a Department of Natural Resources surplus auction. But I digress.

I'm struggling with this meditation project. I was hoping to be further along at this point in my recovery. I desired to be the go-to guy of the local Eleventh Step scene. When people came into an Eleventh Step discussion meeting, I wanted them to whisper to each other about the fact I was there.

They would sit on the edge of their seats, waiting for me to speak. It was these fantasies about my Eleventh Step acumen which had given rise to my desire to master meditation. I had visions of sitting on a log in the wetlands behind the 12 Step Club. People would come visit my Yoda hangout and witness me levitating the Big Book above the mist of the swamp.

Which brings me to my question:

I walk long distances and practice entertaining positive thoughts on these walks. Can I count that as a form of meditation?

The gym I belong to has a sauna. I do stretching and practice positive thinking while I'm in the sauna. Does this count as meditation?

Is it okay to not have a dynamic meditation share at the Eleventh Step meetings? Is it okay to say I've struggled and am making small strides? Even for a person with my advanced years of sobriety?

Silent Steve

*****

Chapter Two
A Believer

I giggled a little and then read it again and giggled some more. Beryl heard me and asked me what was funny. I started to tell her, but my giggles were turning into laughter. She came over and I handed her the letter.

She was reading while I was, hand over my mouth, trying to control myself. I wasn't sure about the appropriateness of it, my spasm of giggling. This was a letter from an alcoholic who had a serious question he was asking and...

I didn't need to worry anymore about the decorum factor because by this time Beryl was chuckling and we looked at each other and both began laughing almost uncontrollably. She handed the letter back to me and went to get Kleenex to dry her eyes. I had to sit down so I didn't fall over and wet my pants.

Though we tried, neither of us could say a word for a couple minutes. Beryl finally regained composure and said, "You should see his other letters."

"Other letters?" I asked her. She handed me the Kleenex box, I needed it, "He's written other letters?"

"Oh yes", she said, "They're not in the Twelve Cabinets. I've got a special file for Steve from Bellevue, Washington."

I stood behind her as she pulled out keys from her purse and unlocked one of her desk file drawers. When she opened it and thumbed through the hanging files I noticed one which had a tab reading, *Steve's Letters To AA.*

She pulled out a thick file and laid it open on the desk.

"These are Steve's letters'" she said, "He's been writing in for the last ten years. Have a look."

So, I did. Beryl had the letters organized chronologically.

*****

May 1977

Dear AA,

I recently attended my first AA dance. They had a mirror ball, blacklights, and the light show from a Jefferson Airplane concert. It was my first clean and sober dance and my apprehension about it showed. My upper body was very stiff, and my legs felt as if they had a rubber'ish nature. It was like I was dancing on bungie cords.

After my fifth can of Tab I relaxed a little and my dancing improved. I then noticed a very attractive woman across the room and I considered asking her to dance. At first, I thought it would be easy to work up the courage to ask her. Then my mind took over the situation and "we" started to think about it. Soon I was fully involved in being sucked down the drain leading to a cesspool of thought.

I had a fantasy vision of what would happen if we danced. In my vision I saw little stars reflected from the beams of the mirror ball bouncing off her in angel like patterns. My fantasy then picked up momentum. The next thing I knew we were married and had built a vast enterprise together. We were the hippest sober couple in the entire AA world. We were gurus, surrounded by our minions.

They came to our Medina mansion on the weekends and did yardwork for us. We had beautiful children. 2.4 to be exact. They were perfect specimens. Both mastered calculus and spoke fluent Portuguese by the age of five. Then the wheels began to fall off the daydream wagon. She divorced me and stole the business.

She went off to live with a guy who resembled something from a Fabio dream. I fell on hard times. I was penniless and had nowhere to go. I ended up living with a sponsee's dog in an unfinished carport conversion sleeping on a piece of memory foam. My doomsday imaginings continued.

One day my sponsee and I were driving back from the 12 Step Club noon meeting and I noticed a couch outside a house with a "Free" sign on it. My sponsee said we didn't have a truck so we couldn't take it. I pointed out we still had the chain in the back of his car we had used towing my broken down 1964 six-cylinder two door Ford Falcon to his place a month earlier.

I suggested we could chain up the couch and tow it back to the house. Heck it was only about a mile. We then hooked up the chain to the couch and connected it to the trailer hitch on the back of the car. Off we went, down the street, towing the couch behind the car. The scene would have resembled that in Italy in 1945 when the Italians towed the body of Dictator Benito Mussolini behind a Fiat jeep.

Mussolini had been executed by firing squad at the end of the war. The couch we were towing was, like the body of Il Duce, subject to the laws of physics. When we went into a turn at a speed of twenty-five miles per hour the couch would travel outside the wake at a speed much greater than the towing car. In that moment I could imagine the Italians watching the little fascist ruler getting whipped into a sharp curve, his lifeless body *bouncing along in the countryside, laying to waste the pretty spring flowers.*

The couch got caught up in some loose gravel and hit a storm drain. It went airborne and came down hard breaking off one of the legs. But it stayed upright, and we managed to get it back to the house in almost one piece.

We sawed off the other three legs and tried our best to balance it with the goal being a comfortable night's sleep. Neither of us had much experience with carpentry so I ended up in a two-season carport, sleeping on a rickety third hand couch, sharing the room with my sponsee's dog.

The dog loved the couch and I never got a good night's sleep. I couldn't make it to work at the 7-11 on time. My nightmarish fantasy concluded with me losing my job and ending up sitting around in a bathrobe watching reruns of The Untouchables and Dialing for Dollars on an old black and white tv with a coat hanger and a piece of foil for an antenna.

Needless to say, I didn't ask that girl to dance. Who needs that kind of trouble?

AA my question is this:

When can I expect my thinking to become less destructive and more inspirational? Heck I couldn't even get halfway through the song "Brick House" without my mind creating a total doomsday scenario.

Steve with nine months

***

AA Reply- May 1977

Dear Steve,

Next time you might consider asking the girl to dance and leaving the results up to God as you understand Him. It is highly likely you will then have a great time.

If you're unsure of yourself, and you hear the opening notes to *Free Bird*, you might want to go outside for a walk. Do your best to avoid the mental rabbit hole one might go down during a seven-minute song.

It takes time, Steve. And time takes time. Go easy on yourself. You are right where you are supposed to be.

Regards,

AA

*****

I was laughing yet again and said to Beryl, "The mental rabbit hole of Free Bird? AA Reply? Who from the office replied?"

She winked at me, smiling, and said, "Well Honey, now you know my secret. Why I keep that file drawer locked."

Still laughing I said, "Oh my God Beryl, you wrote this? And mailed it? Is it ok to do that?"

Still smiling she answered, "Go ahead, Honey. Read the rest."

I picked up the letters and noticed each had a photocopied *AA Reply* paperclipped to it. "These replies? These are all you?" I asked smiling back.

She winked again at me as she sat at her desk to answer the ringing phone. I continued reading.

*****

July 1977

Dear AA,

Well I went and did it. I went to my second clean and sober dance and this time I asked a cute girl to dance. We had a magnetic attraction to each other. She brushed up against me while we were talking. We slow danced to the enchanted sound of the Commodores. Mirror ball reflections bounced off her satin blouse. Lionel Richie sang, "That's why I'm easy, easy like Sunday morning." We exchanged phone numbers and pow, just like that, we started dating. I knew right from the start she was the one for me.

We started planning the rest of our lives together on our first date. We started taking long walks and waxed poetic about a future which included a big house and big AA parties. We went to the park where I read Shakespeare and Rod McKuen poetry to her. I even wrote poetry for her, but for the sake of all things decent I won't include any of the ten sonnets I composed during our first week together.

We went everywhere together, we were inseparable. I stopped going to work for a while. I told her the eight hours I was away from her was too long. My heart ached so much when we weren't together.

I told her we would stay sober together and we would work the Steps together. I prophesized we would only need one Big Book. We would only need one because we would study it together. We would have many sponsees and they would come to our house and do our yard work on the weekends. Wherever our dog popped, they would scoop for us. They would come from miles around just to be with us. The light of our love would shine like ten thousand stars!

We would cook great rib roasts together, bake bread, mend and sew, we would darn our socks in the night when no one was there.

We would do everything under the sun together. Our souls would melt into one being, one spirit, one energy, with one heartbeat.

Then she came to me and told me she needed some space to work on herself. She said we were still together and by doing this work she would be stronger and thus our relationship would be stronger. Then she slowly slipped away from me and I felt a pain so tremendous, so severe that it was to an extent I never thought possible.

When I look back now, I can see I may have smothered her a little during the formative period of our relationship. But imagine how shocked I was when she showed up at the recent Vasa Park AA picnic on the back of Biker Bob's motorcycle! I felt that punch in the gut only true love can deliver. I was completely devastated. I was sick to my stomach. For a while I couldn't eat; I couldn't hold down any food. I thought about ending it all.

I would do a coin toss deciding which bridge to jump from to end my misery. Heads was the Aurora Bridge, tails the Tacoma Narrows.

I was really hoping for tails because the Narrows Bridge has a much wider landing area. Several Aurora bridge jumpers over the years have missed the water and hit boats, docks, and parked cars at the water's edge. In case I decided to jump I didn't want to cause anyone any trouble cleaning up a big mess.

In the end I didn't jump or do anything self-destructive. I talked to my sponsor and he suggested I don't drink and continue to go to meetings. He also suggested I recruit some sponsees because now that I was experienced I would be able to take calls from men gone crazy over lost love. That made sense to me because even though I'm kind of new to AA, I've noticed we drunks seem to take lost love hard.

I have to say though I really, really love this woman and I don't want to see her get mixed up with Biker Bob. He revs up his motor in the 12 Step Club parking lot when he pulls in. He does this just so everyone in the meeting knows he's there. Then he revs it up again when he leaves. He doesn't read the Big Book or work the Steps or talk to his sponsor. He's not good for her.

Despite all the pain I've experienced I can say this was the best relationship I've ever been in. I wouldn't trade anything for the time we spent together. Those were the best three weeks of my life.

AA, my question is this: When can I expect her to return to me? And if she doesn't how long should I expect to wait for the perfect relationship to manifest itself in my life?

Heartbroken Steve with 10 months

***

AA Reply- August 1977

Dear Steve,

AA relationships are as mysterious as the origins of humanity. Ever since God put men and women together, we've been counseling each other about relationships.

Our Big Book says, "See to it that your relationship with him is right and great events will come to pass for you and countless others."

Love is all around us, Steve. And it is important to know there are many variations of love. During your spiritual journey in AA you will encounter love in many forms. Some will be romantic, some will be centered on self-discovery and all will be as unique as you are. Each will become a part of you as you enjoy your journey along the path of lifelong recovery.

Sincerely,

AA

*****

I was chuckling. At this vision I had of *Biker Bob* revving his motorcycle and riding off with Steve's girlfriend but then I immediately felt sadness. Steve was hurt. Really hurt by this girl. I knew the letter I had just read was sent nine years before but something in it reminded me of myself.

I knew that kind of hurt. That pain Steve had described in his letter. A boyfriend I had, Charlie, he'd taken off to LA, right out of the blue with my friend and roommate Carly. Even though I knew he was a two-timing douche and a week later I was happy for it, at the time it still hurt. And hurt badly.

I couldn't help smiling again when I thought of Steve's pain being worth it all because the relationship was the "best three weeks" of his life. He was absolutely nuts. But then again, Charlie and I had been together for only two months and truth be told it was a really fun two months.

In retrospect I laughed about it the same way I'm sure Steve was laughing at himself when he wrote that letter, at least I hoped he was.

In my situation Charlie and Carly were perfect for each other. Both incredibly ambitious and driven. Now I've been told a few times over the years that I'm not hard on the eyes but Carly...she is extraordinarily beautiful and if you saw any summer blockbuster films in the early 1990's then you have probably seen her. She went from television to the big screen in record time. She changed her name telling me *Carly* sounded too "porny".

She'd told me this when calling a year after making it big in Hollywood. Working her Ninth Step and making amends. I'd told her she wasn't too concerned about appearing "porny" when she was stealing my boyfriend Charlie - while roommates she'd had a thing for getting the male perspective from Charlie on her new outfits which were always very revealing. And she regularly had new outfits to show off; she was an unmanageable shopaholic with an unimaginable trust fund.

She surprised me during our call by laughing and agreeing with me. And she went on to apologize for what she had done as my roommate, just up and leaving with no word whatsoever. And doing it with my boyfriend. The fact she had paid our rent for six months in advance before leaving had softened the blow, I admitted to her, laughing myself.

As for Charlie, Carly had dumped him after she'd caught him with her makeup artist. He too however was making it big in film she'd said with a wry sounding chuckle, saying he worked in the production houses of the San Fernando Valley versus the studios in Hollywood.

I can go on and on, I know. Back to Steve's letter. And Beryl's *official unofficial AA reply.*

She'd answered that letter very well, I thought. She really put the hand of AA out there. And reading it brought to mind yet again what an amazing woman Beryl was. She was a once in a lifetime special friend to me. Though at that time I was still getting to know her. And her me I could say, though I think Beryl knew me far better than I knew myself in those early years of my sobriety.

She and Uncle Rick had been together for about three years before I showed up on their couch that fateful night 18 months before. I'd only met her once prior. It was at my mother's memorial service two years before. I'd been drunk. Drunk but polite....God, I remembered telling her that..."Hi, Uncle Rick. Nice to meet you Beryl, I may be drunk, but I am polite, goodbye."

I was obsessed back then with thinking everybody was judging me. Just because I was drinking too much and fairly drunk all the time people acted as if I was a person who drank too much and was fairly drunk all the time. It all seemed terribly unfair - God, I mean wow... writing that out reminds me of the insanity I experienced when drinking.

Beryl was dressed like all the other women at the service. In black, conservative cut dresses and nobody with heels over two inches – except me because I'm short by my family standards at 5'4" and I love 4-inch heels. And I loved wearing what I still call "my little BD's" – which are not so conservatively cut. And it was my mother who died, my mother, so I could wear what I wanted and anyone who didn't like it could just "F-off". That was my attitude in those days.

Even though I was very high at the time I remember well my first impression of Beryl. She was tall, statuesque. Blond, peroxide blonde but very pretty. Her face had smile lines and a few others. She'd lived a hard life at one time, that was clear. Her eyeliner and lip gloss was done well but she really could have used a good foundation, a touch of blush and a quality mascara.

But then again, she seemed to exude something which shone out past the superficial. She had some kind of radiance or an aura. She was special, of that I knew but I was drinking so I didn't have time for further consideration of things like that because my boyfriend of the month – Stuart – having just walked in and feigning the holding of a coke spoon under his nose while snorting loudly, far too loudly the idiot – had given me the universal signal to meet him in the restroom to freshen up our noses.

As I walked toward Stuart, the cocaine and another six months of drinking and drug use which almost killed me Beryl said, "I'll see you soon, honey."

I remember wondering if we'd made plans to get together or some such thing and then I just forgot about it.

***

Picking up Steve's letters I noticed again the paperclipped photocopied AA replies. Each written by Beryl. She'd later told me she'd written the first simply because she couldn't *not* write a reply to that letter, saying she'd never had something like it cross her desk before.

She'd said she was never concerned about "speaking for AA," in that her responses might be misconstrued or misunderstood. Her replies were always short, to the point and stayed on the AA message.

When I'd asked her what Ron H. – he ran the entire office back then – would have said had he known she was doing this she'd replied, "Ron would understand unofficially and been supportive of the idea as long as things didn't get out of control and I didn't become a Dear AA Abby."

In any event Beryl thought discretion – in a file drawer under lock and key – to be the better part of valor. "What Ron didn't know Ron didn't need to know," she had said to me more than once.

"Summer Anne honey," she'd said. "It is intention that matters. I had to work the Steps thoroughly to learn this. Intention is what lies behind all my actions. I find what works well for me is to examine my intentions daily. And that is the Tenth Step, honey."

I loved how Beryl as my sponsor and as my friend, always spoke in first person only telling me what she thought or had done and experienced herself instead of telling me what I should be doing, thinking, learning, and experiencing as a result.

She finished with, "My intention, sweetie - with regard to the replies to Steve - is to provide the helping hand of AA to a fellow alcoholic in need. Yes, I could sign the letters Beryl H., Correspondence Office Manager, AA, NY, NY. But Steve isn't writing to 'Beryl H.', he's writing to AA."

That was all Beryl ever needed to say on the subject and all I needed to hear. She was gathering things from her desk to go meet Uncle Rick for lunch. I had an hour left before leaving for school.

Beryl must have pulled some serious strings to get me back into Columbia. She had told me the Office of Admissions was awaiting my call and the School of General Studies would be a perfect fit for me. I could attend classes part time for now, changing status when it felt right down the road. This allowed me the flexibility for my part time job at the auto parts store offices while also giving me time for my volunteer work at the Central Office with Beryl.

On her way out the door she told me I was done for the day with the filing. I was about to ask her if I could use my time before school to read the rest of Steve's letters, but she beat me to it saying, "Feel

28

free to read the other letters, honey. Just lock them back up for me when you're done."

I thanked her asking her to say hi to Uncle Rick and quickly got back to it. I was dying to see what else this Steve had written in with over the last ten years. I picked up the next letter. It was Steve's third letter to AA in September of 1977 when he was just under a year sober and only 20 years old.

*****

September 1977

Dear AA,

I attended my first Grateful Dead show last week at Seattle's historic Paramount Theater. I took a girl from my young people's group to the show. She's a teenage runaway, was hooking, and was addicted to heroin before she got into a treatment program. We went to the show as just friends. Becky told me she always wanted to be a hippie girl. This concert was the best place for anyone to live out a hippie dream.

There were girls in homemade dresses, revealing their unshaved underarms as they raised their hands, pointing to some unknown Gods lurking in the rafters of the cathedral like music hall. It was like a big cosmic 1960's reunion party. We sat next to a couple named Star and Peace. I thought they could have used a little more creativity when they made up their hippie nicknames. I think he should have adopted the name Fir, Hemlock, Spruce, or Giant Sequoia. Star's grandfather had founded a lumber mill and made millions of dollars. I found it ironic Star, the twenty-three-year-old hippie, had a grandfather who had amassed a fortune cutting down trees which were older than Saint Francis of Assisi. Star looked awesome in his Save the Whales T- shirt.

Peace was a kid from Mercer Island named Jill. She had decided at this show to change her name to Peace and follow the band and Star on the tour. She didn't even call home to tell her mom and dad she was leaving. She just "Peaced out".

I only knew one song by the band and wasn't sure what to expect. I've never seen a band which could turn what looked like certain disaster into something that sounded like pure musical perfection. The concert was like a symphony of patchouli scented improvisation. I was downright amazed by the enchanting sound this band created. Their music was like a rolling wave of thunderous sound.

Jerry Garcia is a virtuoso and his guitar solos lifted me to highs I never thought were possible. At one point it felt like the six strings of Jerry's guitar were in control of the Universe. I'm considering selling all my worldly possessions and taking to the road. I'll follow this band to ends of the earth, or Tacoma, whichever comes first.

Surrounded by tripping hippies and trust fund babies I experienced the whole thing without the aid of drugs or alcohol. Clean and sober tripping I call it. I've seen the light and it shines bright!

Here's my question, do you think I can show other clean and sober people the power of this band? It's like an electric donut dipped in organic coffee.

Steve, trucking up to Buffalo

***

AA Reply – September 1977

Dear Steve,

Though the Big Book never specifically mentions music as a recovery tool it sounds like you discovered something special at the concert. Of course, you can lead by example and take people to a concert. It's all part of the fellowship of the spirit. Learning to do things clean and sober is a great experience. You might want to ease some people into this particular one, however. Not everyone will respond positively listening to a band play seventeen-minute songs. Especially if these are songs your friends have never heard before.

Sincerely,

AA

*****

I paused again with my reading thinking about Steve being clean and sober at a Grateful Dead concert. Well, that was interesting. I was born at a Grateful Dead concert and if I had to guess I was probably the only clean and sober person at that show.

Maybe Steve, along with me as a newborn, was only the second person to attend a Grateful Dead show sober?
I began the next letter.

*****

LETTERS A Twelve Step Journey

Chapter Three
Decisions Made

January 1978

*D*ear *AA,*

Remember that girl I was all upside down over a few months back? We were going to read the Book together and work the Steps together. We were in love and were making plans for a union which would last the rest of our lives. Then she asked for some personal space. She said she needed the space in order to work on herself. If you remember from my letter I was devastated when she showed up to the AA picnic, riding on the back of Biker Bob's motorcycle.

She tried to make a go of it with Biker Bob, but things didn't work out. Bob dumped her for another girl named Metal Martha. Martha wears a different Alice Cooper concert T-shirt every day of the week. She was a hard-core groupie and after having various relations with several of Cooper's roadies, was awarded a lifetime supply of tour shirts. Biker Bob still doesn't have a sponsor, nor does he read the book. He comes to the 11 pm Hoot Owl meeting at the 12 Step Club on a regular basis. He always hangs around talking to people outside the meeting hall. He misses the opening of the meeting and always comes in late.

He always volunteers to share and with total disregard for the topic he goes on about his disability claim. He tells a sad story about how he was banned from the iron workers union for life. Bob and some other union members were implicated in a time clock manipulation scandal. The union backed the workers, yet Bob was suspended and put on probation for sleeping in his van while he was on the clock. Then he pulled a caper which caused the union to issue a lifetime ban. He stole the turkeys that were supposed to go to the youth basketball auction and sold them door to door, spending the proceeds on dope.

He started working for a shady non-union company. He was partying all day with his co-workers and he was intoxicated when he showed up for his swing shift. He sustained a serious on the job injury that day. Now he's trying to make a disability claim for an injury he suffered working for this non-union company. It was an unregistered, illegal company, which had failed to pay their state industrial insurance. But I digress.

My girl had drifted away from the program for a while. She's back now and has a new sponsor. Her sponsor is serious about the program and they are working the Steps. I'm not sure they'll do as good a job as I would have, had we stayed together. But each person must find their own path. I wish only the best for my former heart throb - I can see how beginning a relationship when both of us had less than six months of clean time might not have been a good idea.

Honestly though, I fantasize about the day the two of us may reunite. It's my standard relationship fantasy, including the West Bellevue mansion, the droves of people flocking to us, and as always, I achieve AA fame. The fantasy includes unrequited jet plane love, racing at ten thousand miles per hour in every direction. May all the stars of the Universe shine down upon her.

I am smitten with an insane urge which condemns me to go on loving. When will I find the perfect woman? When will I settle into the perfect relationship? I had thought this was the one. Love is like dope. I just want to recapture that magic feeling from those mind-boggling first three weeks. The most magnificent three weeks of my life I might add.

Here's my question, why am I such a sucker for love?

Smitten Steve

***

AA Reply – January 1978

Dear Steve,

You are not alone. We are all "suckers for love" and as difficult at times as this condition may seem to be, it is far better than the alternative. Keep working to enlarge and improve your spiritual life, Steve. Being true to oneself is a powerful attractor of those who are committed to the same course in life.

Love can be like traveling on a train, Steve. Sometimes we ride in the first-class dining car, living a life of dreams and luxury and sometimes we're back in third class cramped with our baggage along with the baggage of those around us.

Regards

AA

***

October 1978

Dear AA,

I am mad at my sponsor. My sponsor is a guy named Fred. Fred is a grateful recovering alcoholic. Fred says, "Every day I spend above ground is a great day." We hang out at the local 12 Step Club and we are regulars at the 11:00 Friday Night Hoot Owl meeting. I'm sober two years and I've been a little squirrelly lately.

Last Wednesday I had a bad day at work. My boss was being a jerk. I went to the 5:00 Happy Hour meeting at the 12 Step Club and I talked about my bad day and about how my boss hurt my feelings at work.

The meeting topic was meditation or something like that. I don't really know about that stuff. I felt better after talking in the meeting about my day and my hurt feelings. Later that night I was freaking out, I was worried I might lose my job. I don't have much in savings and I have a lot of expenses and I wasn't sure where I would live.

I remembered Fred had said to call anytime, day or night. I couldn't sleep and I was going nuts figuring I would probably end up on the street. So, I called Fred at 2:00 am to talk to him.

I think I might have woken him. He sounded kind of tired when he picked up the phone. I told him I was losing my mind and I had this feeling of impending doom. I asked him what it was. He said, "It's impending doom asshole, go back to bed."

Before he hung up on me he told me the whole "call anytime day or night" thing wasn't really true. He explained to me we say this to newcomers, but we don't really want to be called in the middle of the night. I guess it's part of the AA marketing plan. I figured it was an over-promise-under-deliver strategy.

I still think Fred was kind of mean, don't you? What's with all that, "When the hand of AA reaches out I want the hand to be there for me" stuff? It sounds so good to say it to new people. Is it really

36

just a marketing ploy? Is it kind of like the saying, "One Day At A Time?" Or for those uncomfortable with the term "God", telling them a doorknob can be their higher power? It all sounds good but are all those lures used only to hook newcomers.

I take my life very seriously and I don't think Fred should make light of my anxiety. What do you think?

Steve with impending doom

***

AA Reply - October 1978

Dear Steve,

It is important to remember AA is composed of recovering alcoholics working to navigate through life sober. Your sponsor Fred is probably doing his best in that regard.

We seek spiritual progress rather than spiritual perfection, Steve. One day at a time, staying sober, working the Steps, and staying active with fellow recovering alcoholics is the key to our success.

Regards,

AA

***

December 1978

Dear AA,

I've been attending the Friday night dances at the Renton VFW Hall for a while now. I'm proud to report my dancing has vastly improved.

I met an amazing woman at last night's dance. We shook to "YMCA" by the Village People and grooved to "Sharing the Night Together" by Doctor Hook and the Medicine Show. We then engaged in AA small talk and covered all the usual topics. When the subject of clean time came up, she said something that confused me.

She told me she went for aversion therapy at the Gillette Recovery Center in Burien. She told me they cured her for beer and she feels great. She has lost all her unnecessary beer weight and she's never felt better. She told me they didn't cure her for wine, so she occasionally has a glass of her favorite red. She also had a few jello shots on the Fourth of July, saying it was no big deal.

I'm relatively new to the recovery game and am wondering if this woman is like the boy in the Big Book, whistling in the dark to keep up his spirits.

Here is my question, can this aversion therapy target a certain type of alcoholic beverage? I want to get this information so I can tell her next time I see her.

Steve, confused about her favorite red

***

AA Reply-December 1978

Dear Steve,

The book says, "If anyone who is showing inability to control his drinking can do the right about face and drink like a gentleman, our hats are off to him."

We have heard countless tales of drunks trying to come up with custom diets and plans to control their drinking. Few, if any have proved successful.

Keep on dancing and stay close to your sponsor, Steve.

Sincerely,

AA

***

May 1979

Dear AA,

I was at the 12 Step Club Nooner meeting the other day where I heard something which confirmed some recent suspicions of mine regarding AA slogans.

An older guy named Vance said the slogan "One Day At A Time" was nothing but a business stratagem. He speculated AA founder Bill W. had gone up to Madison Avenue and asked some advertising people for help. He needed a hook to keep people in AA. At least this is what Vance thinks.

Vance ranted on about how "One Day At A Time" is a clever marketing ploy developed in the early days of AA by Bill W. and his cronies. Vance said we say this, "One day at a time bullshit" to new people, so they don't get scared off. Then Vance pounded his fist on the table and yelled,

"This is no goddam one day at a time. This is for the rest of our lives, assholes! It's a lifetime commitment, this sobriety deal. Anyone who tells you different is crazy!"

Vance is deeply passionate about the Program and he usually raises his voice and becomes animated during his sharing at the meeting. *He talks every day for about ten minutes, at every meeting he attends, saying the same thing over and over.*

Here's my question, is Vance right? Is "One Day At A Time" just something they tell us to keep us around? Is it really a commitment for the rest of our lives? I see some value in that but forever seems like a pretty long time.

Steve, one day at a time

***

AA Reply- June 1979

Dear Steve,

No evidence exists of Bill W. ever consulting anyone on Madison Avenue to develop marketing lures to hook potential AA members.

The Book does say, "We, of Alcoholics Anonymous, know thousands of men and women who were once just as hopeless as Bill. Nearly all have recovered." It also says, "We, of Alcoholics Anonymous, are more than one hundred men and women who have recovered from a seemingly hopeless state of mind and body." And with regard to drinking alcohol, "We are assuming, of course, that the reader desires to stop."

Though we can practice our recovery one day at a time and use that philosophy as a diagram for living, our recovery must be permanent and lasting.

Therefore, in that regard Vance has a point, though we hope he doesn't break a bone pounding the table to make it.

Steve, we all have our own courses to travel through the recovery process. For some members, a revolution in thinking and living is profound and sudden, for others it comes slowly, one day at a time.

Regards, AA

***

November 1980

Dear AA,

It seems like everyone is in a hurry to get through the Steps. I see people coming out of thirty-day treatment programs who claim to have worked all the Steps. I question the thoroughness one applies to the task when so new in sobriety. My sponsor told me to take my time and get my feet on solid ground by working the first three Steps. I have made a couple of feeble attempts at doing the Fourth Step inventory. In one attempt I wrote down some stuff on a napkin at Denny's while having coffee after a meeting with Dynamite Doug. Doug had spent too much time working with blasting caps mining nickel in Butte, Montana so he couldn't hear very well. For example, when I tried to tell him about a resentment I had toward my grandfather, Doug said, "Granddaughter, you're too young to have a granddaughter." Along with that attempt and a few others I'm stuck on the Fourth Step.

I have a new sponsor now. His name is Barry. Barry wants me to do a comprehensive Fourth Step inventory. I'm a little long winded and I have a propensity to overexplain things. I've been preparing my Fourth Step on a word processing computer. I've also been doing some therapy and that has helped me uncover many things about my life.

My therapist is a nice lady. She has a cool office in Bellevue. She has a master's degree and charges forty-five dollars an hour. She encourages me to talk about my feelings. We role played and I pretended my dad was the couch pillow. I got angry about some stuff and she said it was safe to punch the pillow. I've heard of this punching the pillow stuff before. People claim it is helpful. I didn't get that much of a thrill out of it.

I've heard the next step up the therapy ladder is at the PHD level. These people charge ninety bucks an hour. My friends in the know have told me you have to be more serious in these offices. There's no pillow punching. You can't beat around the bush with these PHD's. They have a get in and get out quick system. I hope I don't have to escalate to the PHD level of therapy because my insurance doesn't cover it and $45 a visit is already cutting seriously into my long term earnings projections.

I've been writing volumes of prose about my life. This brings me to the concept of the Fourth Step itself. I've heard it's supposed to be a simple list, like the one outlined in the Book. My friend Susan wrote a mammoth computerized Fourth Step inventory. She printed out all the pages on one of those dot matrix printers. Then she lugged it over to her sponsor's house.

They spent several hours going over it. Her sponsor Natalie had said she had a tradition of burning the inventory when they were done reading it. Natalie was accustomed to inventories of two or three pages in length.

The women would set an edge of one of the pages on fire with a match and they would let it burn and then drop the embers in a trashcan. When they tried to burn Susan's inventory, they had to get an accelerant and use a long-necked butane lighter. When they set the 142 page thesis on fire mayhem ensued. Natalie was dancing around her kitchen with a giant bundle of papers on fire. She threw it in her kitchen trashcan and began trying to stomp the fire out. This only fanned the flames more.

Her smoke detector went off, the women were frantically trying to do something about the fire. My friend Susan filled up a soup pot and threw water on the burgeoning inferno. She filled the pot again and threw more water on the fire. Natalie had to reach down to move the garbage can and a pot of water was accidently dumped on her head. After a few more shots of water *they finally extinguished the blaze. Both women almost wet their pants laughing. What had started out as a simple working of the Fifth Step by two recovery sisters ended up nearly burning Natalie's house down. She declared right then and there she would never let a sponsee burn their Fourth Step again.*

I don't want to repeat that scene. I've finished my inventory for the most part. My sponsor wants me to read it to him next Sunday. He said I can't write anymore after we're done. He said if I want to do another Fourth Step I'll have to wait two more years. He just wants me to get the Fifth Step done. He recognizes my tendency to overexplain and be long winded. I'm really looking forward to doing my Fifth Step.

I don't have a specific question other than this. Do you think the pace for working the Steps can be different for each member? Do you think it's counter-productive to apply a one size fits all approach to the timeline for working the Steps?

Steve with a big inventory

***

AA Reply – November 1980

Dear Steve,

Yes. The pace for working the Steps is different for every member. People who work the Steps early in their recovery should be open minded to the idea of coming back and doing them again later.

And to your second question, Yes. The one size fits all applies only to the First Step.

Sincerely, AA

***

September 1981

Dear AA,

My sponsee is a punk rocker named Jim Crisis. He is the lead singer in a band called "Crisis Party".

He bought me a Budweiser King of Beers combo bottle opener/key chain for my fourth AA birthday. He's all punk on the outside, but on the inside he's a kind and sensitive kid who can't sing a lick. He asked me if Bill W. was a swinger because in the book it says – referring to Bill W., "He could see the gay crowd inside." I explained to Jim the different meaning of the word "gay" in the era in which Bill was writing the book.

I was saddened beyond words when I learned Jim had died last week. They found him behind a building in Ballard, stiff, overdosed on heroin, dead.

His mom Marie, was a salty old broad from the Fremont Fellowship Hall. She used to yell really loud in the meeting saying, "If you sons of bitches would shut the fuck up and listen maybe you might hear something that would help keep you sober. Otherwise you're going to end up like the rest of them, drunk, dead, or insane."

Jim was a great kid, but unfortunately, he got up on the horse for one last dreadful ride.

I wish everyone could stay clean and sober forever.

Here's my question, do you think I'll be sitting in a coffee shop thirty years from now and still have occasion to think about Jim Crisis and his mom Marie?

Steve, a sad day

***

AA Reply- September 1981

Dear Steve,

It is devastating when our friends in recovery die.

Our thoughts and prayers go out to Jim, his friends, and family. Jim reached out to you and you became his sponsor while providing the hand of AA to someone who needed help.

Cherishing those thoughts and the time you spent with your friend may not seem like much Steve, but within that experience lies all.

Sincerely,

AA

*****

I had put down the last letter after finishing it. And I began to cry. I didn't know why at the time, Beryl helped me figure it out later.

In 1988, when I was reading Steve's letters for the first time I was 21 years old and had been sober in AA for 16 months. I'd known people who had died from overdoses of heroin and those who had drank themselves to death. And I'd known those who had committed suicide. It was just four months before when it had happened to Keri. She was my first real friend in AA , not counting Beryl , of course.

Keri was a beautiful person with a great sense of humor. She regularly brought me to tears of laughter telling me, as she referred to them, her *lapsed Irish Catholic girl* stories.

She was 22 years old and had been sober in AA for a year. Our AA birthdays were only two days apart. We both were big fans of the local music scene and shared a love for Lou Reed. We had had plans to see Lou in the Village at a small club on an upcoming Friday night.

The night of the show when I thought I was buzzing her in for a quick pre-Lou dinner at my place it was her brother Sean who knocked on my door to tell me she had committed suicide earlier that day. I didn't understand, I'd talked to her the night before and I just didn't understand. It couldn't have happened. This was just her asshole brother playing a sick prank.

But it did happen, and I knew it the second I saw his face when I opened the door expecting to see hers. But like I said, I had talked with her the night before and I had noticed something in her voice which gave me pause to be concerned but I was always concerned about Keri. She was up and down like a yo-yo with her moods. She hadn't given me all the gory details but she had told me things which – let me put it this way - did not endear me to her parents. Looking at Sean and the pain in his eyes I just sat down right in the entryway to my apartment and cried and cried and cried. I wouldn't get up. I couldn't get up. I just cried. Sean called Beryl and didn't leave until she arrived an hour later. She stayed with me that night.

We talked and cried together until two or three in the morning finally falling to sleep on my couch. The next morning Beryl made breakfast and took me to a meeting. Following that I went to her place and saw Uncle Rick who gave me one of his famous bear hugs, tears in his eyes saying only, "Fuck a duck" and then, "Goddam this fucking disease."

I was still hurting. Hurting like I had a knife in my heart. But somehow I knew I was ok. And I felt gratitude for my sobriety, AA and most of all Beryl and Uncle Rick.

And I was angry. Angry at Keri's parents and the upbringing they'd forced upon her with all its horrible dysfunction.

I realized with immediate shame I was also Angry at Keri. For doing what she did to herself and in so, doing it to me. That was the source of my shame – me feeling angry at *what she had done to me.*

She had died but I was the injured party? What a self-centered horrible bitch I was. But I won't get into that now. Let it suffice to say I worked hard and long to pass through my anger and shame finding grace in acceptance and a healthy balance of emotion. And I know without doubt I would have found none of that but for AA in my life.

But at the time I was not quite a year and half sober and my thoughts went back to Steve. I wondered how much he had been hurt by his friend's death. I felt anger toward this Jim Crisis guy who had probably hurt Steve and many others by being an idiot who OD'd on heroin and...

Then I thought, literally speaking out loud to myself, "Summer Anne, what are you doing?"

And this was the beginning of the long haul of me working things out. I realized I was thinking irrationally, thinking on pure emotion and I remembered something Beryl had told me soon after Keri's death. She'd said, "Summer Anne honey, you are not responsible for the thoughts which come into your head. But you are responsible for entertaining them or acting upon them."

She'd also told me early on my mind on occasion was similar to a bad part of town late at night. "You don't want to go there alone. Call me first and I'll go with you."

Of course, I'd laughed at the time thinking it a "haha" idiom but later on I started to kind of get what she had been saying.

What I wasn't getting at all at the time was why I had begun feeling something...something beyond a cursory interest for a person I'd never met and knew nothing about other than what he had written in some goofy, crazy letters to the AA Central Office.

*****

THE AA
guide to hugging

Chapter Four
Looking Within

From 1988 through 1990 I spent two days a week for four hours a day at the Central Office working my volunteer shifts, so it wasn't until I was back in the office a week later before I was able to finish reading Steve's letters.

I'd wanted to take them with me to read at home after school the week before, but I couldn't do that. Beryl had said to lock them back up when done so that's what I did when I finally stopped crying about his friend Jim Crisis and my friend Keri.

Between school, daily meetings and my part time job at the auto parts store office I was busy. This was definitely what I needed back then - and I still do now to some degree - though I am less inclined to make myself busy just for the sake of being busy.

I learned over the years I would use my "busy'ness" to avoid the business of myself; what was going on with me and what was driving my actions and emotions. The Steps of AA and Beryl, always Beryl, my sponsor and best friend helped me discover sometimes more than I wanted to know, but never more than I could handle at any given time. And though it may not have seemed so at the time, everything I learned about myself was a gift.

Beryl had the day off and I was working alone in her office. She'd given me the key to the locked file drawer so I could read the rest of Steve's letters when done with my work.

I was eager to get back to them, so I flew around the office getting all my filing done and everything straightened up leaving me plenty of time to dig in before rushing off to school.

I went to the breakroom to pour myself a cup of coffee hurrying back to Beryl's office. I unlocked the drawer, took out the letters, sat down at my desk and began reading.

*****

June 1982

Dear AA,

In the Big Book Bill says he drank bathtub gin. Was he making gin in his bathtub? Did he keep his bathtub full of gin? Couldn't his wife Lois have just gone in and pulled up the little plug on a chain? She could have easily deprived Bill of his supply. I'm curious about this stuff he drank.

The poet Robert Hunter wrote the line, "Made his way selling red eyed gin." It's from the song Brown Eyed Women. He suggests the man took up this vocation in 1930, after the "Wall caved in."

Considering the effects the events of October 1929 had on Bill, maybe the red eyed gin was more likely what he was drinking.

I need to know definitively because I've already had to improvise my explanation of Bill's bathtub gin to a sponsee who had asked me about it when coming across the passage in the Book.

I told him it was gin made in an old four-legged bathtub. But I'm unsure and I don't want to miss out on or mis-understand a single element of my recovery journey.
Here is my question: What is bathtub gin?

Steve in a tub

***

AA Reply – June 1982

Dear Steve,

The term "bathtub gin" refers to any style of homemade distilled spirits made at home or in nonprofessional conditions.

Because the distilling process requires the sealing of a container it is not likely anyone ever made gin in an open bathtub.

The term is most likely due to the fact the bottles used during the prohibition era were too tall to be topped off with water in a conventional sink. Bootleggers turned to using the bathtub faucet as it allowed them room to fit the large containers underneath the taps.

We hope this will help you Steve.

Sincerely,

AA

***

December 1982

Dear AA,

I was recently criticized at the 11:00 pm Hoot Owl meeting at the 12 Step Club for rambling on during my share.

I was sharing about the Who concert I recently attended. The show was in the Kingdome and even though Keith Moon had died and was no longer with the band it was still a good concert.

Bank Robber Bob said he's going to start calling me Led Zeppelin because I always "Ramble On". I'm worried I will get branded with the AA nickname "Led Zeppelin" which in time will be shortened and changed and will probably morph into just a simple "Zep". I'll have to spend my entire recovery explaining the origins of this nickname.

Many of the members attending the meetings at the 12 Step Club have nicknames. It seems like the idea is to pick the first letter of a name and come up with an alliteration. A few examples are Big Book Bob, Tenth Step Tom, Fifth Step Frieda, Peaceful Pam, Hippie Holly, Serenity Sam, and Humble Hal. A handful of the members have been branded with less than flattering nicknames. These include Negative Nancy, Crazy Carl, Dingy Donna, Dirty Dave, Neurotic Ned, and the best one of all, John the Bastard. Some nicknames are linked to their occupation or another factor in their lives. At the Hoot Owl meeting the regulars are Pat the Plumber, Mechanic Mike, Bob the Barber, Boxcar Bill, Wino Tom, Dan the Dairyman, Hairdresser Harriet, Lou the Cab Driver, and my friend Stockbroker Stan.

Stan ran in a fast crowd and partied hard. He also sold lease partnerships in non-existent oil rigs. His firm asked him to sell stock in shell corporations which had no tangible assets. The principles of the company disappeared one day, never to be heard from again. There was a rumor the CEO lives in a grass hut in the mountains of Costa Rica, but that hasn't been confirmed.

Stan grew his hair out and changed his name to Skyy, yes, with two "y's". Skyy moved to an organic vegetable farm in the Skagit Valley north of Seattle. After three years of living in a converted tool shed he dropped his hippie name and returned to mainstream life as Stan once again. But I digress.

I'm concerned about coming up with a nickname for myself. I need to nip this "Ramble On" name in the bud. I don't want to end up with the nickname Ramble On Steve, or Led Zeppelin, or Zep. I don't want to be lumped into a group with Long Winded Linda, or Ten-Minute Ted, or worst yet, Boring Bonnie.

I've worked my entire adult life in the industries of produce sales and ships chandlery in the Pacific Northwest. Maybe I could use a name like Produce Steve, Ship Supplier Steve or Grateful Steve, Concert Steve, geez I just don't know. I could play the long game and wait. I'd like to be around long enough to be Old Steve, even Fire Hazard Steve.

Here's my question, do you have any suggestions for a nickname?

Steve, in the desert on a horse with no nickname

***

AA Reply – December 1982

Dear Steve,

In the Tri State area, we too know some of the most colorful of AA characters. There's Jersey Jim, Wall Street Walt, Sassy Sally, Hurricane Irma, Windy Wendy, Long Island Larry, Earl the Longshoreman, Gangster Gary, Ivan the Terrible, Mayhem Marty, Limping Louise, Blackjack Benny, Victor the Jockey, Know it all Ned, Hockey John, Dipstick Dan, Connecticut Carrie, Virginia Slim, Humility Harry, and Handgun Hank, to name a few.

Read the Book, go to meetings, work with others, and get to know God as you understand Him and it will all work out Steve.

Don't be too concerned about your nickname. If you must be branded to a rock band, Led Zeppelin isn't a bad way to go. It could be worse, you could associated with Bread, Dan Fogelberg, or Hall and Oates.

Sincerely,

AA

*****

It was at this point in my reading I learned a valuable lesson. It was best not to be actively drinking anything when reading one of Steve's letters or Beryl's replies to Steve's letters.

The Bread, Fogelberg and Hall and Oates references had me spraying my coffee all across my desk as I began to laugh uncontrollably.

I finally calmed myself down, cleaned up my desk and continued on.

*****

February 1983

Dear AA,

I've been sober seven years now. I've been to conventions, conferences, round ups, retreats, and campouts. During these events I've heard some of the best AA speakers of the era. And now I think I'm ready to step up and become a circuit speaker. I'm pretty sure I have that something special it takes to motivate people. And stage fright isn't a problem as I enjoy speaking in front of large crowds.

I drive a lot for my job. This affords me the time to practice my talks during the day whether on the open road or crawling through traffic. I stay focused on what it was like, what happened, and what it's like now.

I even have different pitches prepared for different types of meetings. I have the short participation speaker meeting fifteen minute talk. I have a two speaker thirty minute talk. This talk includes a couple of non-offensive Alanon jokes in case I share the podium with a speaker from that program. To round out my lineup I have a full forty five-minute featured banquet speaker talk.

On top of it all I'm currently available to fly around the country to the big speaker meetings which might be part of any and all scheduled AA events.

My talk is based on the Twelve Steps and adheres to the single purpose of the AA program. There is very little offensive or controversial material in my pitches. And as a bonus I go out of my way to promote the Sixth and Seventh Steps as they seem to get overlooked by so many in recovery.

They are the least glamourous of all the Steps. I do a bit on how the Sixth and Seventh Steps are like the Ringo songs on the Beatles albums. Remember skipping over the Ringo songs? Remember picking up the needle arm and moving it onto the next track of the record? I've tested this Ringo metaphor in my favorite meetings.

Making a reference to the Beatles caused some gigantic laughs in those meetings. I once tried switching the reference to the Keith Richards songs on Rolling Stones albums, but a friend pointed out, "Happy", and "Before They Make Me Run" are darn good songs.

One time I tried the same comparison using the Grateful Dead's Phil Lesh, but it bombed big time. No one really knows who Phil Lesh is. Live he's awful, but the studio versions of "Box of Rain", and "Unbroken Chain" are both gems. But I digress.

I'm available to speak for the big International Convention as well. Thought you might want to know. I'm planning on being sober for a long time. I'm working on a fifty year AA birthday talk. My fifty year anniversary will happen in the year 2026. This could be a problem because it wouldn't conform to the tradition of having the fifty year people share at the convention. I'd say let's do a forty nine year talk at the 2025 convention but I'm not sure forty-nine sounds nearly as cool as fifty. Forty-nine might take some of the luster off my AA bowling ball. Just something to think about.

I'm ready for the big AA stage. I'm ready to step up to podium! Here's my question:

How do I get my name out to the people in charge of picking the speakers? Do they need cassette tapes of my talks? I could do a video on my Betamax and send that along too.

Steve, ready for the circuit

***

AA Reply February – 1983

Dear Steve,

We don't have any resources for you currently. The round ups, conferences, retreats, campouts, etc. you refer to are not affiliated with AA directly.

You might try talking to your local speaker meeting chair-people and ask if they would like to have you up to speak at their meetings. You can write or call the people in charge of the other events and volunteer your services. Sometimes the people in charge of the programs have a hard time finding people who want to speak from a podium.

Bear in mind when you share you are giving service to the event. You don't have to go up there with a polished and practiced speech. There isn't a rating system for AA speakers.

Your enthusiasm is appreciated Steve. Good luck with your podium career. In forty two years when your forty ninth year AA birthday comes around, we'll see what we can do about getting you up to speak at the International.

Sincerely,

AA

P.S. Ringo's *Octopuses Garden* wasn't too bad of a song.

***

July 1984

Dear AA,

It seems like everyone has a mantra and a guru these days. Lots of people are going to EST and Lifespring.

My friend went to an EST seminar. They locked her and fifty other people into a Sea-Tac Airport Holiday Inn banquet room, served gallons of herbal tea but wouldn't let her or anyone else go to the bathroom. Man, that's some crazy stuff right there.

I'm perfectly happy with AA. You can drink as much coffee as you want and use the bathrooms anytime. And I don't want to hire a guru. I investigated it and those guys are expensive!

Here's my question, is AA enough?

It seems like we could have a pretty hip scene here, especially if everyone reached the recovery Nirvana at the same time.

Steve without a guru

***

AA Reply – August 1984

Dear Steve,

It's okay to seek enlightenment outside the meeting halls of AA if you keep your eye on the prize of a lifetime of recovery.

Fads come and fads go, the key is to keep on trucking, Steve.

Regards,

AA

***

April 1985

Dear AA,

There's a lot of talk these days about therapy and the inner child. It seems everyone is in therapy or they're talking about getting in touch with their inner child.

The old timers in the meetings are really up in arms about this trend. A woman named Clara is at the center of the controversy at the local 12 Step Club. She has gone to therapy and discovered her inner child. She talks about it a lot at the meetings. No matter what the topic, she always drones on about her inner child.

Big Book Bob and Tenth Step Tom ganged up on her last night at the 8:00 meeting. They took cross talk to a level I never thought possible. By sharing about her therapy and discovery of her inner child in a meeting she manifested a self-fulfilling prophecy. The old timers shunned and shamed her for the work she was doing. The work she sincerely believes is necessary for her recovery from addiction.

I felt bad for her. She carries a teddy bear with her to the meetings. Big Book Bob threatened to strangle the cute little bear, if she doesn't stop bringing it into the meetings.

I'm wondering if I might have issues relating to my childhood as well. To be honest, I know I have issues. I'm afraid if I ever get in touch with my inner child I might find twins.

Here's my question:

When do I know I need to seek therapy or outside help? How can I tie my childhood therapy into my AA talk and not get drummed out of the 12 Step Club by the old timers?

Steve, wanting a teddy bear

***

AA Reply- April 1985

Dear Steve,

Seeking outside help is not a bad idea for almost any member. If you dive into your childhood issues, please remember to keep the focus on you. You may have been so young you were an innocent victim. Always stay focused on how these issues affect your behavior as an adult.

If you need cover about examining your childhood, you can always take your book out and hit the old timers over the head - metaphorically of course - with the following reminder:

The Fourth Step reads, "We went back through our lives. Nothing counted but thoroughness and honesty." And paraphrasing from the Fifth Step, when taking this Step it is vital to "tell another person our entire life story."

There is also a reference to "the warped lives of blameless children".

Remember you are attending AA meetings, so you need to keep the recovery car in the correct lane. If you try to turn the meeting into an expose' on your childhood, you should expect people to freak out.

We hope this helps. It is a complicated issue. If things become too difficult, take a break, and come back to them later.

Sincerely,

AA

***

March 1986

Dear AA,

I'm working on a new book idea. It's more like a pamphlet than a book. I'll lay out my idea and see if you people want to get in on any of the action with me. We could turn it into an AA pamphlet and you guys could pay me a commission based on circulation. My pamphlet would be called "The AA Guide To Hugging".

This would be a handy guide to which the members could refer when deciding what type of hug is appropriate for different situations. There is a great need for this because the whole AA hugging scene is awkward and there is much confusion and misunderstanding among our brethren. To allay this and create a more comfortable scene for all, the easy to read brochure would define and illustrate the different types of hugs. Utilizing this guide, millions of AA members will no longer experience unnecessary anxiety when it comes time to hug before and after meetings.

Using little stick men and little stick women I would provide the hugger with all the information they need. This is a sampling of the working list of hug types I have come up with:

The tiptoe hug. Both huggers stand 18-24 inches apart and lean into each other with hands around the neck and no body touching. This hug includes a light tapping on the shoulders as well.

Full body press. Usually between a man and a woman. This hug is primarily reserved for our single members. Sometimes these hugs lead to other stuff, sometimes not.

Over the shoulder friends hug. Usually the man stands to the side and hugs over a woman's shoulder thus avoiding any uncomfortable contact.

Man hug. Men hug quickly and then slap each other on the back hard, just because.

Genuine brothers and sisters in sobriety hug. This is a straight on hug and feels good because both people genuinely respect and love each other on a level neither thought possible when they were living their old lives.

The smothering bear hug. The bigger person wraps their arms around the smaller person and holds them very close in a big giant tangled mess of arms and clothes and torso.

Girl on girl hug. Carry on ladies.

There will be a ban on the woman sees the woman across the room and runs up screaming about how long it's been since they've seen each other hug.

The lonely person who hangs on too long hug. Usually a person long denied any physical affection who doesn't want to let go. It feels good to be hugged but now they've turned it into an awkward moment.

The manshake hug. Men do the handshake, then attempt the uncomfortable half hug half handshake which turns into a moment of severe clumsiness. This usually is completed with the hard slap on the back, just because.

Adult child/Alanon safe appropriate hug. Hugger approaches the huggee and asks if it's okay to engage in a safe non-threatening appropriate hug. This is usually the tip toe hug.

I'm working with an artist to come up with non-controversial politically correct illustrations. Each hug will contain a step by step guide for fun hugging. With illustrations this hug guide could run about twenty pages. I know the pamphlets are free but maybe we could push the envelope on this one and charge a buck or two. We could change the meeting preamble to say,

"We have AA literature at this meeting. The pamphlets are free, the books are priced as marked. We can arrange a free Big Book for you if you cannot afford one. This is true for all of our literature with the exception of the AA Guide to Hugging, it's two bucks, no exceptions. See our literature person if you're interested."

This would be a big seller so please consider my offer carefully.

Just think how the recovery community could benefit from this easy to use guide. No more awkward shuffling and side stepping with half hugs launched and failed. Heck, AA's would be hugging like the whole thing was choreographed by the Ice Capades. Go ahead and circulate this idea around and bounce it off your people. I'll be eagerly awaiting your response.

Steve, waiting for a big hug

***

AA Reply- April 1986

Dear Steve,

This sounds like an intriguing idea. Perhaps you could turn it into a video and sell it on late night TV.

Please consult the Twelve Traditions as we don't have any precedent which allows us to form joint ventures with members of the program.

Dream big Steve and swing for the fences. Best of luck with Steve's Guide to Hugging.

Sincerely, AA

***

September 1986

Dear AA,

I have written a draft manuscript of a recovery based story of my life. In the book I tell the story of what it was like growing up in the city of Bellevue, Washington in the 1960's and 1970's. Bellevue was a sleepy bedroom community back in those days, lots of families and station wagons. Underneath the Beaver Cleaver persona this town had a steaming underbelly. There were rumbles at Dick's Drive-in and Herfy's burgers. Underage kids drank their parents booze and drunk drove crazy, all over town.

In my gang we hung out by the tennis courts at Highland Junior High and drank jungle juice from Best Foods mayonnaise jars. Sometimes we drank at six in the morning before ski school, or on Friday nights before the dances in the school gym. We ate mouthfuls of Tic-Tacs in order to get through the drunk teenage dragnet set up by our vice-principle, Henry "Bunny" Howe. Bunny would stand by the front door and try to apprehend us before we made it into the dance. Sometimes we drank Boones Farm, or MD 20/20, or Annie Green Springs, or any other alcoholic beverage a ninth grader could acquire.

Soon after came the drugs and other mood enhancing chemicals and concoctions. My friend P.K. promised he would bring a jar of speed to school one Friday. There was a dance that night and I thought the speed would be a great way to enhance the dancing experience. Ivan Ackerman and I waited that morning for P.K. to show up. P.K. had bragged that his older cousin was a dealer and there would be no problem getting ahold of a jar of crisscross. My friends and I all took crisscross and went to see the movie Fantasia one time at the Crossroads Cinema. I hated the movie but loved that speed.

Ivan and I were shocked when P.K. produced a jar of Vivarin from the pocket of his Peter Kennedy jacket. These were what were called "pep pills". The Television ads proclaimed "V-I-V-A-R-I-N revive with Vivarin." The ads claimed one pill contained the caffeine in two cups of coffee. I took six hits of Vivarin and went to Miss Roe's homeroom. I'm not sure how many pills were in the jar but P.K. and Ivan took them all. The boys became a hot mess and ended up in the nurse's office.

Miss Roe noted I was extra attentive in class that day. I had a hard time sitting still and spent a portion of the three-class block pacing around the room. My head was buzzing, my ears were burning, and my stomach felt like it was riding the Zipper at one of those parking lot carnivals.

I've been participating in some one on one personal therapy. The inner child thing is popular these days. My therapist has a master's degree in social work and charges forty-five dollars an hour. I started going to see her and subsequently told her about my childhood. I told her both my parents were alcoholics and were divorced when I was two. My mom was really messed up from drinking and married two violent alcoholics, got sober and married my stepdad, all before I turned eight. That adds up to four marriages in eight years! My mom told me it was a secret and to never tell anyone. So I never did until I went to the first therapist. I would tell her my story and she would sit there and cry. I thought I was getting ripped off in this arrangement. It seemed unfair I had to pay her to tell her my story and she was the one crying. I asked her, "When do I get to cry?"

It was in these therapy sessions I began the unraveling of the tightly held secret my life was. I really discovered my inner child. He wasn't a bad guy. I always had a feeling that I was weird and different and didn't fit in. I wondered if I had missed school the day the teacher gave all the other kids the secret to life. It was later in another therapist's office I finally put together the link between my childhood, the horrible things I had no control over, and how they affected my behavior as an adult. I had to step outside the conventional AA model with regard to victimhood. By uncovering *what happened in my childhood I had to accept the fact I had been a victim. I had lived what it says in the Book, "... warped lives of blameless children."*

Things were rough at the meetings for a while. There was a tremendous amount of pushback against this whole adult child therapy thing. I used the knowledge I gained in order to become a productive and healthy adult. I discovered I had some anger toward my parents. Some in the program were encouraging people to write letters to their family members in order to let them know about this anger. I never did that. I took responsibility for my behavior as an adult. Uncovering my childhood issues allowed me a chance to do this and it certainly helped that my mom had quit drinking.

She had gone to the bar at the Village Inn restaurant in Bellevue with her third husband. She said she looked into her cocktail glass and then at the guy she had married. It was then she had her moment of clarity. She saw her life for what it was. She realized drinking was her problem. Drinking was the only reason she was married to this guy. Drinking was the only reason her life was such a mess. She walked down the hallway toward the bathroom and dropped a dime in the payphone. She dialed the AA Intergroup Office in Seattle and told them she needed help.

Two men, Ward Lewis and Mike Maher, showed up at the Village Inn and ordered coffee and talked to my mom, Joanne. They got her address and phone number and made arrangements to come pick her up for a meeting the next day. They told her a woman would call her and check in on her as well. The next day a woman named Helene S. called my mom and told her they would be by to pick her up later. A group of people from AA came over and they all went to the Saturday Night Kirkland Study Group. Along with Helene there were two women, Natalie, and Maxine, and two men named Bill Swanson and Lloyd B. They all piled into Bill's car and headed off to the meeting. That was December 5, 1963. My mom stayed sober for the rest of her life. I still have the

Big Book she purchased that night at the meeting. A couple of years later she married Arnie and stayed with him until she passed away in 1994.

These stories should make for a riveting novel. The reader will be hurrying to the bottom of each page in anticipation of getting through the story. Once this book gets on the New York Times best seller list after hitting the bookstores it will be a million seller. I'm one hundred percent confident of this.

Here's my question:

Do you think I should get a car and drive from town to town on my book tour, or should I rent a plane and fly?

Steve with a story

***

AA Reply – September 1986

Dear Steve,

Your story sounds interesting indeed. The art of making your life into a novel can be quite challenging. It sounds like you have a lot of energy behind this project. Remember to be honest and peck away at it, one keystroke at a time. It's your life and your art, be careful of the expectations you place on the outcome. Success can be measured in many ways and not all are related to sales numbers and monetary value. Put your story out to the world and see what happens. Remember to try and keep it simple, Steve.

Sincerely,

AA

***

March 1987

Dear AA,

I heard an interesting story the other night at the Hoot Owl meeting at the 12 Step Club. A guy named Mike shared about a suicide attempt he made in sobriety. I was listening to Mike speak while wondering about how we laugh at stories that would make other people cry.

Mike had reached a point in his recovery where he felt miserable. He readily admitted he was focused on himself and his own problems during this phase of his recovery. One day he decided he was fed up, so he went out to his storage shed and grabbed a rope. He fastened it to the second story balcony of his apartment. He tied a primitive noose around his neck and stood up on the rail of the balcony. He jumped off, expecting this to be the end. But he had failed to correctly measure the length of the rope and the distance of the fall. As his body hit the ground, he heard a gruesome snap sound. He temporarily passed out. When he came-to he discovered to his dismay he was still alive.

He had broken his leg and was laying on the ground in a disheveled state. About twenty minutes later his girlfriend came home to find her boyfriend laying there with a rope around his neck, writhing in pain. He told her he had tried to kill himself but incorrectly calculated the math of his trajectory. She looked at him and started to laugh. Then he started to laugh. As they were laughing uncontrollably, he asked her to hurry up and untie him. He needed to go to the emergency room for his leg. He was afraid someone would see him there and call the men in white suits. By the time he was done with his story we were all laughing in the meeting. He went on to tell us the happy ending.

He had had an awakening there, laying in the grass, with the rope around his neck. He threw himself into working with others and has been relatively happy in his recovery ever since. He said he received a message from God that day. Mike believes God decided it was better for him to break his leg and live so that he may go on to help others.

This story would make most non-recovery people cry. Yet we laughed and in some way could relate.

Here's my question, why do so called "normies" not think this story is funny?

Grateful for my problems Steve

***

AA Reply - March 1987

Dear Steve,

Mike's story is definitely one of the more dramatic a person might hear in meeting halls. We are sure happy things worked out well for him.

To your question, alcoholics tend to act and think in an extreme manner. Often this extreme behavior and extreme thinking is humorous due to the fact many of us can relate personally.

As strange as it may sound to a non-alcoholic, some measure of our progress in our lifetime of recovery work is laughing at ourselves when we understand how ridiculous we have been and may continue to be at times. In time we learn not to take ourselves too seriously.

Hang in there, Steve. Keep laughing and keep up the good work.

Sincerely, AA

*****

Finishing Steve's letters that day left me with a smile on my face and that was exactly what I needed – I'd been a little stressed out over school.

"Steve's AA Guide to Hugging...My God, what a nut," I was thinking as I left the office. On my way to school I thought about what Beryl might say in a reply to his most recent letter; the first letter I'd come across. Steve's meditation letter.

I thought about my own attempts at meditation and where I was in terms of my own recovery. With Beryl's gentle but consistent pushing I'd worked through the Steps during my first year in the Program.

And the Eleventh Step, where was I with that? *Sought through prayer and meditation to improve our conscious contact with God as we understood Him.*

Was I seeking to improve my conscious contact? Did I feel I even had a conscious contact?

I let those thoughts drift away in favor of Pre-Keynesian Macroeconomics which was the topic of my mid-term that afternoon.

*****

Chapter Five
Talking About It

I'm an early riser. Today at 5:15 am I looked in the mirror. I looked into my eyes and spoke out loud.

I do that because it works for me. Keeps me going and along with my daily gratitude meditation I life live one day at a time free of the alternatives. The alternatives...let it suffice to say the alternatives for me are ugly; they do not paint a pretty picture.

One thing I do to ward off ugly alternatives is to tell myself, out loud, that I love myself. That may sound a little strange. It sure sounded strange to me when Alison F. , in the middle of a meeting back in 1994 after I had finished sharing, grabbed me by the hand and literally pulled me out of the church basement meeting room, up the stairs and into the women's restroom. She put her hands on my shoulders looking me in the eye and turned me around, so I was facing a mirror.

Alison was, and still is a force to be reckoned with in my local AA community. She'd been to hell and back through her drinking career and in sobriety. She's been sober longer than any of us in my homegroup. She's always had a good word for anybody and everybody who needed to hear it and at the same time never acted as a coddler or at the other end of the spectrum as a stiff and stoic Big Book thumper. We all referred to her as *A-F*. After the old EF Hutton commercial, "When EF Hutton talks, people listen."

And to this day when Alison - AF talks - people listen. It wouldn't have mattered if she had asked me to stand on a street corner and beat a steel drum, I'd have done it. You just did what Alison said to do when she told you to do it.

She has this voice – it's softened a bit over the years – but back then it was a strong West Indian Creole accent. I couldn't understand a word she said but I somehow knew what she wanted me to do.

Alison, in her Caribbean sing-song voice told me to look in the "meere' tree time a'ever day."

 And each time I was to look into my eyes and say to myself what she told me to say,

"Yah av luv, luv fa ya oin. Ahn' ya' mose' it bay truit, SummaAhn."

It was very difficult for me to do that, to look myself in the eye and say truthfully, "I love you."

It was harder still once I realized why it was so hard. And it can still be hard today at times and I regularly have to remind myself what another force in my lifetime of recovery once told me. Quiet Quince with his own strong accent, South Boston, utilizing his normal colorful lexicon, said,

"Summer Anne, fuckin' people can be stupid, bass ackwards. And alcoholics are the worst. People fuckin' confuse confidence with arrogance. When you are confident, you no longer are confused about that shit, you know what's what; don't listen to those fuckas who tell you different. They're just wishing they had what you have. It's called envy, the fuckin' worst of the seven deadly sins; the sin from which all others arise."

Quiet Quince was anything but quiet and I'm thankful for it because I learned a lot over the years from that crazy Irishman who could go on and on as much as I can.

That may sound kind of weird again but for me, that's more of the Zen Heart of AA , which is really nothing more than people becoming themselves. This creates a healthy independence arising from collective efforts.

Quiet Quince would also often tell me, after meetings when I'd shared of a current struggle and its overwhelming aspects and how I felt like I was stuck in the mud of my path of life not going anywhere, "Summer Anne, for fuck's sake, to be..." He'd always pause there for dramatic effect. "To be Summer Anne, to beeee... is to become. So fuckin' be."

 Then he'd hug me and hang on a little too tight for a little too long and we'd both laugh because in another world...maybe. But not in this one. Though he was a good looking older man the twenty-five year age difference along with him being mentally somewhat of a male version of myself, well...it wouldn't have worked.

To be - no Hamlet reference at all. Simply, To Be. The AA Program has taught me to do that; to be, to become myself and to veer away from what I might think other people might think they want me to be —along with other crazy thinking. Just be myself and keep moving forward. Even during tough times when it seems like every fiber of my being wants to just stop and melt into a couch for a month, or years ago when I still thought of such things, melt into a barstool for a year or forever, AA gave me, and still gives me the strength to carry on.

AA, along with all the people I've grown to know and to love. My fellow AA's, Beryl, Rosalie, Kenny, Henrietta, Barry W., Dick B., Wanda, Willy, Bill P. and Karl M. and so many more all helped me with a kind word or a smile and always their fellowship in this incredible life of recovery from alcoholism.

There I was, just moments ago, looking in the mirror in my bathroom in my apartment telling myself I love myself. In the reflection I saw Ruben – I was dog sitting for my sponsor Darla - look up at the sound of my voice from his favorite snoozing spot on the couch in my office area behind me. He'd seen me do this before. Laying his head down he went back to sleep. It was far too early in the morning for a walk.

While looking in the mirror I noticed the lines on my face. Around my eyes, forehead, and mouth. I thought to myself I was getting older. And I felt good. I was healthy, happy, and grateful for those lines on my face. Yes, age had had its way, but I saw those lines as being there more from smiling than anything else.

And from 1988 onward it was Steve's letters – arriving by mail sometimes monthly and sometimes with a year or more in between – which had created more smiles than any other single thing in my life outside of Beryl and Uncle Rick.

His letters were like perfect little presents appearing out of nowhere and given just to me. Well, me and Beryl. She loved them just as much as I did. The two of us would howl with laughter behind the closed door of her office; the office I moved into when Beryl retired.

Early on in my recovery Beryl and I met once a month to discuss the Steps, my progress in the Program, my trudge along the road of happy destiny. This was the only thing she had ever insisted upon as my sponsor or as my friend. Years later I realized her insistence had nothing to do with what she thought I might need - I was committed to staying sober and would have stood on my head daily if that's what it took to stay that way. I loved her company and loved her and she knew it. I happily would have met weekly or even daily.

She had insisted because she knew I'd wanted it but couldn't yet emotionally articulate what I wanted. And what I wanted was someone in my life to show a consistent long term commitment of concern to my welfare, my mental health and just me in general. It all translates out to me simply wanting what I believe all humans want, to be loved. And love is defined by action. I'm reminded of what the Big Book says in Chapter 6, "Now we need more action, without which we find that faith without works is dead."

I think of traditions – not necessarily the Twelve Traditions of AA – but traditions in general as having possibly begun as simple innocuous acts of repetition. A pattern would present itself, become noticed and then repeated by choice. And before you know it, you have a tradition.

Beryl and I developed our own tradition in just that manner. We met on the first Wednesday evening of the month to discuss our lives, our news of the day, the week, the month and how we were feeling about it and dealing with it. We'd most often meet for dinner at a nearby café we both enjoyed.

From the beginning, during our monthly dinner get-togethers Beryl or I would occasionally bring up something Steve had written in with recently or in a letter past. Though this evoked much shared laughter we'd just as often find a more thoughtful underlying tone in what he'd written. It was clear from his letters he was a Big Book enthusiast. And both Beryl and I were as well. We often turned our discussions into a study of sorts on the Book by relating our own issues to a passage or section contained within. We noticed a year or so into our meetings we had begun to do the same thing with the subject matter of Steve's latest letter. We eventually began bringing a letter with us to our meetings. While continuing to focus on our individual journeys in recovery in relation to what is written in the Big Book, we'd do the same with what Steve was saying in a letter. We'd debate what Step was best encompassed or at issue in the context of his writings. It was an extension of sorts of what I referred to as *Beryl's Twelve Cabinets Filing Method*; a fun mental exercise which helped to keep my mind on the Program. And what I believe is any action which accomplishes a focus on the Program is an action of progress.

Beryl once referred to our upcoming dinner meeting by asking me if we were still on for *As Steve Sees It* on Wednesday night. I laughed at that as it was an amusing take-off on a well-known AA publication which many AA meetings use as a guide to structured discussion. Our *As Steve Sees It* meetings eventually became our *Sorority of Steve* get togethers. Beryl had a theory women in the world were in a sense all just like the first woman, like Eve. All of us doing our best to fit into a man's world. All of us doing our best on a daily basis to accept our daily standing while working to stand taller with the goal of such a thing as a *man's world* becoming a concept which no longer made any sense because it no longer existed. She'd refer to us as two Eves; we struggle not just with our alcoholism but with life in a world of men. Beryl was no far left radical feminist just as she did not lean toward the other end of the sociopolitical spectrum either. She lived in that place not between the two, but above them both. She lived and operated within a place of balance, unflinching truth, clarity and the harmony among all things which cannot help to exist as a result.

Beryl had known how much I wanted to be a member of a particular sorority at Columbia during my first freshman attempt at college. Of course she knew of my inability as well to achieve that goal due to my drinking and cocaine use. Resulting from our meetings she came up with the idea of me already belonging to a sorority. We simply had to name it. So she called it our Society of Two EVES. We thought it to be an amusing and interesting juxtaposition of many things to then refer to this as the "Sorority of STEVE".

It was our secret. It was our bond. Yes, we had AA, our always blossoming friendship and we were officially family once she and Uncle Rick married. We had those things binding us together strongly, but Steve's letters were something different. Something like a Rosetta Stone of a secret language only we knew of, or like the key to a secret little Universe only the two of us visited.

I can go on and on and time goes on. Time went on. Life went on and Steve's letters kept coming. And I continued to read them with Beryl. She would answer them as quickly as she could, penning a reply almost immediately which I would type up and print – two copies, mailing one to Steve and clipping the other to his letter before filing in Beryl's *Steve's Letters To AA* file.

*****

March 1989

Dear AA,

There are a lot of comedy specials on the cable channels these days. Richard Pryor, Robin Williams, and Eddie Murphy have scored big with their shows on HBO. I've come up with a new idea, based on the success of these specials. I'm going to produce a show based on my AA talk. I think the humor in my AA talk will resonate with the non-AA public. A friend who lives in Southern California knows a guy who knows a guy who knows a woman who knows the woman who cuts Martin Scorsese's hair. She thinks he might be interested in directing my special.

He did such a great job on The Last Waltz. He would lend instant credibility to my project. I'm trying to keep my eye on the prize and not wander off and engage in future tripping fantasies. However, I did have one fantasy where the special gets picked up by Warner Brothers and is released in 70mm for the big screen. I make millions and win the Academy Award for Best Film. When giving my acceptance speech I talk about myself too much and forget to thank my grandma for everything she did for me. She gets mad and doesn't invite me over for Thanksgiving. This causes a rift in the family which takes years to repair.

I'm working on the script right now. I'm trying to come up with funny anecdotes about what the life of an alcoholic is really like. I can borrow from many of the funny stories I've heard at the meetings. I'm considering leading with a story of an alcoholic in DT's. He lives in L.A., is having a rough time and sees a herd of mini-elephants running down Rodeo Drive with refrigerators strapped to their backs. I figure my audience will be howling at that story.

I might also do a bit about a man who goes on an ugly binge during the holiday season just before he sobers up. He has a faint memory of cutting the Thanksgiving turkey, eating sweet potatoes and stuffing, pumpkin pie, and telling his sister he loves her and wishes they had spent more time together. He has a strange memory of getting Christmas tree sap all over his hands. His next recollection was New Year's Day. He came out of a month-long blackout and watched the Southern California Trojans defeat the Ohio State Buckeyes in the Rose Bowl. He didn't remember inviting anyone over, yet there he was with friends, watching a gutsy performance by USC quarterback and eventual game MVP Tim Green.

I've been rehearsing my routine and according to a few friends it's quite funny. I'm not currently at liberty to divulge any more of the specifics about this script. As you know, confidentiality is of the upmost importance in this type of operation. I'm practicing the whole thing by working with a three-camera setup. I'm sure Mr. Scorsese can do some good work with the behind the scenes stuff. We may encourage him to do some audience interviews as well.

I'm sure you can see the potential of an HBO special with Martin Scorsese directing. I'm writing this letter just to make sure you're okay with me doing the project. I plan to deliver the entire comedy routine from behind a real podium, just like those used at the speaker meetings. The podium will be faced with a full AA circle in the triangle banner.

I will make several references to AA in my routine. I hope there won't be any issues with copyright infringements. If you feel you guys should be cut in on the action, maybe we can make a deal.

Will you have any problems with me doing the special on HBO?

Steve with a script and maybe a director

***

AA Reply – April 1989

Dear Steve,

We encourage you to study the Sixth Tradition. We don't make business deals with our members. We are not in the business of businesses for profit. Good luck with your venture.

Sincerely,

AA

P.S. Say hello to Marty for us!

***

May 1989

Dear AA,

They discussed the Third Step the other night at the 7:00 pm meeting at the 12 Step Club. Someone mentioned the acid test in relation to our ability to stay sober, keep in emotional balance, and live to good purpose in all conditions. During the discussion, one of the members mentioned the rumors about Bill W. taking LSD in the 50's.

I think the person was referring to a different kind of acid test. My new friend, CharlieBear is confused about all this acid and LSD talk around the tables. He was wondering if he could take LSD on a recreational basis, or in a mind expanding way. He mentioned something about the Santana Abraxas album and its consciousness enhancing values.

I told him I didn't think it was a good idea to use psychedelics in his quest to enlarge and improve his spiritual life. I suggested to CharlieBear that he work to learn to embrace life on life's terms, to approach life with an absolute certainty that altering reality with any mood or mind altering agents is a slippery slope which surely leads us back to full blown addiction.

He's purchased tickets to a big hippie fair in a big field, just outside the city limits of Eugene. His thought is to take LSD only for that one weekend. I told him this would not be wise. And I told him the reference to acid testing is colloquial of the period in which Bill wrote the Book and was not meant to endorse the use of LSD, mescaline, or any other drugs.

Here's my question: did I give CharlieBear the correct advice? That cat has too many questions for one sponsor to answer. He is the poster boy for Overthinkers Anonymous. He makes me look like a Tibetan Monk, deeply engaged in transcendental meditation.

Steve the sponsor

***

AA Reply May 1989

Dear Steve,

Advising a member to not take acid while listening to Carlos Santana or at any other time is the right thing to do. CharlieBear is fortunate to have you as a sponsor, Steve.

Sincerely,

AA

***

January 1990

Dear AA,

One of my sponsees, Lefty Luke, recently did some Ninth Step amends work. Luke was once a promising pitcher in the Pittsburg Pirates organization and even had a cup of coffee in the bigs before a bum elbow ended his career. In 1984 he played most of the season throwing long relief for the AAA Hawaii Islanders of the Pacific Coast League. Luke had an issue with fits of rage when he drank. Many bars and taverns were on his amends list as he was prone to launching beer glasses against walls when he was hammered.

Even with his bad elbow he could still deliver the occasional ninety mile an hour beer mug against brick walls in the years after his career ended. As his sponsor I suggested he go to the restaurant supply store and buy a twenty-four pack of sixteen ouncers. I instructed him to hit the bars and make offers to replace the broken glasses. His effort netted mixed results and he had several glasses left over after he made his rounds. I told him it was the attempt that counted and he had done well to clean up his side of the street. He gave away some glasses to strangers and he ended up with two glasses at the end of the day. He offered those two glasses to me. I took them thinking how nice they might work for my iced tea on a warm summer night.

This experience with Luke reminded me of the gifts we receive in this amazing program. I was able to help guide Luke through his Ninth Step amends. I gave freely of my time in the spirit of service and recovery. Luke was able to put another building block in the foundation of his new life. I cannot count the many ways I love this program.

AA has given me a new pair of beer glasses!

Steve sipping iced tea

***

AA Reply – January 1990

Dear Steve,

We agree wholeheartedly with your sentiment. Yes, AA is a great program. Keep up the good work.

Sincerely,

AA

***

June 1990

Dear AA,

Do you ever have one of those days that stick out in your memory? A day you will never forget, no matter how much sand passes through the hourglass? One of those days for me was June 6, 1968.

Robert F. Kennedy had just won the California primary and it looked like he was on his way to winning the Democratic Party nomination at the upcoming Chicago convention. After giving a victory speech to his supporters he walked through the kitchen of the Ambassador Hotel in Los Angeles. A distraught hotel worker named Sirhan Sirhan approached the Senator with a pistol and opened fire.

In a few precious seconds Mr. Kennedy lay on the floor mortally wounded. I was ten at the time and was entrenched in the camp of Republican candidate Richard Nixon. I had supported Barry Goldwater four years earlier and I was devastated when that old bore LBJ won in a landslide.

I remembered the somber mood the nation was in five years earlier when Bobby's brother had been cut down in his prime by a mad man with a cheap mail order Italian surplus rifle. Against my better Republican instincts, I was pulling for the younger Kennedy to win the White House.

We were reeling from the assassination of Martin Luther King only a few weeks earlier. It seemed the whole world had gone mad. They announced on the news Mr. Kennedy had died after hanging on to life for a few hours. Kennedy's death was too much for me. I told my mom I was too sad to go to school. She was sad too and she let me stay home.

I cried and told her I knew Bobby would have won the election in November. Now the world would be different, forever altered by a handgun in the grasp of a madman. I told her that windbag Humphrey would be nominated now. I didn't like Humphrey much and would have preferred Eugene McCarthy as the Democratic party nominee.

I know you're wondering what any of this has to do with AA or recovery. I'll quit rambling and get right down to business.

I'm pretty sure June 6, 1968 was the day Mr. Pearson, the principal of Stevenson Elementary, gave all the other kids the secret to life. I was absent that day. I was home mourning the loss of Robert F. Kennedy. I'm sure that was the day my life went off the rails. Bobby Kennedy was dead, the world was upside down and everyone else had the secret.

During much of my childhood I felt like a misfit. I felt weird and different, like I didn't fit in. When I picked up that first bottle of Cold Duck in the fall of 1971 it worked like magic for me. When I was drunk it was the first time in my life I felt like I fit in. I felt like I was in the brotherhood of man. The alcohol made me emperor of the entire universe.

I feel like my recovery has been a journey back to that night. The night Rick Greenwood went into the 7-11 and stole the bottle of Cold Duck. He sold it to me for three dollars and I drank most of it. I fell in love with life that night. I've always wondered what was so magical about that night. I've often wondered why the Cold Duck made me feel so excellent. The answer is that in my everyday life I felt so unhappy.

I was under the false assumption I felt this way as a result of missing one day of school. Now that I'm in recovery I'm asking myself why was I so broken? Why did I feel so powerless in my everyday life?

In 1980 I was sitting in the Dairy Queen in downtown Bellevue with Texas Edd. I told Texas Edd when I was a kid I felt weird, awkward, different, like I didn't fit in. He looked at me and said in his Texas drawl, "Steve, the reason you felt weird, awkward, different, like you didn't fit in is because you were weird, awkward, different, and you didn't fit in. It's like alcohol at first gave you a fancy big ole Cadillac with a cowboy boot hood ornament on it to drive around but in the end it took away all the roads for you to drive it on."

Texas Edd went on to explain alcoholics drink for power. He told me we drink for power because we don't feel like we have any power in our normal lives. Alcohol makes us taller, smarter, stronger, faster, better dancers, greater lovers. It gives us the illusion of ultimate power. He reminded me the Book says, "Lack of power, that was our dilemma."

He said if we replace God for alcohol then alcohol gives us the power we need to solve all our problems. This is true for a brief period, until alcohol no longer works and becomes the cause of all our problems.

He told me the concept of learning the proper use of power is one of the main goals of sobriety. We learn to balance power in harmony with our ego, our instincts, and our desires. We use the Twelve Steps to maintain a balance of our newfound power.

What Texas Edd said made me feel better about the day of school I missed in 1968. Alcohol gave me the power I needed to be anything I wanted to be. Recovery for me is a quest to find power within and to learn how to use it effectively. The proper use of power, that is the goal. And I can't get there without examining my childhood.

I brought this up in a noon meeting at the 12 Step Club a couple of days ago. The chairman was a guy named Railroad Ron. I guess he used to work on the railroad. He said this childhood nonsense has no place in the real AA. He said, "You won't get away with crying about your childhood in my AA. Not in my AA, or in my AA meeting!"

All I can say is I was an intense kid and I went through some intense stuff. I also told Railroad Ron to mind his own business. I started wondering if I have a different book than the other members. Maybe mine is missing some pages or maybe there are some missing Steps I've never read before. The Book I have tells me to go back through my life. Nothing counted but thoroughness and honesty. It also informs me the Fifth Step isn't done until I've told another person my entire life story.

This is a theme in my recovery I tend to beat like a dead horse. I've gone over this countless times with sponsees and friends. Once

Railroad Ron was done with his rant I started talking again. He tried to cut me off, but I managed to tell everyone in the meeting I was proud of the work I had done on my childhood. I said if anyone in the meeting wanted to talk about it afterward I was available.

A few people were brave enough to approach me and I was surprised when a woman thanked me for sharing. She said she didn't have the courage to bring it up the topic in meetings. I told her the work is personal and it was her choice to talk about it or not in the meetings.

AA, here's my question:

I know I've written in about this before, but do you think the childhood stuff is legit?

Steve, sad about 1968

***

AA Reply - June 1990

Dear Steve,

Yes, it's legit. Bear in mind, your raw honesty might be too much for some of AA's old guard to handle. There are those who have built up reputations of being people with all the answers. Along comes this whipper-snapper Steve, talking all kinds of "nonsense".

Railroad Ron may never soften up to you. But many AA's will, and these are the people you need to share your experience, strength, and hope with, Steve.

Sincerely,

AA

***

February 1991

Dear AA,

I was sharing a story about an experience I had recently at a Grateful Dead show. They are the best band in the world, and I have attended twenty-six of their concerts over the years.

I related this experience at the 11:00 p.m. Hoot Owl meeting at the 12 Step Club. I shared how I have been going to these concerts for years and have never used drugs or alcohol at any of them. Fourteen years of Dead shows, never a single toke, shot, hit, or a snort.

Toxic Tom cut me off in the middle of my story. He started yelling and said if I was at one of those concerts with all those damn hippies, all smoking grass and taking LSD then I must have gotten a contact high. He demanded I surrender all my AA coins and reset my sobriety date. He said just being in close proximity to the "heathen hippie scum" was sufficient grounds to support his argument.

I understand Toxic Tom is by his own nickname, Toxic. It's a fact the smoke at the indoor concert venues was as bad as the haze that used to hang in the old Aurora Fellowship hall back in the 1970's. The outdoor venues do allow a certain level of breathable air, though I did see the largest cloud of dope smoke ever when Ziggy Marley opened at an outdoor show one summer.

Here is my question:

Is Toxic Tom a douche for cutting me off? I was just trying to show newcomers we have not become a glum lot. There is lots of life to live out there! Oh, and I swear Jerry smiled at me at the big show in the big field just outside the city limits of Eugene last summer.

Steve, playing in the band

***

AA Reply-February 1991

Dear Steve,

Don't let guys like Toxic Tom bum your natural high. It sounds like you are out there living life and doing your best to share your experience, strength, and hope. Tom's anger is likely the product of an issue which has nothing to do with you.

Remember to show compassion and pray for Toxic Tom. Maybe he can learn from you and who knows, maybe you from him, Steve.

Sincerely,

AA

***

March 1991

Dear AA,

I met a guy the other day who hadn't read the Book at all. He has five years of clean time and says he doesn't need a book to stay sober. He said his sponsor, Angry Arnie, told him Bill W. sold stock in a bogus shell corporation to raise funds to publish the original Book.

Angry Arnie has a posse of guys who hang out at the 12 Step Club with him. They go around spouting Arnie's crazy philosophy. So, I have deputized myself and I now attend the 11:00 pm Hoot Owl meetings these guys frequent. I go in there with my Book and all my AA guns ablaze. I'm not going to let these guys infect the mind of a newcomer.

The Book is the single greatest asset in my recovery. I'll be plugging the Book to everyone in my recovery community until the day I die.

I imagine myself as a modern day AA Marshall Matt Dillon throwing AA bad guys through the swinging doors out into the dusty streets. Here's my question, do you have a gift shop where I can buy an AA Sheriff badge, and an AA Sheriff cap gun and cap gun belt? I'd wear them to every Hoot Owl meeting at the Club.

Steve the Enforcer

***

AA Reply – March 1991

Dear Steve,

We don't currently carry any of those items in our gift shop. You can deputize yourself and you can fight for what you believe in. That fight is noble and commendable.

Remember, AA also has the Twelve Traditions in place to protect the Program. No one has ever successfully broken through the fortress of protection the Traditions provide for the safe-guarding of AA's long-term survival.

Sincerely,

AA

***

August 1991

Dear AA,

I have been in a reminiscent mood lately thinking about old stories and adventures. One of the events which comes to mind is something I billed as the Ninth Grade Keg. In mid-May of 1972 I began collecting spare change from random students at Highland Jr High. One day my homeroom teacher, Miss Roe, asked me what the big bulge in my jacket pocket was. I dumped the change out on the desk and she helped me count it. Pat Roe was a former gym teacher who had been called up to teach homeroom upon the untimely death of one of the faculty. By 1972 she had not taught gym for several years. Even though she didn't report to the girls locker room she still donned her gym teacher green jumpsuit. She had a whistle around her neck and a pack of Pall Mall straights in her pocket. She had a giant laminated wood paddle which was used to maintain law and order in her classroom.

We counted sixteen dollars in change, and she asked, "Steve, what are you going to do with this money?" I told her I was going to donate the money to the ninth-grade class so we could buy our vice-principal, Henry Howe a present. She looked at me with a Pall Mall and coffee stained smile and said, "I don't believe you are going to buy that bunny rabbit a present."

I told her the truth. I told her I was going to buy a keg of beer and throw a party in the woods. Miss Roe told me she didn't like beer too much. I asked her if she liked whiskey. She smiled the same smile, laughed, and said "Oh yeah, I love whiskey."

I was close enough to my goal of twenty-two dollars. I decided to throw in the last six dollars myself from the money I earned cleaning offices in downtown Bellevue for Jet Janitorial. With the stake of twenty-two dollars I could get a keg of Blitz Weinhard and pay the tap deposit down at Tom's Tee Pee Tavern.

You might be wondering how a fourteen-year-old ninth grader could just waltz into a bar and buy a full barrel keg of beer. I had worked all the arrangements out with a local recluse. His name was Andy Thomas and he was a twenty-three-year-old fellow who lived in his parents' basement. Their house was a regular hangout in our neighborhood. Andy, his brother Rainbow, and his friend Fountain hung out at the Thomas family home every day. There was always some kind of party going on there. The basement was a trippy place with black lights, black light posters, giant speakers suspended in macramé, tropical birds everywhere, marijuana, LSD, the smell of incense, and stained-glass wind chimes hanging from the rafters.

Andy went into the Tee Pee and bought me the keg. For payment he took five bucks into the Prairie U-Mark It Grocery and bought five eighty-nine cent bottles of Boones Farm Strawberry Hill. He and Fountain and Rainbow were having a wine tasting that night. Andy drove back up NE 24th Street and when we reached a barricade me and a couple of buddies hoisted the keg out of the back of Andy's mom's convertible Mercury Comet.

The barricade was in place because there was a major construction project going on. The state was proceeding full speed ahead on the extension of the 520 freeway. Beyond the barricade on NE 24th there was a vast territory of unoccupied woods and backland. I saw this area as the perfect location for an outdoor keg party. I had taken my construction team into these hinterlands the day before and we had cleared a large area. Our party site was under some power lines and was a safe distance away from any nearby homes.

I was fourteen and had accomplished quite a feat. I had raised the twenty-two dollars, found a hermit to make the buy, located and cleared the party site, and through word of mouth had marketed the party among my classmates at Highland Jr High. When a group of us ninth graders lifted the holy keg of Blitz

Weinhard out of the Comet I was temporarily overcome with emotion. For a fleeting moment I knew how Howard Hughes must have felt when the Spruce Goose lifted off the water. The keg represented my life's work up to that point. The keg of Blitz, lifted up and out the backseat, set down on the ground, was my Spruce Goose.

Andy handed me the taps and told me to protect them with my life. I handed the taps to my tap man, Mark Olson. Mark assured me he knew how to tap a keg. I assembled my transportation crew and we started to slowly roll the keg down the precipitous grade of NE 24th Street. The keg was heavy and started to gain momentum. One of the boys slipped on some gravel and fell. The keg then broke loose and began rolling down the hill. It took a sharp left turn, hit a curb, and went temporarily airborne coming down hard like that ski-jumper in the opening clip of ABC's Wild World of Sports. Squirrels and rabbits dove for their lives as it blazed a path toward the bottom of the ravine far below. It came to rest in a tangled bramble of sticker bushes. I looked down into the ravine and saw my life's work in ruins. At that moment I knew the meaning of the phrase, "The thrill of victory and the agony of defeat."

I immediately went into problem solving mode. I sent a recon team down into the ravine to retrieve the keg. This was no time to panic. We would bring the keg back up to the road and take turns carrying it to the party site. In the words of my stepdad I looked at one of my posse and said, "Hey, get on one end of this would ya." We finally got the keg to its resting place at the party site. Mark Olson tapped the keg with the same precision Dr. Barnard had used to transplant the first human heart. Mark looked at me and said, "Okay man, hand me a cup and let's get this party rolling." This was where our ninth-grade keg party hit a major snag. I had been hyper focused on the process of engineering, site preparation, purchasing, procurement, finance, and marketing. In my zeal to get the party organized I had never thought to acquire any cups. So there sat a full barrel keg of beer, with the taps, and we had no cups.

I organized another recon team led by Richard Ward, son of a local radio personality. Richard grabbed two of his most trusted servants and they took off down the power line right of way toward the sprawling Safeway distribution complex. In a short time they returned having rummaged through a few dumpsters. They showed up with three empty coffee cans. One Maxwell House, and two Folgers. In 1972 coffee was still packed in full three-pound cans. These cans were not the little thirteen-ounce wimpy things they peddle today. I took the Maxwell House can, looked inside and saw a few grounds hanging around. I put it under the keg and pulled on the tap. The trip to the bottom of the ravine had jostled the contents of the keg. I filled the coffee can with pure beer foam. I let it settle a little and poured some more foam. Finally I could not wait any longer, so I sucked down an entire dumpster coffee can full of foam. It was, to borrow a slogan, good to the last drop.

The party was a raging success. At its peak we had forty revelers partying in the woods of Bellevue. Some older juvenile delinquents showed up in a stolen car and joined us ninth graders. Many of us had brought camping equipment and were spending the night in the clearing. I am the world's worst drunk camper. I woke up about 6:00 am, shivering and lying in the dirt next to my sleeping bag. I had partied hard the night before, drinking myself into a stupor and a blackout. Now the hangover tiger was stalking the campsite and he pounced on me the minute I woke up. With a head full of cobwebs and goblins I managed to lug the empty keg back to Andy Thomas' house where we boys split up, all returning to our respective homes.

When I got back to the house my stepdad looked at me and looked at a big paint tarp and said "Hey, get on one end of this would ya." He was painting the house and pointing to a ladder handed me a wire brush and ordered me to start scraping under the eaves. Paint flakes fell into my dilated red eyes. The ladder teetered and the world whirled around in circles. I rode that demented carnival hangover horse the rest of the day. Then I had that thought every alcoholic has....... I felt like I was dying, but it was a small price to pay for that hour of fun I had had the night before. But I digress.

Even with a full keg of beer I feared there wouldn't be enough for me to drink. I was a fiend for that alcohol. I insisted I get the first two full coffee cans out of that keg. My heart was pounding, my head racing, I settled down a little only after I started to feel the effects of the alcohol. When I was up on that ladder the next day and the world was spinning and I felt like death I had one thought, I can't wait to get drunk again. Over my drinking career the hour of fun got shorter and the emotional and physical damage became worse. I was truly a drunk's drunk. John Barleycorn himself had become my best advocate.

Which brings me to my point. The ninth-grade keg was a turning point in my drinking career. It marked the day when drinking stopped being fun and became an obsession. I had become a full-fledged alcoholic at age fourteen.

Writing this story reminds me of why there is no doubt in my mind I am an alcoholic. When the old timers in meetings say they spilled more on their ties than I drank I remind them we wore no ties at the ninth-grade keg party. I drank foamy beer from coffee cans found in dumpsters and as a result instead of feeling like I belonged at last I felt once again like a drifter, a loner, separated from the crowd. The dark cloud of death hovered over me for the first time at that keg party. I am eternally grateful my obsession to drink was removed at such a young age. I was given the gift of sobriety and am honored to share my story with others.

My question is rhetorical and perhaps unnecessary, but here goes: If alcoholics apply the same ingenuity, energy, and organizational skills to their sobriety that they did to their *drinking don't you think everyone would have a chance to succeed at this sobriety deal?*

Steve, climbing out of the ravine

***

AA Reply August 1991

Dear Steve,

Alcoholics for the most part tend to be very creative, energetic and industrious people. This can work in our favor with regard to the lifelong journey of recovery we must embark upon to become sober and remain sober. But unfortunately there is another element which may be the most important component in an alcoholic's efforts. In Chapter Five of the Big Book it is stated, "Rarely have we seen a person fail who has thoroughly followed our path. Those who do not recover are people who cannot or will not completely give themselves to this simple program, usually men and women who are constitutionally incapable of being honest with themselves. There are such unfortunates. They are not at fault; they seem to have been born that way. They are naturally incapable of grasping and developing a manner of living which demands rigorous honesty. Their chances are less than average."

Stay true to thine own self, Steve.

Sincerely, AA

***

January 1992

Dear AA,

I was reading the Book recently with a sponsee. We were covering Chapter Three and came across the example of the man who drank after a long and successful career.

I made sure to emphasize to my friend the perils of holding out reservations about returning to drinking after a layoff. The man in the story stops drinking for twenty-five years and retires at age 55. He resumes drinking upon retirement, goes to pieces quickly, and is dead within four years.

We sure learned a lot from this chapter. This is my question, what are carpet slippers?

Steve with sixteen years and two sponsees

***

AA Reply – February 1992

Dear Steve,

We are glad you are sharing the Book with the people you work with. This is essential to long term recovery. Regarding the reference to carpet slippers this is what we came up with:

carpet slipper
['kärpət ˌslipər]
NOUN
carpet slippers (plural noun)
a soft slipper whose upper part is made of wool or thick cloth.

Keep up the good work Steve. Your thoroughness will pay big dividends in the long run.

Sincerely, AA

***

May 1992

Dear AA,

My sponsor recently told me pain can be a touchstone for spiritual progress. I've heard this many times in meetings over the years. I realized I wasn't entirely sure about the word "touchstone" and exactly what it meant. So I consulted the Merriam-Webster folks and this is what they had to say:

Touchstone – nòun
Definition of touchstone:
1: a fundamental or quintessential part or feature
2: a test or criterion for determining the quality or genuineness of a thing
3: a black siliceous stone related to flint and formerly used to test the purity of gold and silver by the streak left on the stone when rubbed by the metal

I read this as meaning the absence of pain would be measured as positive spiritual growth. I have noticed a subsiding of my pain as I have worked the Steps over the years.
When the Promises began manifesting as truths in my life, they became the touchstone of my spiritual progress. I have always had a love-hate relationship with the Promises. I'm now starting to love them more than hate them.
I'm working with a few sponsees right now and trying to nudge them in that direction. It feels good to pass along what I have learned from those who so freely gave of their time and energy.
I've always been hesitant to say I am grateful to be an alcoholic. This concept is starting to make sense to me now. It signifies by

admitting I was powerless I have discovered unlimited power in an infinite Universe. By connecting with this power, the pain has been reduced in my life.

Is it okay to say I'm grateful for my alcoholism?

Steve, rounding the curve

***

AA Reply – May 1992

Dear Steve,

Yes. It is absolutely ok.

We wish you the best as you come out of the curve and begin a straightaway. Keep up the noble effort, Steve.

Sincerely,

AA

*****

Chapter Six
Willingness And Hard Work

In 1993 I finished school, receiving my MBA from Columbia. I couldn't have done it without Beryl and Uncle Rick. Both of them would say the same to this day, that it was me who did it. That it was me who stayed sober, went to meetings at least five days a week, worked the Steps, sponsored newer members in AA and continued volunteering my time at the Central Office until they finally hired me as a full time employee.

Beryl would never let on who she talked to or what she said to get me back into school early on in my recovery. But I knew she talked to somebody because I was on an academic scholarship and had failed all my courses in my first three quarters at Columbia before dropping out at 19 years old. I knew they were not too keen on giving me a second chance.

I was more willing to believe I had received my full-time position at the Central Office on my own merits due to my years of volunteering and my hard-won MBA. But keeping that job after my boyfriend used my position and access to steal almost a million dollars from donation accounts was something Beryl was entirely responsible for. And as well she was entirely responsible for me obtaining the necessary bonding following the incident which the Trustees rightly so insisted upon as a condition of my continued employment.

All in all that era of my life, the 1990's, was very trying but equally rewarding. The 1990's...My heart was broken only twice, which seems to be a decadal average for me, good lord. But throughout all that and everything in between, Steve's letters continued to arrive and Beryl's replies kept going back out to him. And both of those were absolute rays of sunlight during times difficult and great in my life.

*****

March 1993

Dear AA,

I went to the backroom meeting at the 12 Step Club last Sunday night. They have a weekly meeting there chaired by a nice woman named Rose. She has the group read from the Book and then conducts a discussion meeting about the reading. I noticed a reference to a longshoreman in the chapter we read. It goes something like, "Show any longshoreman a Sunday supplement which describes exploring the moon by means of rocket and he'll say I bet they do it someday."

Did Bill have a thing against the longshoremen? Did he spend his life in the buildings of Wall Street looking down at the shipyards in Brooklyn? Did he thumb his nose at those hard-working men? Was Bill Wilson a snob?

I have spent most of my life around piers and wharves. I worked as a salesman among the commission houses of Seattle's Western Avenue. The firm I worked for was involved in the export of fresh fruits and vegetables. They were also engaged in the business of ships chandlery. What's a ship chandler you ask? Well it's the world's second oldest profession. Christopher Columbus probably had a ship chandler who arranged for the rope, sails, provisions, medicines, and any other needs for the voyage of the Nina, Pinta, and Santa Maria. This chandler then presented a bill to Isabella and Ferdinand which they probably waited one hundred and twenty days to pay. Did you know Ben Cartwright of Bonanza fame made his fortune as a ship chandler in Massachusetts before he headed out west and bought the Ponderosa?

I've worked around those wharves and docks most of my adult life. The longshoremen were some of the hardest working, rough and tumble guys I ever saw. Back in the days of break-bulk cargo they worked long days down in the holds of those ships. They hauled up banana stalks the size of hanging beef while fending off snakes and spiders from the jungles of Costa Rica. Years ago in Tacoma a sling snapped, and four men were killed by the falling cargo. This was known as Black Tuesday and was memorialized as a non-working holiday for many years.

In my days on the docks I met some very interesting people. The men and women I counted as customers had literally sailed to the four corners of the globe. Some of the most interesting stories I had ever heard were told by the various and assorted crew members of the freighters, ice breakers, research ships, king crab boats, coast guard cutters, catcher processors, oil tankers, and others ships and vessels I helped provision. I'll write a book about the business someday. Sorry, it won't be one of the books I will try to market through you guys.

By the way, I wanted to point out the inconsistencies in the song 'Brandy' by the band 'Looking Glass.' As I mentioned I've spent close to a lifetime around ports and docks. I know a lot about this stuff. In the song, Brandy, "Works in a port on a western bay that serves a hundred ships a day."

Do you realize how big a port would have to be to serve one hundred ships a day? Think of how many sailors and longshoremen and truck drivers would be frequenting the bar where Brandy worked. She would be inundated by the advances of these men. She would be slinging drinks to lonely men, stranded in a port, some of them thousands of miles from home. Brandy would make millions off the sexual harassment lawsuits alone. Not to mention how much she'd make in tips.

And in the song she serves them whiskey and wine. I can't imagine a longshoreman, after a hard day of working in a cargo hold, coming into the bar and ordering a glass of chardonnay. They would want strong drinks for men that want to get drunk. But I digress.

So here's my question:
What's Bill got against longshoremen?

Steve on a ship, loading wheat for Egypt

***

AA Reply – March 1993

Dear Steve,

We certainly don't think Bill Wilson held any kind of vendetta against longshoremen. Bill celebrated the fact AA's came from every walk of life. Our membership – then and now - represents a cross section of society. The term *longshoreman* might have been used to make a reference to everyday people. The longshoreman in the example is shown evidence of some futuristic adventure involving interplanetary exploration. He then says, "I'll bet they do it someday."

In 1935, when Bill wrote the passage, the future was ahead of them and everyone felt anything was possible.

102

Steve, easy does it. By the way, your work around the ports sounds like an exciting and rewarding career.

Many regards,

AA

***

December – 1993

Dear AA,

I was thinking about New Year's Eve, 1973. I Started out drinking Jim Beam at the Eastgate Safeway with Bob Bendix, William Sanders, and Richard Marks. I drove Richard home and damaged my tailpipe backing out of his driveway. Ironically, he lived about 500 yards away from a church where I have regularly attended AA meetings for the past fifteen years.

That night I had a twelve-pack of Rainer for myself, and four or five bottles of Cold Duck to boot. We partied in Cherry Crest, a neighborhood at the north end of town. I drank a lot. I mean a lot.

We ended up at the House of Pies in downtown Bellevue. I don't know how we got there. I was driving but I still don't know how we made it there. We might have gone to Dick's Drive-in next door first, I'm not sure. Everything was like a dream. I remember saying things I shouldn't have said to the waitress.

Six of us piled into my 1951 Plymouth. I remember driving down Bellevue Way and throwing empty Cold Duck bottles out of my car. Being a lefty pays off when the activity is tossing empty champagne bottles at Uncle Harold's Quality Key and Cycle. I have a faint memory of William stumbling up to his front door after I dropped him off at his home.

I drove the entire route, House of Pies to Woodridge and back to Cherry Crest in a total blackout. Lost time I will never recover. I could have run ten cars off the road, I'll never know. At this point in my life I was a menace to society. Alcohol robbed me of all reason, judgement, and sanity. I was completely insane. I was sixteen years old. I tried everything to reduce my intake and thus make drinking fun again. Nothing worked. I was at the end of the road. Thank God I bottomed out so early in life.

Tonight I celebrate my seventeenth consecutive sober New Year's Eve. I am grateful, grateful, grateful.

Here's my question, was I really spared the last ten or fifteen years of literal hell the rest went through? I'm sure I wouldn't have lived ten more years. I had a premonition death was imminent. It was like a dark cloud of death was hanging over my life.

P.S. My Plymouth was a flat head six with six-volt power. I had a 12-volt battery sitting on the floor in the back seat. I used it to power my eight-track player which most often had Led Zeppelin, Houses of the Holy playing. I always wondered why the song "Houses of the Holy" wasn't on the Houses of the Holy album. Do you think they pressed a million copies of the album and then realized they screwed up? I wonder if someone from the record company called and told the band? The band probably said, "Oh that's okay. Just put it on our next album, Physical Graffiti. We're Led Zeppelin, our songs are about mystical forests and Hobbits. No one knows what the hell we're saying anyway. Most of our fans are like that guy Steve from Bellevue, Washington. They sit around and get baked and listen to our records and try to figure out what's going on. They'll never notice the Houses of the Holy thing."

Steve, sober for seventeen New Years

***

AA Reply – January 1994

Dear Steve,

Way to go, congratulations! It sounds like you were granted the gift of sobriety at exactly the right time. God – as you understand Him - is amazing that way.

Sincerely,

AA

***

October 1994

Dear AA,

I'm working with a couple sponsees. I've told them about the letters I've been writing to you over the last seventeen years. They both have written letters they too want to send in.

I've told them it's unlikely they would get a reply soon since you probably get bags of letters from people like us poured out on your desks every day and if I mailed them in they might get an earlier reply because I always seem to get quick replies.

I've enclosed both letters with this one. Thank you in advance for reading them. You'll see what kooky guys I have to deal with as a sponsor...whew. I don't know how these guys find me.

My question is:

If you have a chance would you please answer their letters and send the replies back to me?

Thanks, Steve with kooky sponsees

Letter from Tim T.– Kirkland, WA October 1994

Dear AA,

This is Tim T. here. I've been sober now for almost six months. My sponsor Steve told me it might be a good idea for me to write in because I'm not getting the answer I want from him.

I've had a rough time trying to find the right AA woman for me.

So far, as soon as we get together, they all seem to want to help me do a Fourth Step. I've repeatedly told these women I've already done my Fourth Step. Maybe I'm not getting it across well as I've been known to mumble.

My question is do you think it would be a better strategy to go out with a girl who has at least 60 days sober?

These 30-day gals are driving me nuts.

Sincerely,

Tim

Letter from Dan S.– Seattle, WA October 1994

Dear AA,

This is Dan from Seattle. I have five years of sobriety and am excited about life. Or well...I was.

I've recently become aware of a bump on the back of my neck. Right below my head. I'm pretty sure it's a tumor and clearly a malignant one because who ever heard of a neck tumor that wasn't?

I want to go out like a man, like Raspy Ralph did dying last year of emphysema at 87 with 48 years of sobriety. He never complained, whined, or even shared about his condition for the whole last year of his life at meetings. At least I'm fairly certain he didn't; he was hard to understand between his fits of coughing and even harder to hear when he had his full-blown oxygen face mask on.

I'm not saying I want to smoke cigarettes right to the end as did Ralph - who showed all of us how much more important not drinking is versus not smoking. And besides, I quit smoking over three hours ago so it's not an issue for me.

I've realized and accepted I'll never be able to get married, raise children, and have a rewarding career or become an AA Circuit Speaker - and I would have been great! But more importantly I've been thinking about others and not myself. Specifically, my sponsees.

There are 14 at last count and maybe 16 if Karl and Kandi come back sober from Ozzfest in LA next week - I don't hold out high hopes for them...sponsoring a newly married couple who are into heavy metal is tough!

I mentioned this cancerous bump to my sponsor Steve. He felt the bump on my neck, then he noticed he also had a tumor in the same area on his neck. He freaked out and went to the local library and logged on to one of the county computers. He conducted a Netscape Navigator search concerning the bump on the neck. Within a few seconds Steve received all the information one human could ever consume about the bump at the back of his neck. He came back to me and explained it is something called the Atlas bone. He said not to worry because everyone has an Atlas bone. Steve said I could relax and go on with my life. Wow, that internet thing is an amazing tool.

However, I have to wonder if everything will be ok when a guy like Steve tells me to relax. This is a guy who can create a relationship, lose everything, and end up sharing a couch with a dog, all in the moments after he chickens out of asking a girl to dance. Though I do appreciate his efforts on my behalf I still have lingering doubts about the results of his Netscape Navigator search. I'm going to conduct a search on the Internet Explorer. I don't trust that Netscape product at all.

All in all, it may not be that easy to escape from these woods. Well it's more like a forest, the dark forest of big ugly neck bumps. Alas, life was once so promising.

So, my question is what sort of legacy should I offer to my sponsees on my deathbed? I currently have over 97 hours of my recorded thoughts on cassette tapes which I know will be of great use to them. However, a few of my sponsees now have computers and CD players. I've heard about these digital transfer processes. But they may be expensive. Should I stay analog or go digital? I want to keep my costs low to hedge my bets in the unlikely event I survive.

Sincerely,

Dying Dan

***

AA Reply – November 1994

Dear Steve,

We are sure you can offer great guidance to your sponsees. It may be best that you answer the letters yourself.

Sincerely,

AA

*****

It turned out Steve had taken Beryl's suggestion literally and had written his own *AA Replies* to his sponsees' letters. We found this out because he mailed in copies of those replies a week later. Here they are:

*****

Steve's "AA Replies" to the Tim T. and Dan D. Letters

Dear Tim,

What does the "T" stand for? Terrible? Really? You're having sex with girls with 60 days of sobriety? What does your sponsor say about that?

We took your case to the Supreme Allied AA Behavior Council and they agreed you should be censured for your actions. Take the cotton out of your ears and put it in your mouth. Go to meetings, work with newcomers, listen to your sponsor and leave the girls alone.

***

Dear Dan,

We have been reading Steve's letters for many years. He is a shining beacon of hope in a stormy sea of recovery. Sure he's a little kooky and off the wall but that shouldn't stop you from following his direction and respecting his vast wealth of knowledge and experience.

If he says the neck bump is in fact the Atlas bone and nothing to worry about then you should heed his advice and count your lucky stars, because you have an entire galaxy of them.

You are a lucky man to have Steve as your sponsor.

*****

Included was a letter from Steve letting us know he might be available in the future to assist us in crafting the many replies we must surely be mailing out every week in response to the hundreds of letters like his we were receiving.

He also said we were "free to pass them around the office and bounce them off the CEO of AA if in fact we had a CEO."

Reading Steve's *AA Replies* to his sponsee's letters had Beryl and me in stiches of laughter for weeks. For years after Beryl and I would joke about the *CEO of AA* whenever an opportunity presented itself.

It was January of 1995. A new year had begun. There was a fresh dusting of snow on the sidewalks. I followed it all the way to the office where I found waiting for me in the mail another letter from Steve.

*****

January 1995

Dear AA,

You said there was no way to make a normal drinker out of an alcoholic. You said science may one day accomplish this, but it hasn't done so yet.

Are you in touch with science? Do you know if they're still working on it?

Thanks.

Steve, curious about science

***

AA Reply- February 1995

Dear Steve,

We haven't talked to science in years. We are fairly sure they are not working on it anymore.

Hang in there, the journey can be tough and filled with difficult questions. The rewards reaped daily living sober are worth it all.

Sincerely,

AA

***

February 1995

Dear AA,

In the Book you say a prosaic steel girder is a whirling mass of electrons. Duh. I learned all about that in my high school sophomore year from Mr. Tom Fackenthall. He was a trippy dude who made methane out of chicken shit and taught physics at Interlake High School.

My question is this. What's a prosaic steel girder got to do with not drinking?

Steve the physics major

***

AA Reply - February 1995

Dear Steve,

A prosaic steel girder *is* nothing more than a whirling mass of electrons.

In order to build the Empire State Building we had to have faith the electrons would hang together and hold up the building.

Though we may not understand the electrons, and how they stay cohesive, we must have faith to go to the top of the Empire State Building.

We hope this helps.

Sincerely,

AA

***

May 1996

Dear AA,

A guy named Hippie Ed made an outlandish claim last night at the Hoot Owl meeting at the 12 Step Club. His claim referred to something Bill W. had done a long time ago. I'm pretty sure Ed made it up.

Hippie Ed is the guy who spent four hours separating the white tiny time pills from the colored tiny time pills in a bottle of the cold medicine Contact. He and his friends read a story in High Times magazine which made the claim if you mixed the white tiny time pills with ground up Valium and snorted it, you'd get really high.

Ed was also once arrested for traveling southbound on northbound Interstate 405 without the aid of a motor vehicle. In the depths of his alcohol and drug induced malaise he concocted a plan to blow up the city of Bellevue, Washington.

He hated Bellevue and all the materialistic waste it stood for. After having a heart to heart talk with a family member Ed came to his senses. He took an honest look at his life and saw it for what it was. Ed was living in a house with no power, no running water (except on rainy days) and no front porch.

During a party they had overloaded the front porch with too many people. It collapsed and mayhem ensued. Cooler heads prevailed and they decided to drag the refrigerator out from the kitchen and drop it by the front door. The refrigerator was useless because the house had no power. As Ed was climbing up on the refrigerator to enter the house, he had a moment of clarity. He saw his life for what it was. His life was a total mess, he considered how insane it was to think he could blow up a town the size of Bellevue. In his moment of clarity he decided to blow up nearby Redmond instead, because it was smaller. But once again I digress.

In the meeting Hippie Ed said Bill W. had taken LSD back in the 1950's or 1960's. If this is true, my opinion of Bill W. just went way up. Man, that Bill was one hip cat!

I'm planning on attending The Happening in Oregon this summer. It's in a big field, just outside the city limits of Eugene. It's a huge event featuring forty-seven Grateful Dead tribute bands. There will be lots of dust, heat, sweaty hippies, free love, and a giant camping area. Here's my question,

Can I take LSD at The Happening and still preserve my AA birthday?

Heck, Bill did it

Steve, seeking enlightenment

***

AA Reply – May 1996

Dear Steve,

There have been ugly rumors swirling around for years about this. What we know is during the era in question some doctors did experiment with small doses of Lysergic Acid Diethylamide to treat depression. Bill W. - as with anyone else - had a right to the privacy of his medical conditions and/or treatments for them. Thus AA has no position on the issue. We can offer the following thoughts.

If your vision is one of Bill sitting on a bean bag chair, next to a lava lamp, listening to jazz records with Dr Leary, then your vision is incorrect. Bill wasn't hanging out in Greenwich Village with a bunch of LSD dropping intellectuals. Though he may have been at Washington Square Park in 1962 when Joan Baez and Bob Dylan played a set together on a Sunday afternoon.

You might ask yourself what the long-term consequences would be of taking LSD at The Happening. The Book refers to the individual who sets out to celebrate with the best intentions in mind. The disastrous result of the celebration usually outweighs any positive intention the person had going into the relapse.

One of our local friends is heading out across country to go The Happening. Her name is Alice and she came of age right in the prime of the Haight Ashbury scene. She's in her mid-40's and has long dyed purple and gold hair. Look for the yellow balloons and you'll find her. She'll be holding Twelve Step meetings for Dead Heads in recovery.

Sincerely,

AA

***

February 1997

Dear AA,

I'm in my twenty first year of sobriety. I've developed what I call the 'Ninety-Day Method' for reporting my sober time. For the first ninety days following my sobriety date I say, "I just celebrated twenty years." Once the ninety day threshold has been met I then say, "I'm in my twenty first year of recovery". It makes me sound more credible.

I have developed some other unique insights into this recovery thing and am considering writing a book about my perspectives on the subject.

Here are some working titles for my manuscript:

"I'm Okay, You Bite the Big One"
"The Power of Occasional Positive Thinking"
"The Idiots Guide To Sharing In AA Meetings"
"Shut the Heck Up and Listen to Me"
"Zen And The Art Of Rebuilding Your Motorcycle In The 12 Step Club Parking Lot"
"The Missing Steps, 4a and 4b, 10a, and 13"

Is there a protocol for getting my book accepted as AA approved literature? I read an article about some company that sells books from a giant warehouse in my hometown of Bellevue using modems and computer connections. I don't think that system will ever be profitable. I'll need to sell my books in one of those 12 Step shops, or in the lobby of the 12 Step Club.

Steve with a headful of ideas that are driving me insane

***

AA Reply – February 1997

Dear Steve,

Approved AA literature is extensively reviewed and must meet content and messaging guidelines. Based on your titling options it is likely your submissions would not meet the necessary requirements for publication.

But never say never, Steve. Keep writing, have fun, stay loose, and hold onto your sense of humor.

Sincerely,

AA

***

August 1997

Dear AA,

I was talking to a friend the other day and a tough topic came up. My friend is disillusioned with the program and is considering stopping her participation in AA. She has reached a point where she sees the people of the fellowship as the face of the program. She thinks AA is a cult and she's tired of people giving her unsolicited advice. She's been sober a little over ten years (she's in her eleventh year). She's noticed some members talk big talks in the meetings but don't really live their lives according to their own dogma. She said she wanted my honest advice about what to do. I told her one of my stories.

In the church where we held my home group there was a long hallway with offices and rooms we never used. I once thought there were secret rooms back there reserved for AA. At some point in your recovery the old timers would take you down to the secret room and tell you the truth about recovery and AA. As you reach different levels of enlightenment, they would reveal more about the secrets of long-term recovery. There was one room where they took you and told you the fellowship and the program are two separate realities. This would be the room where I learned the journey is personal and I had to detach myself from the fellowship and take ownership of my own recovery.

I explained to my friend the rooms were strictly metaphorical and represented the alcoholic reaching different levels of enlightenment. I suggested she think of each stage of awareness and learning of new knowledge as the opening of a secret door. Her journey in recovery could be thought of in terms of a long hallway with many doors.

I told her I will always participate in AA, for the rest of my life. I attend AA because I enjoy it and because I get a chance to pass along to the newcomer the message so freely given to me. I explained to my friend I needed to go outside AA to acquire some of the necessary tools for my recovery. I also explained to her the people who make up the fellowship are part of my solution but shouldn't be considered my solution in its entirety. I told her recovery is a personal journey for me and I am committed for my lifetime.

There came a point when it became necessary for me to detach from AA and accept the fact the journey was personal. She shook her head and said this confused her because she had never heard anyone in the program say something like this. I pointed out some people leave AA after becoming disillusioned with it. Most often they had had bad experiences with people in the fellowship and stopped going to meetings. This is where the cult myth comes in. Some people in AA say you can't stay sober without meetings. The disillusioned member then quits going to meetings concluding if the AA's were wrong about so much, maybe they were wrong about the drinking thing too.

I told my friend this was the great trap we never want to fall in. We are members of the "never again" crowd. Could we survive and stay sober long term without AA? Maybe we could, maybe we couldn't. I continue to participate because I feel attendance at AA is part of my long-term recovery. Staying on the path of spiritual growth and never forgetting - each day - I am an alcoholic who never wants to drink again are also integral parts of my recovery.

I also told her another great secret of the secret rooms; over time you will develop a small tribe of long-term friends to share your recovery journey with. Though you may meet hundreds or thousands of people over the span of time, these few close friends will be with you for the rest of your life.

By the end of our coffee session I had told this woman several different versions of the following ideas:

AA is not a cult unless you let it become one.

AA is a vital resource for recovery, but it is not the end all.

You must learn how to survive the fellowship in order to survive the disease.

Regular participation affords us countless examples of what happens when people don't take their alcoholism seriously. The "slippers" and "relapsers" do our research for us.

Recovery is a personal journey which requires a mix of working with people and going off and discovering things by ourselves.

I don't want to lose my friend to alcoholism. I'm afraid if she strays away, she'll never come back. I reminded her the solution is better than the problem. I have bonded with this woman, and I love her. When I say the word love I mean like the way someone loves the state of Connecticut, or the Grand Coulee Dam, or Mt. Rainier.

So here is my question:

Am I obligated to reveal the secret rooms metaphor to as many members as possible? If we talked about them more wouldn't we save a lot of people a lot of heartache?

Steve worried about his friend

***

AA Reply – August 1997

Dear Steve,

The Fellowship and The Program are two separate entities as you put forth so well. Studying The Traditions may help your friend better understand this necessary aspect of life as an AA member.

A person's experience, strength and hope shared honestly is as unique as the person speaking it. It's difficult to determine what the truth or reality is for others even though we may have discovered it for ourselves.

Steve, the best teachers remain open and willing students.

Sincerely,

AA

*****

Chapter Seven
A Little Help From A Friend

W e didn't receive any letters from Steve for six years. When we finally did, this was what arrived in the mail.

*****

August 2003

Dear AA,

Today I am writing with a heavy heart. Julie was one of my favorite people the meetings at the 12 Step Club. She was a junkie and a drunk (the two seem to go hand in hand) and fought a valiant fight to get clean and sober. She struggled for many years to get some clean time.

121

She was once a respectable Bellevue housewife and gave birth to two beautiful children. She had a few years clean and it looked like she was on her way to the promised land of recovery. Then she lost her sobriety a few years ago.

Julie's family tried everything they could to get her help. Lately it seemed like she had lost her grip on reality. Early last Wednesday when the club kitchen manager Hazel pulled into the parking lot, she noticed a car parked in a back corner.

When Hazel approached the car, she discovered Julie, lying motionless in the driver seat. Her eyes were open, and her hands were riga-mortised to the steering wheel. She had OD'd sometime in the night, after the Hoot Owl meeting.

All of us regulars at the club were devastated by Hazel's discovery. I'm mad at God and I don't understand why Julie couldn't get clean.

Here's my question: Why did God pick me to get clean and sober, and not pick Julie? I want to go back in the time machine and save her.

Life is so precious, why did she have to lose hers?

Steve, shocked and bummed beyond belief

*****

Beryl and I both cried. Yes, for Julie whom we'd never met and yes for Steve whom we'd never met. We cried for other people too. People we knew and loved who'd died on 9/11 or after - because of 9/11.

Most of all we cried for Uncle Rick. It had been almost two years and I don't think either of us had ever fully grieved our loss. A husband and best friend for Beryl and for me, my uncle. My uncle who never tried to take the place of my father who died too young from alcoholism. My uncle who never looked down on me even at my worst. My uncle who had saved my life by introducing me to a life I'd only dreamt of before. My uncle who'd introduced me to Beryl.

He'd been down near the towers that morning. He consulted with FDNY teaching Qi-Gong exercises at station houses. The guys loved him and from the chief on down all found the practice of breathing and focused awareness merging with fluid body movements helped the guys out physically and mentally.

He'd been leading a session when the calls came in. That had happened before, and he'd never go on any calls. He wasn't a fireman or paramedic. He'd just pack his gear and leave or stick around if it was a *treed cat* call since the guys would be back soon and then they'd resume the class.

But that morning was different. Calls were coming into every station and when Uncle Rick heard what was going on he followed the trucks on foot arriving fifteen minutes later. He'd called Beryl from a payphone to let her know what was happening telling her things looked bad and he was going in to see if he could help.

That was the last time she heard his voice.

It seemed like everyone lost somebody that day. And Beryl had cried that night and the next day and then she was done. She wouldn't let her grief overshadow what she might be able to offer another in need. A lot of people were in need in New York. A lot of people all of a sudden had no husband or wife, father or mother or uncle or aunt when the night before they had had those people in their lives.

Beryl was a great behind the scenes organizer and she knew many people in all the right places to make things happen. She never wanted credit for anything she did, and she wouldn't want me to talk about it even now, so I won't. But I will say when she passed away seven years later in 2008 it seemed as if half the Who's Who of the City were at her memorial service.

I knew Beryl was well known around town and I was by no means her only sponsee. She worked with many AA's so I expected a large service. I certainly didn't expect some of the people I saw there and especially those who offered me condolences saying my name as if we had known each other for years. It was all very surreal.

I'd known, we'd known, she didn't have much time left. The chemo had had no positive effect and she didn't want to go another round with it. I didn't blame her for not wanting to; the first round had taken more of a toll on her than had the cancer.

We spent the last two weeks of her life together at her home. The office of course was incredibly supportive offering me a month off. I didn't take the full month but instead only the two weeks I had with Beryl. And following her passing I went back to work. I needed to keep busy. And by then I was no longer needing to keep busy to run from my feelings or anything else. I simply needed to keep busy to continue to move forward in my life.

I go on and on. I guess I digress. Like Steve. And to me, digression is not a bad word. I think you can – well...I can at least –I can learn much about a person from their digressions.

Take Steve, yes he's neurotic but he has a great sense of humor. I know he's laughing at himself. And for me, along with many if not all AA's, I have to laugh at myself. I do my best to not take myself too seriously because really, I mean really...does anybody know what the heck is up with this journey of life we are all on together?

I'd asked that very question of Beryl once. She'd replied,

"In the face of all the mystery surrounding existence I do the best I can with what I have."

And with Steve, I know he's a got a great heart and I know he is driven, just like me, to continue to move forward.

It was summer of 2003. Beryl and I worked together to write the reply to Steve's letter about Julie. We referred to it from then on as the *Julie Letter* because it not only marked the return of Steve into our lives after a six year absence but it marked a change as well in Steve. He still wrote of his goofy ideas and he was still candid about his thoughts but there seemed to be more gravity with which he spoke.

*****

AA Reply-August 2003

Dear Steve,

We are very sorry to hear of the loss of your friend. It always seems so random and unfair when our loved ones in recovery lose their battle with alcoholism and or drug addiction. You said in your letter Julie was one of your favorite people. It is natural to feel angry at God for taking her soul across to the other side.

Just remember, before Hazel made her grisly discovery, before Julie's family found out she had passed, before you and your local recovery community knew anything of her demise, and as her soul ascended to heaven, God alone was the only one who knew of her fate. God was indeed the first to cry.

Rest in peace, Julie.

Sincerely,

AA

*****

A year and a month passed before we received Steve's next letter. Following that the letters began arriving on a more regular basis again. Whenever I'd see the familiar lefty scrawl on an envelope while sorting through the department's mail it was like getting an early Christmas present.

*****

October 2004

Dear AA,

My friend Pete and I met a transcendent old hippie in Hawaii on our high school spring break in 1974. Tony lived on the third story of an old run down hotel apartment called the Polynesian. It was a four-story building located on Kalakaua Avenue, right in the heart of Waikiki.

We'd first seen Tony on his balcony above us leaning on the railing and drinking a beer. Pete got his attention and made a simulated gesture of smoking a joint. We were down on the street below and Tony signaled with his fingers, three, three, four. We climbed the stairs of the old ramshackle building and found room 334 was open. We walked in and there was a David Crosby looking character sitting on the couch, sipping on a can of Primo beer.

He said, "Come on in boys. You interested in acquiring some of the island's finest grass?"

We both nodded in the affirmative and I asked Tony if he had anything we could light up right away. He took out a pack of Zig Zags and rolled up a modest sized doobie. I thought it was a little smaller than what I was used to. The big clobber joints I rolled back home resembled a prehistoric club Fred Flintstone would use to knock out a saber tooth tiger.

Tony sparked up the joint and took a big toke from it. He passed it to Pete and after taking a decent hit Pete passed it to me. Right away I noticed this weed had a distinct smell to it. It smelled different than the Mexican stuff we smoked back on the mainland.

We smoked the joint and I asked Tony to roll another. He suggested we should wait a little while because we were going to be surprised how powerful this stuff was. I told Tony we were on vacation so another joint would be okay as neither Pete nor I had any pressing appointments.

Tony rolled a perfect joint. It had even density all the way through. The rolling paper was twisted perfectly at each end. When I lit it up, I touched the match to the end of the paper, and it burned evenly all the way through.

Tony told us it was Acapulco Gold and he'd have more coming in soon. It was forty dollars an ounce and he asked if we would like to make a purchase. I noticed I was getting higher than I had ever been before, thus I told Tony to hold us an ounce and we'd be by on Easter Sunday to pick it up.

Pete and I thanked Tony for the sample of his product. We said goodbye and went down the stairs. The Lollipop strip club was located on the street level of the building and I greeted the bouncer when I reached the bottom of the stairs. I thought he looked smaller than a normal bouncer. In fact, everything in the world looked smaller to me.

We hit the coffee shop restaurant at the Hilton Hawaiian Village where I ordered a plate of French fries. This was the moment in my life when THC met with my OCD. In one continuous motion I mowed through an entire plate of French fries. Pete didn't even eat any of his, he just watched me.

He watched me systematically separate the fries on the plate and line them up in rows, based on length. I had matched up all the fries by size then dipped them in the ketchup and ate them. I rearranged another load and got them ready to dip. All the ends of the fries had to be even before I dipped them. Pete was so high he got caught up watching the slaughter taking place on my plate. Pete ended up with no appetite, so I assaulted his plate of fries with the same Blitzkrieg attack I had used to eat mine.

We left the Hilton and walked down to the Royal Hawaiian. I took special note of the fact the stop signs were shorter, the people were shorter, the buildings were shorter, everything was small.

We sat on the sand in front of the Pink Palace and I held out my hand and looked at my fingers.

I told Pete to hold out his hand and look at his fingers. I said, "Look at your hand, we're nothing but animals. We're animals, on a planet, hurling through space at 67,000 miles per hour. If it weren't for gravity, we'd just fall off the planet and float through the eternity of space forever."

Pete was a little freaked out by all the planets and gravity and animal talk. That night was the apex of my drug career. It was pretty much downhill from there.

We returned to Tony's pad on Easter and picked up an ounce of the Acapulco Gold. Tony rolled me a few of his gold medal joints for the road. We smoked two joints with Tony, and he told us all about life at the Polynesian. We went out on Tony's balcony and hung out for a while. Once again, I noticed how everything on the planet seemed to be in twenty five percent reduction.

Diamond Head looked smaller, Kalakaua Avenue looked smaller, and the thousands of people on the street on Easter Sunday looked smaller. Tony waved down to the floor below where another resident was out on his balcony.

The man Tony waved to was a gruff, portly looking fellow with a joint in one hand and a can of beer in the other. Tony told us the guy's name was Lou and he was from the East Coast. Lou had come to Hawaii because he thought he could hide out from the law. He hadn't considered the fact Hawaii was a state, not a foreign country. Lou was a wanted man in his native New Jersey.

Lou yelled some unbecoming remarks to a couple as they were crossing Kalakaua. He implied the woman could come up to his apartment and he would show her a good time. The man flipped Lou the bird as they walked under the awning that extended out above the entrance to the Lollipop.

Lou got mad and climbed up on the railing of his balcony. He jumped down with a plan of landing on the awning and hoisting himself down on to the sidewalk to apparently confront the guy who flipped him off.

We watched Lou jump and in what appeared to be a slow-motion hallucination he disappeared through the awning. Lou jumped off the balcony and went right through the roof!

We were so stoned it took us several minutes to process what had happened. My eyes had seen Lou jump and then disappear. The message was sent to my brain, yet I couldn't process what had happened. After what seemed like an eternity Tony became frantic and started running toward the stairs.

We all ran down to the street level and stumbled out of the building to find fiberglass chunks all over the sidewalk. There was sunshine pouring in through a hole Lou had blazed through the awning. He was leaned up against the building and was gasping for breath. He had a roach clip in one hand and a crumpled-up can of Hamm's in the other. Lou said in a faint voice "I blew it man, I really blew it."

The bouncer from the Lollipop said he had heard a big explosion and then watched a body bounce off the sidewalk. He said Lou had scrambled to find his roach clip and then crawled over to where he sat now, the can of Hamm's never leaving his hand.

Tony and I helped Lou up to his feet and got him back into the building. Lou slowly crawled up the stairs saying something like, "I need to get back inside before the cops come."

Pete ran up to Tony's room and grabbed the weed and we hit the road. We smuggled the bag back to the mainland and carefully rationed out the fantastic green drug over the next couple of months. I kept a bunch of the seeds and grew quite a crop over the summer of 74.

Here's my question:

When we were at Tony's the first time, I managed to suck down two cans of Primo. The second time, when we watched Lou crash through the fiberglass awning, I drank several bottles of Miller

High Life. Based on those facts can I add this story to my AA drunkalogue?

It's a weed story but I did drink a few qualifying beers. Are the beers enough alcohol to include it in my story? Does AA have a formula for this stuff? I don't want to piss off the old timers.

Steve taking a trip on Acapulco Gold

***

AA Reply - October 2004

Dear Steve,

It is a single purpose program. You are from the generation where there are few alcoholics who did not use some or most of the host of drugs which have tragically become so widespread. If your story is focused on how you recovered from alcoholism and not on how you recovered from weed, then it would be appropriate to share.

It's a darn good story.

Sincerely,

AA

***

March 2005

Dear AA

What's the deal with this three-minute time limit? Last night at the 7:30 meeting at the 12 Step Club they called on Angry Arnie.

He started complaining about the limit saying it would take him five minutes just to tell us how "goddam stupid" a three minute sharing limit was. He was really revved up about it.

He went on and on and before too long the timer went off. The guy timing the meeting was in a good mood and he used the opening guitar riff from Deep Purple's "Smoke on the Water" as the signal to stop talking.

This made Arnie even angrier than he was before he started. Arnie yelled at the timer guy and told him he didn't much like Deep Purple. He told a story about taking Orange Sunshine and seeing Deep Purple at the California Jam in 1974. It was the David Cloverdale era and apparently Angry Arnie preferred the Ian Gillian incarnation of the band better. He added he liked Cloverdale's next band, Whitesnake. He saw them in '88 at the L.A. Sports Arena while high on Purple Microdot. Anyhow, I digress.

Arnie went on well beyond the sound of the timer. He never got to share about the topic. The second time the sound of "Duh-Duh-Duhhh, Duh -Duh ta Duh" went off, Arnie got angrier and stormed out of the meeting. He spun his tires in the unpaved parking lot. The meeting hall was showered with pieces of gravel as he sped away.

My question is this, three minutes seems too short, do you think we should extend it to five?

Smoke on the Water Steve

***

AA Reply – March 2005

Dear Steve,

The AA Fourth Tradition states, "Each group should be autonomous except in matters affecting other groups or AA as a whole." That about says it all.

Go to the business meeting and see if there is a consensus among the members of your group to extend the time limit. Keep up the great work, Steve.

Sincerely,

AA

***

July 2005

Dear AA,

Thirty one years ago this week I was treated to a free nights lodging and a complementary bowl of Kellogg's Corn Flakes by the kind citizens of Richland, Washington. At dawn they transferred me in handcuffs to the Freddie English Home for Wayward Children. I was locked in solitary confinement and was waiting for my dad to come bail me out.

The day before, as we drove eastbound on I-90 we rose to a crest at Echo Glen which offered a beautiful vista of Mt. Si dead ahead to the east. We were smoking a bowl and enjoying some ice cold Millers in the bottle. I remember thinking life could never get any better. It was a sunny summer day and we were on our way to the Tri-Cities of Kennewick, Pasco and Richland, Washington to watch the hydroplane races. 'We' being my older brother along with his frat brother at the University of Washington. I remember thinking how great it was to catch a buzz at 9:30 in the morning. I thought the day would keep getting better and better. Imagine my dismay when at 11:30 that night the steel door of the jail cell

132

opened and I was greeted by a crazy cat standing there in his underwear. He was screaming about his civil rights and the constitution and a bunch of other nonsense. Welcome to the Richland city jail on Atomic Cup weekend, young man. This guy is going to be your cellmate for the next six hours.

When the heavy, poorly painted door clanged shut I entered a whole new realm of awareness. I was a luxury kid from luxurious Bellevue. Here I was locked up in a cage, an animal among animals. Underwear man kept up his yelling until the wee hours of the morning. They never let him exercise his rights and stuff. There was a quiet guy sitting on a cot and he was all melancholy and all. When the sun rose the next morning they took the three of us juveniles outside in handcuffs. An officer who was right out of central casting for the Broderick Crawford Story drove us to the home for wayward children. I remember watching the sunrise and thinking to myself what a beautiful place the Tri-Cities was.

When we arrived at the joint old Freddie English told me all he had was a solitary cell. Officer Crawford turned the light off from the outside. Just like that the single light bulb hanging from the center of the room went out. There I was, locked in solitary in the arm pit of the world. Richland, Washington. It was 5:30 in the morning and I was hungry. The police had confiscated my tub of Resers potato salad and my package of "Art Oh Boy Oberto" Pepperoni upon my arrest. I pleaded with them to let me keep the potato salad. They said I could have somehow injected drugs into the package.

When I look back now it must have been pretty exciting for those guys to arrest two frat brothers and a sixteen year old, all with idyllic Bellevue, Washington as the hometown on the I.D's. In the dark, in my cell, I began to shout a demand for an opportunity to exercise my civil rights. Old Freddie came down the hall and turned on my light saying, "Okay Mister Abby Hoffman, do you want some breakfast?" I asked for Sugar Frosted Flakes and was instead treated to a bowl of regular Corn Flakes. I demanded, as outlined in the United States Constitution, to exercise my right to make a phone call. Old Freddie sighed and in a few minutes he came back to inform me my dad was there to pick me up. I remember it was about 8:30 a.m. on Sunday morning. That meant my dad must have been woken up in the middle of the night by the Richland police. He had probably left the old Lake Hills house around 3:30 in the morning on his cross state adventure. He was there to liberate me from the tyranny that was the City of Richland.

When I was freed from my jail hell I offered some of the long term residents a piece of my gum. They all shook their collective heads and said they weren't allowed to take anything from outsiders. Freddie shook hands with my dad and they opened the door and I stepped out into the sunlight a free man. Free at last, free at last!

I was indeed free at last. I only drank one more time after that weekend. And that was a few weeks later when I was with my friends hanging out in the field behind Cherry Crest Elementary. We were standing around smoking weed, drinking beer, doing nothing, and listening to Led Zeppelin on the eight track playing out of someone's parked car. As I hoisted the quart bottle of Schlitz beer to my mouth I suddenly put it down and decided right there at that moment I would never take another drink. I've been sober ever since.

AA, here is my question:

I attend a men's meeting every Wednesday night. There are a lot of rough and tumble guys at the meeting. Last week they were talking about prison and jail. Several of those guys were in some really rough joints. A few guys did hard time in federal penitentiaries. All I ever got charged with in the Richland caper was "minor on the loose without a guardian." Do you think my jail story is bad enough to share ?

Steve with a case of bad envy

***

AA Reply – July 2005

Dear Steve,

The trudging of the *Road of Happy Destiny* we speak of in AA may often be better described as a trudge up a down escalator. When we work hard we move upward against those forces which would otherwise move us downward when we apply less effort. When we slow or stop we may stay in one spot briefly but we will no longer progress upward and invariably will begin a downward motion.

For many recovering alcoholics, the escalator is the *old thinking* of a mind long accustomed to such self-defeating notions. The Program offers us new ways to think which promote new ways to see life and new ways to attain true victory. And true victory is victory over old ways of thinking which do not promote progress. Our trudge up that down escalator becomes easier in time and eventually becomes no trudge at all but rather a comfortable striding along the path of life.

Let go of the bad envy. You are a member of AA because you say you are.

Sincerely,

AA

***

November - 2005

Dear AA,

I have discovered a book, written by some cat named Webster. I feel it is almost as important as any of our sanctioned literature.

I am working with some guys and we are going through the Seven Deadly Sins and studying how much they can block our spiritual enlightenment. I feel it is important to gain as much knowledge of these sins in order to put them in a proper perspective.

That Webster dude did a good job of laying out the work before us. The word we are working on this month is envy:

envy
['envē]
NOUN
a feeling of discontented or resentful longing aroused by someone else's possessions, qualities, or luck.
"she felt a twinge of envy for the people on board"
synonyms:
jealousy · enviousness · covetousness · desire · resentment · resentfulness ·
[more]
VERB
desire to have a quality, possession, or other desirable attribute belonging to (someone else).
"he envied people who did not have to work on weekends" · "I envy Jane her happiness"
synonyms:
be envious of · be jealous of · begrudge · grudge · be resentful of

It's amazing how that one word, and its definition, sums up so much of what troubles me as a human being.

When I study the definition, it drives me to discover my true self. It sends me into an introspective tunnel of colors, images, and feelings. Envy is like a giant mirror that reflects me back onto myself. Out of necessity, for survival, and to prosper as a human being I must constantly investigate the mirror of envy.

I am committed to a rigorous and comprehensive study program. The goal of which is to gain a better understanding of my human nature and how I relate to the world and its people.

Here is my question: How early in a newcomer's recovery journey can I ask them to join me on my magic carpet ride of understanding in a search to find enlightenment in a world that seems so unenlightened?

Steve going deep in recovery

***

AA Reply – November 2005

Dear Steve,

You've likely heard the old saw, "When the student is ready the teacher will appear."

You have already shown your ability to teach and to learn. One of our members refers to this as the Zen Mind of AA. Or maybe it's the Zen Heart of AA. I'll have to ask her.

In any event, quite possibly carrying the torch of enlightenment in a world darkened by a lack of such is akin in its way to the AA concept of attraction rather than promotion.

Sincerely,

AA

***

February 2006

Dear AA,

I was sharing the other night at the Hoot Owl meeting at the 12 Step Club. The topic was the Second Step, so I talked about something I did once that proved I was in fact insane.

It was 1975 and I had traveled to L.A. with friends to see Jethro Tull play in the Forum. They were touring in support of the Minstrel In The Gallery album. They were playing the album in its entirety and the concert was backed up by a full psychedelic light show. In order to get into the mood, I took half a hit of four-way windowpane.

About halfway through the concert I freaked out and thought the Los Angeles Forum was a giant flesh-eating insect. I swear there was a Lakers game going on at the same time. Jerry West was in the twilight of his career; he hit Kareem with a beautiful pass and Jabbar launched a perfect sky hook over Willis Reed.

I eventually tried to crawl under my seat, but I didn't fit. I ended up in the medical tent and my girlfriend was sobbing uncontrollably. They took me to USC Medical and tried to sedate me.

That was a lot of acid, man. It took me a few days to come down. I lost the love of my life as my girlfriend said I was just too darned high. She said she didn't want to watch me die. I asked her if I could have back my Thick as a Brick album which I had previously loaned her. I told her I was going to need it to survive.

As I was sharing this story, honestly, from my heart, the chairman cut me off. It was that darned Bank Robber Bob again and this time he told me I was overexplaining myself.

He went on to say no one cared about my acid trip at the Tull concert in 1975. He suggested I start a new 12 Step group and call it "Over-Explainers Anonymous". He said I could have a thirty-

minute time limit. He even suggested I might collaborate with James Michener to write a twelve hundred page Big Book.

Bank Robber Bob really hurt my feelings. I never even got a chance to explain Thick as a Brick was the second Tull album to feature Jeffrey Hammond Hammond on bass. He had joined the band after Glenn Cornick departed between the release of the Benefit album and the Aqualung album. But I digress.

My question is this, don't you think Bank Robber Bob was being mean to cut me off?

Steve the Chronic Over Explainer

***

AA Reply – February 2006

Dear Steve,

You really love rock music, don't you? Sounds like you were at some of the classic big arena shows in the 70's.

Meetings may not be the best place for you to relate your stories of attending rock concerts. Many meetings have a sharing time limit now so you can hardly get started, especially if you try to share about Pink Floyd's Dark Side of the Moon tour.

With regard to Bank Robber Bob, he has his own row to hoe and often when others direct frustration at another it is due to an unresolved issue the angry person – in this case Bob – has yet to deal with. Most often the anger has nothing to do with the person it is directed toward. Stay on the high road, Steve. Work to develop compassion toward Bob. He may be envious of your wide and varied experiences seeing many of the day's great bands while he served a prison term for bank robbery relegated to a *live music* format of only weekly viewings of the Captain and Tennille TV show.

Keep up the good work on your side of the street, Steve.

Sincerely,

AA

*****

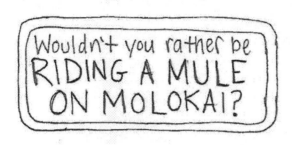

Chapter Eight
Working And Living

Beryl was diagnosed with Acute Myelogenous Leukemia in March of 2006. She didn't want her condition to be known outside of our small circle of close friends and co-workers. And even now, after her passing of over eleven years ago she wouldn't want me to discuss too much of this, if any at all. I will honor her wishes. I will always honor her wishes.

Nine years ago – just over a year after Beryl's death - I traveled to Hawaii to visit Jordan, an old AA friend who had moved to Molokai the year before. We had shared a love for walking the city. We also did a few week-long hikes along the Appalachian trail together.

I enjoy exercise and solitary time as I often hike alone. Jordan is one of the few, if not the only person who I could comfortably backpack with. I've tried with others and a lot of chatting while hiking is not what I'm looking for. Jordan is the same way. In fact, we'd often separate after taking a break and meet up at our campsite near the end of the day. This would give us hours to be alone with ourselves and our thoughts. And we could stop and take photos, have a visit behind a bush or whatever without interfering with each other's hiking flow. For me, as a hundred and twenty pound woman carrying a thirty five pound pack on a ten mile hike through mountains, getting into a flow is critical. When I'm in my zone I want to stop and take a break only when I want to stop and take a break. Jordan was the same way.

Jordan lived in a condo on the eastern side of Molokai. Right outside her door there were some beautiful trails along the cliffs she and I hiked together. I'd been more quiet than normal for the two of us. We'd talked a little about Beryl's passing and how I was dealing with it all; was I moving on as Beryl would want me to and so forth.

I told her the truth. No, I was not moving on. I wanted to but couldn't seem to find myself in a world without Beryl. One night while out on her lanai Jordan suggested I go on a tour of Kalaupapa, the once leper colony which had become a National Park.

She knew I'd rather do it on my own and had already made my reservation for a guided tour of the area. The next morning she dropped me off at the top of the trail which is the only way in and out except by air. The sea cliffs of Molokai above Kalaupapa are the highest in the world. To say the views and surroundings in every direction are magnificent is an understatement of epic proportion.

In any event, I am not bringing up Kalaupapa to discuss the wonderful solitary hike down and up. It was the guided tour at the base of the trail. It was led by an older gentleman who at the age of five years old in 1947 had been plucked out of his schoolroom in the middle of the day and shipped off to Kalaupapa. The school nurse had identified a sore he had on his cheek as leprosy and in those days there was no going home and packing and saying goodbye to your family. They took you right then and there. I won't tell his story here. I will say I was profoundly moved by it and moved by him as a fellow human being.

The history of Kaluapapa is long and deep. The recently canonized Father Damien wasn't the only person to have done great deeds in converting the tragic anarchy of the isolated leper colony into a community of people who worked together to build a better life – which was no easy task considering the circumstances. He was helped by others. Mother Marianne was one of those.

When thinking of Beryl since she passed I also think more and more about Mother Marianne. Beryl, like Mother Marianne, was a humble angel of God. Neither desired accolades in this life or the next for their tireless service to humanity.

***

Beryl and I received together a few more letters from Steve over the next year. Each was a gift. Each supplied laughter which had years before morphed into timely and fulfilling discussions of the issues Steve had brought up in his latest letter.

It seemed as if each additional letter served to form another link in our bond together as friends, confidants and what had grown into sisterhood. Beryl was my big sister and I was her little sister. And we were, the two of us, The Sole Sisters of the Sorority of Steve.

*****

June 2006

Dear AA,

I heard a speaker at the Winter Celebration mention the possibility of the existence of hidden messages in the Big Book. He thought they were planted there by the original authors. The speaker had struggled for years with the problem of compulsive over-thinking. This is a problem I've dealt with as well.

143

The speaker mentioned something about a black light and reading between the lines in the Book. He even thought there might be some missing Steps as well. I'd be very curious to find out about this.

Does the AA gift shop have the secret Big Book and the special black light?

There was a body builder who hung out at the 12 Step Club a few years ago. He was trying to win the Mr. Seattle competition and became obsessed with weightlifting. He even went so far as to have all his teeth pulled so he could get a clean straight pair of choppers to enhance his smile for the competition. While he was in between dental procedures he had a temporary plate which would shift while he shared in the meetings, making him tough to understand. He too struggled with his recovery and was miserable most of the time. He was convinced there was something he was missing in the AA literature. He mentioned the existence of a secret Twelve Step decoder ring.

Does the AA gift shop sell the secret Twelve Step decoder ring?

Steve looking between the lines

***

AA Reply - June 2006

Dear Steve,

There are many characters in AA. There are no special Big Books with hidden messages. There are no missing Steps which will be revealed using a black light. There is no AA secret Twelve Step decoder ring. The AA program lays out a simple set of spiritual tools at your feet. You can find the right wrench to fix any nut in AA.

Sincerely, AA

***

October 2006

Dear AA,

I've been thinking about my legacy in the local recovery scene. I plan to be around for a long time. Unless God has predetermined a bolt of lightning for me. There's an old guy, Old Fred, who regularly attends meetings at the 12 Step Club. He has a posse which includes a complex tree of sponsees, grand sponsees, and great grand sponsees. When he gets up to receive his birthday coin at the local meeting his entourage resembles that of a boxer or rapper. They must extend the time of the meeting to accommodate the thirty minutes it takes for all his people to get up and praise him. More time is consumed as Fred reminds all his people of the fact most of them were nowhere, had nothing, no hope, no life, until they connected with him. Fred also has a chair at the 12 Step Club he always sits in. His people show up early and protect this chair to ensure no one else sits in it. Sometimes when I go to the Hoot Owl meeting and he and his posse are not there I sit in Fred's chair.

I'm working on ways to improve my image and legacy in the local AA community. I have memorized many passages from the Big Book. There used to be an old guy named Mike who chaired the Saturday night birthday meeting at the 12 Step Club. Mike could recite the entire preamble and How It Works from memory. He would also recite the Traditions from memory. His skills were impressive. That's the kind of AA prowess I'm aiming for.

My plan is to stay around long enough to build up my own posse and thus my legacy, and to ultimately gain permanent possession of Old Fred's chair.

My question is this, I'm not sure if my motives are pure. Does that matter when it comes to staying clean and sober?

Almost Famous Steve

***

AA Reply – October 2006

Dear Steve,

If you're motivated to outlast Old Fred and thus gain AA stardom, then you're on the right track. Anything which keeps one moving forward in recovery – and does no harm to others, of course - is a good strategy. One day however, if and when you achieve local AA fame you may find yourself wondering why anyone would ever want to be anyone else's guru or posse leader.

Sincerely,

AA

***

May 2007

Dear AA,

I attended the 7:30 p.m. Sunday meeting at the 12 Step Club last week. A man named Niles said he was there because he was addicted to emotions. I was a little surprised he was at the AA meeting sharing about his addiction to his emotions.

Now I'm not trying to knock anyone who is addicted to their emotions. I've heard they even have a Twelve Step group to deal with that stuff. In recovery I remember the old timers telling us not to get emotionally involved in our first year.

Think about that statement, "Don't get emotionally involved." We are by our own admission alcoholics; we get emotionally involved with everything. I've heard men who have done hard prison time in Atascadero, Soledad, and Walla Walla, cry like little babies when they talk about their failed relationships. They can organize an entire tier in a federal prison but let them go out for one coffee date and they can come completely unglued.

Don't get emotionally involved with what? Shoes? Tennis? Golf? Stamp collecting? Comic books and cast-iron cookware? We could increase the list ad infinitum. This man said he was addicted to many other things as well. He attends many Twelve Step meetings to help him with his myriad of addictions.

For his eating disorder he said he attends Overeaters Anonymous. I didn't see anything out of sorts with his size. He seemed normally height weight proportioned to me. He mentioned his OA sponsor had told him to go to our Sunday night AA meeting. Some smart ass in the OA meeting wanted to bet Niles fifty dollars he wouldn't go to the AA meeting. Niles' Gambling Anonymous sponsor, who was also an overeater, stepped in and said that wouldn't be a good idea.

Niles' GA sponsor is a guy named Todd. Todd lost his family fortune in Vegas and took solace in hitting the $1.99 breakfast buffet at the Circus Circus. Todd also has an overpowering addiction to movies. He is specifically addicted to movies starring Ethel Merman. He watched the movie the Poseidon Adventure and he rewound and watched one scene over and over. It was the scene where the heavy-set woman attempts to swim to safety. Imagine his dismay when he watched the credits at the end and discovered it was Shelly Winters, not Ethel Merman who played the role in that movie.

Niles said his OA sponsor invited his GA sponsor and his Emotions Anonymous sponsor to the OA potluck. Wow, my head was spinning. What do you take to an Overeaters Anonymous potluck?

Niles went on to share how he had become addicted to checkers. He played checkers until he lost his job, all his money, and his self-respect. Niles would wake up each morning and resolve not to play checkers at all. Soon he would take to the streets with his little checkers box tucked under his arm. He would wander around until he could find someone to play checkers with.

He became belligerent and often violent when his opponent would call an end to the game. Soon he was held up to ridicule, darkness descended upon him, he lost all hope. He and his wife and their two children were living in the carport of a relative when the family did an intervention. Each member of the family got a chance to tell Niles how his obsession with checkers had affected his life, and in turn how it had affected their lives. He admitted he was powerless over checkers and agreed to get help. He promised to stay off the streets and he vowed to beat the checkers demon. He would recover, he was willing to go to any lengths.

He went cold turkey off the checkers and was doing well until the family went out for dinner to an Italian pizza restaurant. When he saw the red and white checkered tablecloths, he began to breath heavily. He became lightheaded and his vision blurred. He slowly gained his composure and called his Overthinkers Anonymous sponsor.

His Overthinkers sponsor showed up with Niles' Compulsive Boardgame Players Anonymous sponsor - along with his companion service parrot - and eventually Niles settled down and was able to eat his spaghetti and meatballs. He called his OA sponsor and they discussed his obsession with ordering the extra meatball, the garlic bread, and the spumoni. He didn't get the garlic bread and meatball, but secretly ordered the spumoni which he snuck into the bathroom and ate.

My first thought was this guy has more sponsors than the Super Bowl. He would have to carry a three-ring binder in order to keep his Fourth Step inventories straight. I wondered how hard it would be to keep all his anniversary dates organized. He must fill up the entire tray with Twelve Step birthday coins when he goes through a metal detector. I wondered how he kept all his sponsors' phone numbers listed in his cell phone. He probably lists them as sponsor, Twelve Step Group, and then name. It would look something like this:

Sponsor - People Who Obsess About the 1909 Penny Anonymous - Doug-206/555-1909
Sponsor- Husky Football Anonymous-Joe-206/555-1111
Sponsor-Fingernail Biters Anonymous-Shirley-425/555-9999

I was thinking of the ways this guy could have multiple relapses in one single motion. Let's say he bets a guy in GA he won't bite his fingernails. Then he sneaks off alone and eats a hot fudge brownie delight from Dairy Queen. He accidently gets some brownie material under his fingernails. Not wanting to waste good food he bites his fingernails to get the full value out of the brownie. In one motion he loses his anniversary in three programs. He slips in OA, GA, and FBA, all at the same time. But I digress.

It seems like there are a ton of Twelve Step groups out there. I hope each organization may help its members in the way AA has helped millions of seemingly hopeless drunks. My original point of this correspondence was to ask how appropriate it is for people with non-AA related issues to attend closed AA meetings. So here's my question:

I worry our newcomers may become confused if they hear people talking about their addiction to the board game Monopoly, instead of talking about how they overcame their obsession with alcohol.

Is it just me or will AA's single purpose message get watered down if we allow people with other problems to attend our meetings?

Steve, with only one sponsor

***

AA Reply – June 2007

Dear Steve,

Each group has but one primary purpose, to carry the message to the alcoholic who still suffers. People with poly-addictions and other problems may attend closed meetings. But everything has its place, thus when one shares in an AA meeting about their obsession with building a hotel on Marvin Gardens or taking a ride on the Reading Railroad someone needs to step up and defend our program.

Our fellowship will not survive if we allow our message to become diluted. Keep up the good work Steve.

Sincerely,

AA

***

October 2007

Dear AA,

I met a nice lady at the 12 Step Club. We met at the 5:00 pm Happy Hour meeting a couple of weeks ago.

I've been careful about starting relationships since my past attempts at romance have turned out badly. I've been doing some intense Step work with my sponsor. I've been working with newcomers and have helped guide a few guys through the Steps. I'm feeling pretty good about my progress.

This lady is attractive, and we seem to share a lot in common. I asked her if she wanted to go to Denny's for coffee after the meeting. We had a great conversation. We continued to do this together for a few weeks.

We seem to have run into a snag in our floundering relationship. Things had been heating up between us when the topic of sober time came up. She said she felt intimidated because I have thirty one years and she only has nine months. She mentioned her probation and ongoing legal hassles.

With regard to dating I've heard there is a formula people use which is half your age, plus seven. So for instance, a fifty-year old could date a woman aged thirty-two.

My question is this, does AA have a mathematical formula for dating in sobriety?

Steve , dating a girl with a blow and go

***

AA Reply – October 2007

Dear Steve,

AA relationships are more mysterious than the origins of the universe. There is no exact formula. Though if both parties are working on their individual programs things tend to turn out for the better.

For further thought one may consider the fact many AA's now enjoying healthy intimate relationships have arrived at that point by not letting greed, lust or envy direct their decision making.

You know the answer, Steve. There is no math involved.

Sincerely,

AA

*****

It was April of 2008. I had brought from the office a letter to Beryl's apartment. Beryl was living the last days of her life. She had chosen hospice at home. Along with myself and her nurses she had around the clock care.

I'd moved in taking as much time away from the office as necessary; I'd stay with Beryl until the end. She was my family. All that was left of it.

Looking back now, my mother and father were both gone. My grandparents had passed away long ago; I'd never even known my father's parents. Uncle Rick had been gone for over five years. I'd never married and though Donny and I talked often on the phone and would get together for dinner when he came into town our relationship had turned into more of a close friendship like that I had with Rosalie.

I still spoke to her regularly – once a week after the Sunday meeting, East Coast time. She'd moved back to Burgundy with her wife Marnie and ran a successful restaurant on her family's vineyard. She'd done well with Marnie. They were happy together and Marnie had accepted with some grace the fact as a female American chef in France she might never receive a Michelin three star rating – regardless of her wife's family wealth, heritage and the connections which came with that.

It had almost destroyed their marriage. The first three years after leaving New York had been difficult on the two of them.

Starting the restaurant began with ease and fanfare but that only lasted as long as Marnie didn't exert any *American* ideas on menu selections, meal styling, preparation and presentations. And for any chef, that was a recipe for disaster.

Marnie was no dummy, is no dummy and she knew there would be somewhat of an uphill battle to become established and respected. But she didn't – nor did any of us – consider the possibility of a consortium of chefs in the neighboring towns and hamlets organizing a blacklisting of anyone who chose to work with her. And it all happened literally overnight. A Friday night's full reservation list arrived to be greeted by an apologetic Rosalie explaining the restaurant had to suddenly close due to an employee walkout.

Marnie was understandably terribly upset and like every other temperamental chef in the world she was not averse to express her anger via the hurling of expletives and the occasional sauté pan across the kitchen.

Rosalie told me when we spoke the next day, she had thought this was it, it was over. Their marriage, their new life in France together along with their joint business. It was all over.

Marnie was in full fury in the kitchen with Rosalie trying to calm her. They had only three hours before people began to arrive for drinks and then dinner. Marnie was cursing the French and their attitudes about American Cuisine and Americans in general. Rosalie, worn out from the circular arguing and Marnie's tirade finally said, "Fwack a Dwack. Fwack a dwack, Marnie".

Rosalie told me Marnie had stopped yelling to say, "What? Fwockawhak?" Rosalie had apparently never used Uncle Rick's signature line with Marnie before. She explained to me she said it over and over, "Fwack a Dwack, fwack a dwack" but Marnie just wasn't understanding.

By this point in the story hearing Rosalie over the phone telling it, we were both in tears with laughter. Finally Marnie understood and Rosalie said it was as if all the stress which had been building over the last year just evaporated. Uncle Rick from the Great Beyond had helped two more people in need of it

The two of them laughed and decided together they would open on time serving nothing but Marnie's American French Toast along with a vast assortment of fresh jams and jellies, sauces and brulees to accompany it and anyone who didn't like it could just go fwack a dwack.

The breakfast for dinner was received well and the two of them began brunch sittings which have become quite popular. The local walkout was lifted and Marnie is slowly becoming accepted in the community of chefs as a force d'être compté avec of sorts.

I can go on and on and in this case I think, no...I know it's to distract myself from writing – and in so doing, reliving to a degree – my last days spent with Beryl.

Immediately I am compelled to call my sponsor Darla, to ask her help in discovering why all these years later I still push that time out of my mind when thoughts of it arise. I want to write an inventory of exactly what it is I am feeling and what's my best educated guess as to what's driving those feelings. And I like writing inventories. I've become rather prolific at it over the years. I don't do it daily as the Tenth Step suggests but I write them at least weekly.

Darla recently suggested to me I might be writing inventories to avoid dealing with the very issues I am identifying in my writings. That wouldn't have made any sense to me at all if not for the fact it made perfect sense. More of that mysterious and beautiful Zen Heart of AA.

Two days before Beryl died and left this world I had gone to the office to pick up a letter. A letter from Steve. I had previously told my assistant Jon to keep an eye out for anything with a Bellevue, Washington State return address. He'd texted me that morning to say a letter had arrived the day before postmarked from Seattle with only the name *Steve* along with a return address in Bellevue. I told Beryl I was going out for my morning run and would be back soon. I wanted to surprise her.

When I returned an hour later I walked into the living room where she lay on the couch. With an outreaching of my arms followed by my best attempt at a stage bow I stated the Sorority of Steve was now in session. Beryl was smiling back at me and doing her best to clap her hands – she had been very weakened by her condition – she said, "Read on, honey, read on."

I sat down next to her, opened the letter, and read aloud.

*****

April 2008

Dear AA,

I have my hands full with my new sponsee. His name is Dan, but we call him Danger Dan, or Dangerous Dan. He's an intense guy, an overthinker blessed or cursed with enormous intelligence. He's taken up the game of golf and it's become quite a problem.

He has an obsessive, compulsive, addictive personality. This personality combined with a game like golf has opened an institutional size can of worms. He has taken up residence with the lovely lady, Strawberry Jane. She's known as Strawberry Jane because she grew up on an organic berry farm in the town of Monroe, Washington. Her grandmother, Betty Nelson, provided the land which hosted the Sky River Rock Festival and Lighter Than Air Fair in the summer of 1968.

Jane and Dangerous Dan live in a simple 1930's white farmhouse near the banks of the Skykomish River. Jane loves Dan and at first, she supported his need to get out and play golf. She is prone to obsessive and addictive behavior herself, so she took up crochet to pass the time while Dan golfed. Strawberry Jane has now knitted together enough sweaters to supply half the homeless women in King County.

I went golfing with Dangerous Dan and his golf gang last weekend. What an adventure it is to go golfing with a bunch of guys from the Program. Dan has been playing every weekend and practicing every day in between. Golf is an exceedingly difficult game to master and Dan is a perfectionist prone to fits of rage.

This toxic conflagration of difficulties and emotions came to a fateful conclusion on the fairway of the 12th hole. It's a 385-yard par four with a wide entry and a straight path to the green. There is a small lake in front of the green however, you can drive the ball straight down the fairway and then take a second shot over the water to the green.

Dan had displayed some mounting frustration with his game on the earlier holes. At one point he missed an easy three-foot putt for par on the second hole par 3. He stomped on the green and called his ball a "No-good cock sucking motherfucking son of a bitch whore."

He tapped in the second putt , took the ball out of the cup, and threw it up in the air trying to hit it, baseball style, into the woods. Instead of hitting the ball straight on he fouled it off and it ended up in a nearby sand trap. He stomped into the bunker to pick up the ball and stepped on the rake and it flung up, hitting him square on the kneecap. He picked up the rake and threw it. He then stormed out onto the fairway to retrieve it, carrying it back to the bunker to rake the trap furiously. He then picked up the ball and threw it into the woods. He muttered something about the ball and "its mother and its father and its sister too."

As his sponsor I felt I needed to have a little talk with him. I took him aside and suggested he might be a little too caught up in the intensity of the game. I suggested he might be missing the entire point of what we were doing out here. He admitted he was getting a little wound up and he professed his desire to calm down and just enjoy the fresh air and the camaraderie of being out here with the guys. He said he wasn't obsessed with golf, he thought he could quit any time he wanted, he just needed to settle down a little and everything would be fine.

On the next hole he hit his drive tall and far down the fairway with a bit of a hook. Unfortunately, the ball trailed off at the end of its trajectory and followed its hooked path into the woods where we could hear it hitting several trees. Dan tossed his driver straight down the fairway, hammer style and we could see the sun shining off the shaft as it traveled a good twenty yards making a "whoosh, whoosh, whoosh" sound as it flew through the air.

Dan then stomped around saying, "Worthless cocksucking piece of god damn horseshit driver. I paid a hundred bucks for that no-good chicken shit piece of god damn son of a cocksucker."

I rolled my eyes and told Dan he could hit his second shot from where his driver landed since he'd never find his first shot deep in the surrounding forest. He was seeing red and didn't find my comment very funny.

When we reached the 12th hole Dan wasn't saying much. He hit his drive right down the middle of the fairway. He was in pretty good shape for his second shot. All he had to do was hit the ball over the water with his seven iron and he could get it on or near the green.

He lined up to hit the ball and he topped it and the ball took a weird flight path. It went up for a while and then turned straight down and went splash, straight into the water. He calmly took another ball out of his bag and dropped it on the ground. He hit this shot off the heel of the club and the ball took off, about five feet above the water. It hit about mid-lake and skipped like a stone, almost, but not quite making it to the other side sinking about three feet from the far shore.

Dan became animated and irate and stomped up and down, beating his seven iron into the ground. He then ran to the water's edge and launched his club, tomahawk style, straight up in the air. It came down with a splash about 25 feet from the shore. He then yelled, "No good monkey fucking sack of rats ass pig fucking piece of god damn shit seven iron. Rust and rot at the bottom of that no-good cocksucking mother fucking lake you stinking fucking piece of shit."

He then stormed back up to the rest of us, stopping by the 150-yard marker. Looking up at the green, he said, "That's no god damn 150 yards. Who the hell measured this fucking piece of shit golf course?" Dangerous Dan then grabbed his six iron and dropped another ball. He took a full swing, at first it looked like he made good contact with the ball but I immediately noticed a big divot came up with the shot. Apparently he had gotten under the ball a little too much. The shot went high up and at first it looked like he got just enough of the ball to carry it over the water. He was waving his arm like Pete Townshend at the Monterey Pop Festival yelling, "Carry, carry, carry you no good piece of horseshit ball!"

His pleading was to no avail and we saw the ball make a dreaded splash about two feet from a safe landing just across the lake. We had all hit our shots over the water. In fact, my ball had made the green and I had about a twenty-foot birdie putt coming up.

Dan went completely off the rails when his third shot went in the water. He again ran down to the lake , this time carrying his golf bag. He then spun around like a discus thrower, running toward the edge of the water. He slipped , stumbled, and dropped the bag, its clubs spilling out on the fairway as he slid down the slippery bank into the water.

He jumped out of the water, put all the clubs back in the bag and launched everything, bag, clubs and all into the lake. There was a big splash and the bag and clubs disappeared in what looked to be about ten feet of water. From where the rest of us then stood atop the green you could see the bag sitting at the bottom of the lake. Dan, dripping wet, joined us up on the green and looked down at the bag at the lake bottom saying, "God damn son of a motherfucking whore, kicked in the balls with steel toed boots, no good piece of fucking cat shit golf clubs."

As his sponsor I felt it fell upon me to tell him his keys and wallet with driver's license and credit cards all now lay at the bottom of this nameless little lake at the River's Bend Golf Course in nowhere Carnation, Washington.

Dangerous Dan was about to become Deep Sea Diver Dan as he had to go into Mike Nelson mode and dive in and retrieve his golf bag. He waded in and dove headfirst and came up with the bag on the first try. It was a hot summer day and he professed none of this was a big deal because everything would dry off soon. Since he was already soaking wet, he dove in a few more times and came up with about a dozen new golf balls.

Nobody was behind us needing to play through so we shot the bull waiting for Dan to wring out his shirt and shorts and dry off a bit. We all then, Dan included, shared a decent laugh about the scene. We let Dan drop a ball on the fringe of the green and after three putts he managed to sink the ball into the hole.

Somewhere on the 14th fairway I realized Dan had never done the deep-sea dive for the seven iron that he first tossed into the lake. He said, "That thing is a no-good piece of shit anyway, I never liked it. Let it be gone from this world forever at the bottom of that no-good cock sucking lake".

After we wrapped up our round, I drove back to the strawberry farm with Dan. On this drive I laid out to Dan the fact golf was a measuring stick for his life. I pointed out he was obsessed with the game and he was currently too emotionally unstable to ever expect to be a very good player. I suggested he spend more time hanging out on the banks of the Skykomish with his strawberry love, Strawberry Jane.

But I digress

Here's my question:

It seems like people in recovery tend to go headfirst over heels, wild and crazy, ten thousand miles an hour into activities with the *same addictive energy they pursued their other destructive addictions.*

Is it possible to achieve balance in life? Can I/we find things we enjoy without destroying everything in our wake?

It seems like we should be able to learn to exercise moderation in some areas. I know I've become more aware of when I'm obsessing about things.

Steve, with a full set of clubs

*****

I believe I can say as objectively as possible, that I am a relatively happy person. I have a good sense of humor and have enjoyed much fun and laughter with friends and family over the years. I can say the same for Beryl. In short, we both laugh regularly and genuinely.

It took us a half hour to get through Steve's latest. The scenes he described with his sponsee on the golf course literally had me convulsing with laughter. I fell to the floor and cried with it. I had to force myself up because I was worried about Beryl, that Steve's letter might kill her.

She was shaking her head and holding her big smile giggling after yet another coughing fit caused by her laughter. She said, "Don't worry, I'm okay honey. And dying of laughter wouldn't be a bad way to go out."

We spent the rest of the day talking about everything from Beryl's early days in the Program, and some of the characters she'd known in the meetings in those days, to all that had changed in the Central Office over the years and how we both strongly agreed AA to be likely the most impactful and successful social endeavor of the 20th Century.

We discussed Uncle Rick and how much she loved him and how grateful she was for every moment with him and more so her gratitude for the fact she lived those moments as fully aware and present as was possible.

Beryl told me every single thing wonderful in her life since 1965 – when she stopped drinking and became a member of AA - she had experienced because of the simple fact she had stayed sober and to the best of her ability, daily worked the AA Program.

We discussed my love life and its ups and downs and how I was beginning to feel less in need of a romantic partner yet still wanted one; but I had no sense of urgency or feeling of a lack of completeness without one.

Throughout our long talk that day and the silences we shared in between topics, Steve's latest letter kept coming up and we'd laugh all over again. I had set the letter down, for the tenth time or more. We were quiet for a while. I was smiling, content, happily lost in thoughts of a thousand different things. I was beginning to doze a bit. Beryl jarred me out of it saying, "Summer Anne honey, you'll have to write the replies from now on. The replies to Steve's letters."

Beryl knew me well, better than anyone else. She knew I'd fall apart if she brought that up; the need for me to write the replies to Steve which would be for one reason and one reason only. That being Beryl would be gone.

I found out at her memorial service she'd had my assistant Jon hold Steve's latest letter for two weeks instructing him to send me the text of its arrival when she knew her time was close at hand.

She knew me well. Steve's letters were ours. Beryl's and mine. And the thought of her not there to write the replies, to share the letters with, to have more conversations brought up by whatever Steve had been writing about and how Beryl chose to reply... The thought of her no longer there; to share together each and every envelope wrapped present postmarked in Seattle and sent across the continent...she knew I'd fall apart so she waited. She waited until a point in time in which I would not fall apart. I might cry – and I did – but I didn't fall apart because I knew Beryl and I knew my assistant Jon. I suspected the latest letter might have been

161

delayed a bit and I suspected why Beryl might arrange what she managed to arrange.

I looked her in the eye and told her yes, I knew I would have to write the replies and I would do her proud.

*****

Chapter Nine
Living And Working

It was late in May of 2016. I was nearing a milestone in my recovery. Thirty years of sobriety. The big Saturday Night Alive But For The Grace of God meeting chairperson had asked me to speak. Of course, I accepted though I just didn't feel up for it. 500 people or more regularly go to that meeting on speaker night which is held the last Saturday of every month.

"I always answer 'Yes' when asked to be of service in AA," Beryl had often said to me. Come to think of it, she'd said it to me just about as often as I had said to her I didn't want to be coffee maker at the Monday Madness meeting or clean-up person at the Tuesday Tonight meeting or GSR of the Friday Night Steps Group.

I absolutely did not in any way, shape, or form want to be chairperson of the Sunday Morning Lapsed Women meeting – I didn't care for women only meetings at the time. And a women's meeting by that name? I wasn't even sure I knew what it meant...a lapsed woman? Huh?

Over time, as with everything else I've applied myself toward in my journey through life as a member of AA, I figured it out. Figured it out for me, that is. Today the Lapsed Women meeting is my homegroup and there is nowhere I'd rather be on Sunday mornings. And every service position I'd ever taken on was rewarding in more ways than I can count.

I guess I've been fortunate. And willing. Always willing to turn my will and my life over to the care of my higher power. And She, He, It – doesn't matter – often spoke through Beryl. Beryl...God, I miss her. I miss her so bad sometimes it physically hurts.

Beryl never once ordered or directed me to do anything. She only suggested courses of action. Most often discussing what she had done in a similar situation. Only if I pressed her, would she speak of what she herself might do in my situation. In the end she always left it up to me to decide my own course.

And I made some mistakes; some small and some not so small. The larger mistakes had names. Brooklyn Bobby was one. He broke my heart. And almost my career, my ability to work for the organization I love.

After everything came out, even though I was entirely vindicated, it must have taken every last favor Beryl had owed to her to keep the Trustees from making sure I never worked for any non-profit again much less the one they sat on the board of.

Bobby and I were together for almost five years. We'd met when I was still going to school and working part time in the corporate office of a chain of auto parts stores. He was in charge of IT for the company. He was a hard worker and very smart. The company had fifty stores in the five boroughs and ten across the river in New Jersey. Bobby implemented state of the art point of sale and inventory systems which were a vast improvement over the previous systems.

Bobby would often come pick me up after work. He was very personable and was always chatting it up with someone in the office while I was finishing for the day. In getting to know my co-workers, especially our own IT people, he had gained access to the donation accounts. 857,000 stolen dollars later he was caught after leaving a digital paper trail in my name.

Then there was Donny. He was a street dancer, making it big after getting clean and sober at 16 years old. Like Bobby he was great with people and along with his talent and dedication established himself as a name in the dancing business. He worked hard and auditioned every chance he had for every gig available. He danced for the hottest stars in pop music for ten years.

Donny made great money and was one of the very few in that industry who didn't blow it all on fast living. He was sober and in the Program but being on the road so much he didn't make it to that many meetings. This may have contributed to how and why our relationship ended but then again maybe not. We all have our own path and who am I to critique his and how it may or may not have been better trod upon?

He knew early on his dancing days were limited – it's a young person's game – so at 22 years of age he paid his own way into Juilliard, graduating four years later with a BFA in dance. All the while still working and summer touring. Following Julliard, he continued to dance for the day's pop mega-stars, but choreography was his true love. Along with Bruce in San Francisco I discovered.

It was the year before, 2015. Donny had flown to San Francisco to work on a music video for a rising new star. I was looking forward to his return having arranged a romantic dinner at our favorite date night destination. A rooftop restaurant in the neighborhood Rosalie, a close friend from the program, operated in late spring through summer. She and her partner Marnie were going to pull out all the stops making it a night to remember.

There'd been some distance developing between us, me and Donny, but we'd discussed it - well, we discussed the need to discuss things - before his trip and I was sure everything would be just fine, better than fine but great. We both had strong programs and long term sobriety. Of course everything would be great.

In fact, I was so sure things would go right I'd spent a thousand dollars on a new dress and shoes. Rosalie would call them fmp's that would do Amy Winehouse proud. Rosalie and I shared a love for her fabulous singing voice and a sadness for her tragic alcoholic demise.

When my phone rang the night before Donny's return from San Francisco and I saw it was him I thought he was calling to say good night and tell me how much he was looking forward to arriving back the next day.

Instead he told me he'd fallen in love with Bruce and would be staying in San Francisco indefinitely. Bruce, a man. A man named Bruce. Bruce, he'd told me, was a local producer on the shoot who he'd known through the business off and on for ten years.

I didn't know what to say except "What?" over and over. And to ask him who in the hell in today's world comes out as gay at 51 years of age while living for years with his girlfriend.

He'd answered that he did. Then he broke down and cried. He cried while I sat there stupidly staring at the phone in my hand, listening to him cry. "Fuck a duck," I said and hung up.

The next morning I called Rosalie to cancel the dinner reservations. When I told her what had happened she immediately came over to my place, made me breakfast, sat with me for a couple hours leaving at noon and insisting I dress up and meet her for dinner at the restaurant. She could take the night off, she'd said. Her partner Marnie was a chef and pretty much ran the restaurant, kitchen, and floor. Rosalie was the face of the restaurant, greeting patrons and chatting them up throughout the evening.

"Rosalie, you need to work, it's your restaurant and this is the beginning of your season and," she'd interrupted me telling me to shut up, she owned the business and the building below it and could do whatever she wanted and she wanted to take the night off and have dinner with me.

That evening she joined me not as the owner of the restaurant taking some time for her friend but as a friend taking time for her friend, Marnie making sure nobody disturbed us. We had a great dinner and dessert and sat under the stars on a warm Manhattan night talking and drinking coffee until three in the morning.

When the subject of Donny came up, early on, I had cried but my tears quickly turned to tears of laughter when Rosalie with her heavy French accent kept saying, "Fwack a dwack, Summer, fwack a dwack." She'd known Uncle Rick having been a close AA friend of mine for over 20 years. That girl has always been able to put a smile on my face, making me laugh and that night I needed it like never before.

***

When I awoke that Saturday morning, the day of the speaker meeting, I didn't want to get out of my pajamas and even go outside for my morning walk. I didn't want to go to the coffee shop I went to on most Saturdays before and after the 11 a.m. Brunch Busters meeting.

Out of nowhere, Steve the crazy letter writer popped into my head. I wondered if he'd ever felt the same, if he'd ever had a day where he just didn't want to face the world, face life, but knew he had to pick himself up and do something. Something productive that would give him a boost to get out there and back into life.

Slow down girl, I told myself. I was putting all my own feelings into the persona of a person I'd never met. It didn't matter why Steve wrote his letters to AA. Well, it did matter but it didn't matter that I didn't know the reason for it. Well maybe that did too and, fuck a duck, maybe he could just tell me some day.

Right then I had an overwhelming urge to write my own letter. My own letter to AA.

I sat down. I'd been pacing back and forth across my apartment. I was a pacer, doing my best thinking while pacing. Or the other way around maybe. My best pacing while thinking? I didn't need to get caught up with thoughts of pacing and thinking right then. I knew that. I also knew I wouldn't have known it if I hadn't been pacing and thinking while doing it so I shouldn't be so quick to stop thinking about my pacing. In fact, maybe I should get up and pace some more so to get my thoughts straight on this letter...

Fuck a duck, was I as crazy as Steve? No, he was definitely crazier than me. I smiled and laughed out loud, surprising myself. And started typing.

***

May 2016

Dear AA,

My name is Summer Anne. I'm an alcoholic and I don't know what to say. In some ways I feel like I've got nothing to show for my life. My 50 years of age. No husband, no idyllic marriage, no children coming home from college to summer in the Hamptons at our vacation house.

My last boyfriend I was with for eight years. I thought he was it. The one. I thought he was going to ask me to marry him. I thought I might even say yes if he did. It turns out he was thinking about another man. A man named Bruce.

Bruce... why is it so many gay men are named Bruce? In fact, do I know any Bruce's who aren't gay? There's Bruce at the office, he's what you'd say...well, what he says about himself; if he was any more flaming than he is you'd have to call the fire department.

There's my good friend Bruce A. from the Tuesday Night meeting. Central casting gay with his tight jeans and Freddy Mercury mustache. And Bruce the barista at the coffee shop.

We've gotten to know each other over the last year. He's a nice kid. He and his boyfriend want to go shopping with me.

How could I have not known? In looking back and being truly honest with myself I guess there were some signs. His Judy Garland T-shirts? Well, maybe. But what straight guy wears a Liza Minelli T-shirt? And professional dancer or not you only watch Cabaret so many times unless...And speaking of movies what straight guy chooses Barbara Streisand films for a movie marathon weekend? I like Babs, who doesn't, but Funny Girl and Funny Lady followed by Bette Midler in Beaches, Dolly Parton in 9 to 5 and Olivia Newton John in Xanadu?

***

I stopped writing. I didn't have a question. Steve always had a question. And I realized I might be digressing. Steve would know. He's an expert digresser.

He'd been writing in for forty years. Forty years. I've thought of him before of course. I've been answering his letters for the previous eight years since Beryl had passed away. And I've been reading his letters and her replies to him for almost thirty years.

There had to be some therapeutic value to writing those letters. Between the AA Program, the letters and whatever else Steve did he was staying sober. Maybe the letters were a way to reach out which was different in some way from what we do in normal daily life.

And this letter I was writing.. who would I send it to? I was the AA Steve sent all his letters to. I was it. AA for Steve...fuck a duck, if he only knew.

But then I knew. My letter would be to Beryl. She was my AA to write to. And I realized I had a question. I continued on. With my letter to AA. My letter to Beryl.

*****

Donny...I felt it just today...today while writing about him in this letter. In remembering our break-up. Thinking back on it I realized I felt hurt by it. Duh...of course, that's basic but what I'm talking about is how I remember it today, in a retrospective sense.

And today, right now as I write this I remember it as me being hurt and not me being hurt by him. At first, last year when this all took place the pain I felt was all wrapped up in him and what he did to me. Did to me to hurt me. And the feelings associated with it were an incredulous disbelief mixed with anger followed by resentment and more anger.

Thank god for the Program. For AA and the Steps. They have changed me, woken me up to become aware of patterns of thinking and how those lead to patterns of perception. I might have become trapped in a self-defeating downward spiral of anger and resentment and I've seen what that does to a person. It turns them bitter. Bitter about life and love and possibility.

And becoming bitter scared me more than drinking. So, I did what I knew I needed to do. I stayed sober, went to meetings, and most importantly stayed close to my most trusted AA friends because as I understand them they understand me.

And, and this is a big "and"...I stayed true to myself to the best of my ability and as a result I experienced a psychic change in my thinking.

It may not sound like much but to me it's a big deal. A fuck a duck really big deal. Donny didn't hurt me. He was and still is, simply living his life. Being himself. A child of God. A child of his God, your God, God's God. He's no different than me or anyone else. We are children of God. Doing the best we can with what we have and who we are.

My lingering resentment along with its simmering anger toward Donny has vanished. They are just gone. And in their place is acceptance. And love.

So my question to you AA, to you Beryl is this: What do I do now?

Ken Davies and April McKernan

*****

I'd finished my letter. Then I looked at the clock. Perfect. I had plenty of time to get ready and get on over to the big Saturday Night Alive speaker meeting. I was looking forward to it. I was looking forward to sharing my experience, strength, and hope.

The next day I slept in an hour longer than normal for me on a Sunday. I'd been up late the night before. The meeting had gone well. Though I was at first a bit nervous speaking in front of so many – I'd later heard there were over 700 people there – I quickly felt at ease. Even though I'd rarely gone to this meeting I knew I was at home there. I was one among hundreds who just like me were committed to recovery from alcoholism.

The best part of the night was after the meeting. I'd gone to coffee at an all-night diner with a group of people from the meeting and an hour later after many laughs and more coffee, pie, and ice cream than any of us needed they all left to go home for the night. All but one. A young woman in her twenties new in the program who hadn't said much stayed behind. The two of us talked for another hour finally leaving to go our own way for the night with plans to meet again to talk some more the following Saturday.

It was Sunday morning, my favorite time on my favorite day of the week during my favorite time of the year. After breakfast I changed out of my PJ's and into one of my favorite summer dresses. A dress Beryl had bought me ten years before. I hadn't worn it since she passed.

I was about to leave my apartment but quickly turned on my heels in the hallway, went back to my office and sat at the desk. I had a reply to type. The official *AA Reply* to my letter of the day before. I knew what Beryl would say to me. I opened my laptop and began typing.

***

AA Reply – May 2016

Dear Summer Anne,

The answer to your question is simple. And straight from the Zen Heart and the Zen Mind of AA.
You are living your answer.

With much love,

AA

*****

I walked down the street. On my way to my homegroup meeting. With a smile on my face I started skipping, a 49 year old woman skipping like a kid right down West 12th. I stopped at the first corner taking in everything around me. The sounds, the smells, the blue sky and warm sun overhead.

Writing letters to AA was pretty darn good therapy. I thought of Steve, wondering if it was as beautiful a day in Seattle and maybe he too, at that very moment was looking up into a blue sky on a warm morning. I also thought of where I was at that moment. The here and now of it, so to speak. The contentment I felt and the ongoing gratitude I had for my state of mind which had long before let go of thoughts I expressed in meetings in my early years. Thoughts primarily of "How do I get from here to there?" *There* always being some ethereal point in the future where everything in my life would be just....you know, just perfect. Whatever perfect was. Letting go of those thoughts has been one of my greatest victories over self, over ego, to this day. Today and for some years now I know for me there exists only the *here* and the now. The *there* is not a place where I live. I'm reminded of Quiet Quince again. He told me life is about our actions in the now and the results of those actions are where God lives. I can go on and on.

Beryl once told me I was a mental wanderer. That was the only time I can recall I ever differed with her on a personal assessment of me. I told her no, I was not a mental wanderer. I was a mental *wonderer*. She thought a moment looking at me and smiled, saying "Summer Anne honey, I stand corrected. A *wonderer* is exactly what you are and every life you touch is richer for it including, of course mine."

***

Backing up a little, it was the *here and now* of August of 2008 when the next letter from Steve crossed my desk. I'd been dreading it because I knew it would bring back all the pain of my loss of Beryl. I also knew that life goes on and I must go on with it.

Without allowing myself to ponder those thoughts for too long I opened the letter and read.

*****

August 2008

Dear AA,

I rushed out of work last week and went to a meeting. It was a Saturday night and I went to the big speaker meeting in my hometown. I arrived there just as the meeting was starting and managed to secure one of the last seats in the auditorium. I took my jacket off as soon as I sat down. I had come from my business, a local pizza restaurant.

It wasn't until I took my jacket off, I realized I was wearing a Mac and Jack African Amber Ale T-shirt. Dave, the local brewery rep keeps our staff regularly stocked with a fresh batch of T-shirts.

We wear them as a way of promoting our local breweries. These shirts are perfectly proper for the pizza joint. But here I was, sitting in an AA meeting, with a beer shirt on.

I wondered what would happen if someone saw the shirt and it set off a craving for alcohol. My mind drifted off into one of its doomsday fantasies. I was thinking about ten years in the future... I would be at a meeting and I'd hear the speaker say:

"I was four years sober and had put my life back together. I had regained the trust of my wife, my kids, and my employer. I hadn't had any cravings or compulsions to drink in a long time. I had a few sponsees and was in the process of leading a couple of guys through the Steps.

"Then I went to the Saturday night speaker meeting in Bellevue and I saw a guy wearing a Mac and Jack African Amber Ale T-shirt. My next thought was something like, 'Well I've never had Mac and Jack before. Maybe it will be different. Maybe I won't get in a fight or go to jail if I drink this brand of beer.'

"I then made the fatal mistake of picking up a Mac and Jack beer and thus began one more trip to the asylum. I ended up in a Skid Road mission with a guy named Reverend Jim. Legend has it he was an ex-Seattle cop who had flunked out of the seminary. He applied for a theology school but was turned down. He finally gained his collar and robe when he discovered the Church of Lunar Awareness in a Google search. He ordered a robe, inflatable pulpit, collar, bible, and a master's degree in theology from their internet gift shop. Reverend Jim took me under his wing and helped nurse me back to life. We would go up to Gais Bakery in the mission van and load it up with day old bread. Then we would drive around and hand out Kaiser rolls and bagels to the downtrodden of Seattle's streets.

"I've been sober ten years now and have built a whole new life. I have a new wife, and we're expecting a baby in the fall. I went back to school and got my master's degree in psychology and now

work in the field, helping people who struggle with this horrible disease.

"It took me a long time to get over the resentment I had against the guy who wore the beer shirt to the meeting that night. I couldn't help but blame him for destroying my life. When I look back, I should have been able to handle seeing the guy in that shirt. Still I wonder what ever possessed him to wear a beer shirt to an AA meeting.

"Oh well. I now stand on firm bedrock upon which a happy and purposeful life is being built. If I go to a meeting and see some clown wearing a T-shirt that says, 'Miller High Life, The Champagne of Bottled Beers' I'll be able to handle it."

Can you imagine how I would feel when I heard this guy speak? All I would be able to think about was that night over ten years before, and how I should have kept my jacket on.

I'm careful now to wear neutral colors to meetings. I did wear a 'Save the Whales' shirt when I went to an AA picnic on Vashon Island. I was trying to impress this hippie girl I met down at the Pike Place Market. I had thought maybe we could get some bees and make honey on the island.

The thing with the Market girl didn't work out, though she was cute and was also a great dancer. But I digress.

Here is my question:

Am I responsible for someone relapsing if they see me at a meeting wearing a beer shirt? I kind of suspect I'm not. I once received a Budweiser King of Beers key chain bottle opener combo from a punk rocker named Jim Crisis for my fourth AA birthday. I never once pondered the possibility of drinking a Budweiser because of it.

Steve with a beer shirt

*****

Up to that point in my life, the reading of Steve's latest letter, I'm not sure if ever there was a single thing more opportunely delivered and received.

I laughed. I cried. I laughed again and cried again. Both of my assistants came into my office and asked if everything was ok. I assured them things couldn't be more ok than at that very moment.

I shooed them out and immediately wrote my reply. Beryl would be proud.

*****

AA Reply – August 2008

Dear Steve,

You are only responsible for your own sobriety and not that of others. It's probably best not to wear beer shirts to AA meetings, though.

Many Regards,

AA

Chapter Ten
No Stopping Now

I had felt satisfied about my first reply to a Steve letter. Satisfied. But there was a gentle nagging I should assert more of myself and less a voice of what I thought may sound like an all knowing AA Oz.

And wouldn't I be the female version of that little middle aged man behind the curtain; offering sage AA wisdom to a man who had nearly ten years more sobriety and AA experience than me? Beryl had eleven years more sober time than Steve so she could get away with it and as far as I was concerned she wasn't pulling levers behind any curtains. She was the AA Oz and she was up front and center and wait a minute...aren't we all? Aren't all of us AA's potential fountains of wisdom to each other. And most of us never even knowing it?

There have been numerous occasions over the years when someone has approached me in a meeting and spoken about how something I shared in a meeting two years before, five years before, ten years even had resonated with them to the point of altering their recovery for the better. And I've heard almost everyone I know in the Program speak of the same thing of having had the same experience.

In fact, I myself have heard people say things which greatly impacted the way I thought about an issue to the point where it literally brought about a change in my thinking and from that a change for the better in my life. In one case, I ran into one of those people and she swore up and down she hadn't been the one to say what had inspired me, that it must have been Melinda A. or Jen H. since it was the sort of the thing those two would say.

It's not that I wanted to....again for lack of a better term, *manufacture* anything wonderful for Steve – or for that matter anyone else. I simply wanted to be myself more than a voice of AA which while still being myself might be less myself. Though I felt somewhat confused about this issue, I was clear on one thing and I knew it was the only thing I needed to be clear on. To thine own self be true.

The letters continued to arrive over the next eight years - from 2009 to 2016 - and as I continued to learn and grow in the Program and in my life in general, I would become more and more true to myself.

*****

March 2009

Dear AA,

I have a dilemma which I felt warranted a letter. When I first got sober, I asked Fifth Step Frank to be my sponsor. He's a regular at the meetings at the 12 Step Club. He has a regular chair he sits in. He has a pack of sponsees which surround him at the meetings. I think I may have outgrown Fifth Step Frank.

I started going to meetings in churches and other locations in my hometown of Bellevue, Washington. I met an interesting guy at the Union Club lunch meeting. He's blind so he needs rides to meetings. He got sober and his sordid past caught up with him. He was convicted of crimes he committed in his drinking days and he spent ten years in prison on McNeil Island. He celebrated sobriety each year he was at the federal penitentiary which is in the south Puget Sound.

After he got out of the joint, he went blind due to complications from diabetes. He claimed to have once been a hit man in Philadelphia. He said he was forced to make a career change after he went blind. He said it played hell on his aim. I asked Blind Nick to be my sponsor.

We got in my car and he pulled out a twenty-dollar bill and held it up. He said in his Philadelphia Godfather voice "Is this a twenty?"

I told him it was indeed a twenty. He took a breath and just like Marlon Brando said, "Let's go to 7-11 and I'll buy you twenty dollars' worth of booze." He went on to say, "I think you're too young to make it sober long-term, Steve." He snapped the bill with both hands and said "What do you think? You want to go to 7-11 and buy a few racks of Miller?"

I said no, I didn't want to go to 7-11 and get beer. I told Blind Nick I was done with drinking forever. I was willing to go to any lengths to stay clean and sober for the rest of my life. I explained to him my sobriety was all or nothing. I told him I would never do any street drugs. I told him I had changed my AA birthday to the last day I smoked weed. Well it was Lebanese hash, but I digress.

Nick directed me to the 12 Step Club in Bellevue. I led him into the club, and he bought me a Big Book. He handed me the book and said, "Since you turned down the offer for the free beer, and you now have a book, don't call me in the middle of the night bellyaching about how you want to drink."

Nick said "I'll be your sponsor kid. We've already done the First Step. I still don't think you'll be able to stay sober at your age."

We bought that Big Book in 1976, I've been sober ever since. Nick was my sponsor for a few years. He was quite a character. His sponsor had had serious colon cancer. He had a colostomy bag that he had to use for the rest of his life. Nick was sitting next to his sponsor at a meeting one night. When they called on Nick to talk, he said "I'm blind and my sponsor doesn't have an asshole. Between the two of us we never have a shitty outlook on life." Half the people laughed, the other half cried. That's my kind of humor.

A girl asked Nick to dance at the regular Friday AA dance at the VFW hall in Renton. I was with a girl and we were dancing right next to Nick. They were playing, "You Really Got Me" by a new band, Van Halen. When the song was over, I told Nick he was a heck of a dancer. He leaned up to my ear whispering and asked me if the girl he was dancing with was a good looking babe. I told him she was gorgeous. He smiled a big Blind Nick smile and snapped his fingers and kept right on dancing into "Brown Eyed Girl" by Van Morrison.

Nick's work with me on the First Step was solid. I had told him I was ready to surrender. He told me he didn't think I would stay sober because he knew by saying that I would take it as a challenge. He was from the old school of AA. He didn't want to waste time trying to talk people out of drinking. He wanted to work with people who had truly hit bottom. I had truly hit bottom, even though I was so young.

I am forever in the debt of Blind Nick. He passed away several years later. I miss him.

Which brings me to my question:

I made the commitment to go all in on sobriety. I've never wavered on this commitment. Do you think this old time AA hard core approach to the First Step will work with today's AA's?

Steve, all in on sobriety

***

AA Reply – March 2009

Dear Steve,

It really comes down to different strokes for different folks. Some people will respond to the hard-core approach, some won't. People start attending meetings for different reasons. Not everyone you meet will be convinced they need a life of sobriety. Most people come to this awareness slowly. Others come to it by way of a burning bush.

It sounds as if Blind Nick was quite a character. I'm sure you are grateful for the time you spent with him.

Sincerely,

AA

***

November 2009

Dear AA,

I've been clean and sober for several years now. I have reached that point described in the Book where I feel safe, protected and in a position of neutrality.

When I first joined, I swear every person in attendance at the meetings was one hundred and four years old. The old farts would look at us younger people, shake their finger at us and go on and on about how lucky we were to have joined when we did. They would drone on about how they had spilled more alcohol on their ties than we ever drank.

They made me feel guilty for having discovered clean and sober living before the age of thirty. Now I've noticed a reversal in fortune has occurred. When I go to meetings the young people look at me and say, "You old people are lucky you got here when you did."

These young people go on about how our weed was weak powered Mexican ditch grown garbage. They remind us of the old days of seeds and stems and ninety dollar a pound bags of leaf. They laugh when I tell stories about how the seeds inside the joint would explode and a live cherry of ashes would land in our laps. And how we had to try and put out this fire while driving our Chrysler K cars at 55 mph on the freeway.

The same kids would go on to lecture us old folks about the perils of today's drug world. It's crazy out there with the crack, meth, heroin, oxy, and everything else.

What the hell happened to the days of drinking Annie Green Springs, smoking eight joints, popping a few reds, and listening to Tales From Topographic Oceans by the band Yes?

By the way, when I worked at the produce terminal on Occidental Avenue back in the 70's I got some killer speed from the long-haul truckers. We would buy these tiny pink pills from a crusty old trucker named Red.

Red called them "L.A. Turnarounds". I asked him one day why they were called by that name. He looked at me through bloodshot eyes that hadn't blinked since he left Salinas and said, "Because you take them, drive to L.A., turn around and drive back."

I popped one of these pink pills before a Grand Funk Railroad concert. We smoked so much Mexican weed that I fell asleep during the drum solo. But I digress.

I'm not sure if I discovered sobriety just in the nick of time or if I missed out on the cool new drugs that are destroying lives at a staggering pace. It's like I'm jealous because I never did meth.

Maybe that makes me not cool enough to be sober. Here's my question, why did I get sober when I did?

Steve the pink pill popper

***

AA Reply – November 2009

Dear Steve,

People who are coming into the rooms today face issues regarding what seems to be best known of as *dual addictions*. An addiction to alcohol and any or all of a host of street and prescription drugs. This is a source of frustration to many traditional members. Many of them want to keep the druggies out of the meetings. But the AA member who has not at least dabbled with drugs is hard to find so it is likely this issue will sort itself out. Our focus on the issue of alcoholism and providing support to those who wish to recover will necessarily include members' other addictive and destructive behaviors engaged in during their drinking days. And these behaviors, more often than not, include the use of drugs.

It must be acknowledged there are complex layers involved in today's recovery world. To your question, insofar as timing goes it would seem to ring true you got sober when you did because it was the perfect time for you to discover sobriety.

Whatever you took or didn't take doesn't really matter. It is important to really listen to the stories of those new people. They are telling the *yets* which may be waiting for any of us were we to relapse. The pink pills you bought from Red might kill another member. The crack the other member is doing might kill you.

Sobriety is a treasured possession, hang on to it and cherish each day you live free of the clutches of alcoholism.

Regards,

AA

***

June 2010

Dear AA,

I have an eccentric sponsee named Logged In Larry. Boy, is he a handful. I gave him some pointers on AA nicknames and he came up with his nickname alliteration.

Larry is one of the few people I've shared my letters with. I have been reluctant to tell people about the correspondence I have with AA. I've not spoken of it because I'm sure you're overwhelmed with hundreds, if not thousands of letters daily or weekly.

I told Larry to write a letter and I promised him I would send it to you. Larry wrote the letter during the 5:00 Happy Hour meeting at the 12 Step Club. He was on a conference call conducting trades on the Australian commodities market. He was typing furiously on a Bluetooth keyboard while muttering into another Bluetooth about pork bellies, corn, and wheat futures. Larry is the world's foremost authority on multi-tasking. Here is his letter:

***

Dear AA,

My name is Larry L. I have an issue which my sponsor Steve suggested might prompt a letter. It is my hope you will provide a solution which will enlighten those with whom I have a conflict.

184

The issue has to do with people at the AA meetings I go to at the local 12 Step Club. They are becoming irritated with me. Their irritation is irrational.

I regularly share about how busy of a guy I am, and I've been going to meetings at the Club for two and a half years now, ever since I became sober and entered the AA Program.

I'm a busy guy and it's important I stay logged into my devices so I can update my calendar and not miss online meetings and conference calls. I must also consider option opportunities with equity and commodity futures. And my high-speed trading algorithms need monitoring, duh ...whose don't?

My fellow AA's at the meetings have become increasingly agitated with me and I don't understand it. I'm on Bluetooth and speak quietly with a hand over my mouth when conferencing so I don't know what their problem is. I'm a very successful multi-tasker and can share my experience, strength and hope while on two conference calls, facetiming a virtual meeting, entering buy and sell orders and puts on the three laptops I position perfectly around me so as not to get into others' personal space.

The meeting room has plenty of electrical outlets and I only use two plus one extension cord and only one power strip. The other day at a Businessperson's Nooner meeting people got upset, blaming me for the coffee being cold saying it was me overloading the circuit when the Club is using coffee pots from the 1960's which are so inefficient they require a dedicated hydro-electric generating plant to operate.

The last time the circuit tripped from a coffee pot overload I was blamed again. The power outage had negative effects on all of us. The people in the meeting complained of sipping the harsh cold coffee. In this room of selfish, self -centered drunks nobody was concerned at all I couldn't execute a buy option on Dow Futures which was a lock for a 2-day ROI of 12%.

I really love AA and it has turned my life around. And these Businessperson Nooner meetings fit perfectly into my very busy schedule. When drinking I was pulling in only $400K - post tax - in a good year and now sober I've averaged over $2.7 Mil annually in pre-tax revenue - I'll attach spreadsheets to illustrate exactly which of the Program's Twelve Steps I worked, when I completed them, and how I best enhanced my margin positions and overall bottom line.

Back to the issue at hand. I'm at my wit's end with these people at the 12 Step Club. My arbitrage people investigated buying the 12 Step Club. At all three Board Meetings I've attended over the last three months they have voted unanimously "No" to a sell. Several of the board members are regulars at my noon meeting. I think they are all out to get me. What do you think?

Sincerely,

Larry L.

***

You have now had a chance to see inside the complex mind of Logged-in- Larry. He has no clue how strange it looks when he is all plugged in and logged on in the meeting room at the club. The manager has gone to the board members to try and come up with a solution. I explained to Larry he couldn't buy the club based on its bylaws.

I've pleaded with the club manager to let me try to reason with Larry. Last week during the noon meeting he made a six-figure profit on a day trade. He had opened his laptop and noticed a short position in a highly speculative tech company. Their prime product was a cutting edge AI talking computer program which was supposed to speak utilizing proper Queen's English. Upon the rollout the voice sounded like that of a customer service rep for Comcast. This caused panic selling as investors ran for the hills triggering a pre-programmed transaction point resulting in a

$265,000 profit for Larry. Larry jumped up out of his seat and started running around the room seeking high fives from the attendees.

It reminded me of the time I went to the Fremont Fellowship Hall and a guy was listening to a football game on a transistor radio. When his team scored a touchdown he erupted in yelling and cheering, right during the meeting.

I'm walking a tightrope with Logged in Larry, I'm not sure what to do.

Do you think I should apply a strong dose of tough love on this guy?

Not Logged on Steve

***

AA Reply – June 2010

Dear Steve,

We can't give advice about how the 12 Step Club should manage its meetings. It seems like having a person wired into the stock exchange and logged into multiple devices would cause a considerable distraction.

Try gentle persuasion with him first. If that doesn't work, then you may have to interrupt his signal.

Sincerely,

AA

***

February 2011

Dear AA,

I recently attended the local Winter Celebration convention in my hometown. The keynote speaker was a guy named Bob. He told a harrowing tale of drinking and drug abuse. In the worst days of his drinking and using he absconded with his daughter's Girl Scout cookie money.

She had gone out and done a great job of selling cookies. She had outsold every Girl Scout in King County. Bob stole the cookie money, bought a rock of blow and a case of champagne. Immediately following he met a couple of wild women with an appetite for cocaine. He then rented a room at the Golden Kent Motel.

He spent a crazy weekend at Longacres Racetrack with the women, the coke, and the ponies. He came-to on the floor of the fleabag motel room on Sunday morning. The cocaine, champagne and wild girls were gone, along with all the Girl Scout cookie money.

His daughter never recovered from the cookie debacle. By the time she was twenty-five she could be spotted shuffling into the local K-Mart. She would drive her Chevy II station wagon into the parking lot at 9:30 am. She would come into the store wearing a bathrobe over her pajamas. She'd walk in with bath slippers and curlers in her hair. She arrived at 9:30 because that was when the first batch of corn dogs came out of the deep fat fryer. She would get two corn dogs and push a cart through the store buying assorted plastic knick-knacks.

The same year Bob was somehow put in charge of the Little League baseball uniform money for his son's team. The uniform money was blown in a lost weekend at a motel in Bellevue with some seedy characters.

The son never lived down the shame of his team being uniform-less the entire season – the kids had to wear jeans and white t-shirts with their names written on them with a felt tip marker. He started stealing cars at fourteen and ended up in reform school by age fifteen. Later he lived in the family basement and would lock himself in his bedroom spending hours playing video games and writing an extremist right-wing conspiracy blog that had fourteen followers. He had hijacked the neighbor's Wi-Fi signal by paying the twelve year old kid next door five dollars a month for the password. This deal was consummated while he and the neighbor kid were outside burning an ant hill with a magnifying glass.

The son cut a hole in the bottom of his bedroom door so his mom could shove plates of food through the opening. Later he expanded the opening to accommodate Pizza Hut pizza boxes. Finally he had to shave off an additional three inches when Pizza Hut introduced their thick crust pizza and crazy bread.

Bob's wife ended up in a straight-jacket and occupied a rubber padded room at a local sanitarium.

It was at this point I leaned over to the alcoholic next to me and said, "Man I wish I could have been as screwed up as Bob."

I realized I aspired to be as screwed up as the worst drunk in the room. I felt inferior for not being inferior enough to belong to AA. I felt like I was joining a biker gang or prison gang. I felt like I had to be really screwed up in order to gain membership. I had what I call a case of "bad envy." I was jealous of the speaker because he was more screwed up than I was. His story was so bad he was insured legendary status in AA. Here's my question, am I screwed up enough to be in AA?

Jealous Steve

***

AA Reply – February 2011

Dear Steve,

All of us have our own journey. The speaker's story indeed does sound harrowing. We hope it has a happy ending. We hope the family healed along with Bob. Maybe the daughter shed her bath robe and her corn dog breakfast and enrolled in college. Maybe the son became a serious journalist. We hope Bob's wife received the help she needed.

Your story is your story, Steve. It is as unique as you are. Regarding *bottoms*, we all have to identify our own. When members share of what constituted their alcoholic bottom they offer each other a list of *the yets* any of us may experience if we were to drink again.

Happy trudging Steve.

Sincerely,

AA

***

August 2011

Dear AA,

I have low self-esteem coupled with an overwhelming unrealistic sense of self-importance. I'm not sure if I am deserving of AA membership, but just in case I am, I want to be exceedingly popular.

When I was asked to speak at a local podium meeting, I didn't know if I was worthy of being the speaker. I was awfully nervous before I went up there to share my story. I had lingering doubts about whether I could sufficiently motivate the crowd of people.

I fantasized the people would write Yelp! reviews of my talk. The day-dream went something like this:

*One Star ***

"This guy would die if he were to come upon a still pond in the forest. He would starve to death looking at his own reflection in the water. Worst speaker I've ever heard. If you're working with any newcomers don't ever let them hear this guy. After the meeting I went up to the chairperson and gave him a piece of my mind. Steve hates AA! I hate him!"

SerenitySam449

*Two Stars ****

"Blah blah blah, this guy almost put me to sleep. Steve was a one-star speaker all the way. He only gets the second star for his funny stories about the 1970's Mexican weed. Ninety bucks a pound and full of stems and seeds. Macramé suspended Advent doubles and Grateful Dead Mars Hotel album hallucinations. Hilarious stuff."

BettyHead7989

*Five Stars *****

"I had tried everything to get sober. The pathway to my front door is paved with ninety-day coins. I was prepared to give up forever, this was going to be my last meeting. Steve's talk turned my whole life around. After hearing him talk I'm happy, joyous, and free! Best AA speaker ever. He should write a book, I'd buy it."

SteveBeliever1

*Three Stars ****

"He talked a lot about what it's like now, I liked that part. He seems a little negative about AA. He talked about the Beatles, Disco and Roger McGuinn's 12 string Rickenbacker guitar. He mentioned McGuinn was inspired to buy the Rickenbacker based on seeing George Harrison's solo during the song, "I Should Have Known Better" from the movie Hard Day's Night. Did he ever work the Steps? He never mentioned how many sponsees and grand sponsees he has. Not the best speaker, not the worst."
NinthstepNan21

I compiled a 2.75-star average. The first guy obviously didn't dig me too much. Another person loved me and two others seemed not to care one way or the other.

I need to do some work on my AA image. Here's my question:

Maybe I need some type of advanced rehab. Are there any professional facilities or life coaches specializing in AA image enhancement?

I'd really like to get on the speakers' circuit. I'm not sure I deserve it, but if I get a chance, I want to be the best!

Steve with Yelp! Reviews

***

AA Reply – August 2011

Dear Steve,

To thine own self be true. Honestly share your experience, strength, and hope.

Assume people like you. As far as assumptions go, that one is better than most. As always, relax Steve. Breath deep, take it easy and continue having fun.

In closing, we're not aware of any coaching or treatment programs which help AA's enhance their image.

Sincerely,

AA

***

January 2012

Dear AA,

I had an interesting discussion with my friend Joe last week. Joe has been attending meetings for about two years and has noticed a remarkable improvement in his life. He came into the program on a deferred prosecution for DUI. He told me a story about an experience he had at a meeting. Joe said he was wondering if he would have time to share in the meeting. It was a First Step discussion meeting and he was hoping to connect with some of the new-comers. In a previous discussion I told him about a formula I use in the meetings. I multiply the amount of people by the three-minute timer and compare the total to amount of time left in the meeting. Joe calculated the time, based on the Steve formula, and determined there was plenty of time for him to share.

When the police administered the breathalyzer test, he had registered a .014 blood alcohol level. Joe was busy planning what he would say in the meeting and he decided to throw out his blood alcohol number. The chairperson was a regular at the meeting and called on a few of the popular people first. The first person talked about a DUI and boasted of a .016 blood alcohol level. The next person talked about rolling bowling balls through the car wash, lost hubcaps, losing two wives, and bragged about blowing a .023. The next person got kicked out of Lollapalooza, snuck back in, and got kicked out three more times. He also was a multiple drunk driving offender and proudly declared he had an average reading of .024 on his three convictions. He bragged about his cumulative average much like the parent of an honor roll kid brags with the bumper sticker.

Can you imagine a parent with a bumper sticker "My kid blew a .024?"

Can you picture a meeting where the president of the Rotary Club, when announcing this month's guest speaker says "Charlie has a great talk prepared. Charlie is a respected business leader in our community. He has taught his family the virtues of building a strong community. He is a man of unparalleled values, morals, and integrity. Hey Charlie, what did you blow on the last DUI?"

My poor friend sitting there with his measly .014 felt like a misfit in AA. Only in AA can a person feel inferior for not having been MORE drunk when they got pulled over. Finally the Wally Cleaver of the group said he registered a perfect .040. He died three times before they could stabilize him at the hospital. He spent a week in intensive care under strict twenty-four-hour supervision. He was transferred to detox where he wore a straight-jacket and heart monitor for a month. His talk was so inspirational they asked him to speak at the group's gratitude dinner.

When Joe got his chance to share, he told a funny story about how he pissed in a dryer while in a blackout. That got a lot of laughs and he resigned himself to the fact his DUI would never impress anyone in AA. He expressed he had regrets that his story doesn't sound as bad as the other members. I reminded him of the same thing I remind everyone. Your story is your story is your story. Hitting bottom is a personal journey for every person. I told him about the one big question to ask yourself. How do you feel about yourself when you're drinking? If you've had enough, then you've had enough. I told him to listen to the stories and eventually *he'll hear almost everything that could have happened to him. I say almost everything because some stories are so weird and far-fetched it's possible you would never do those things, no matter how drunk you were.*

I heard a guy tell a story once which caused me to rethink the idea of the "yets" people speak about in meetings. In the depths of his despair he joined a religious cult. He didn't join the group because he had an affinity for their particular view on the concept of God or Jesus or anything spiritually related. He joined because the group owned a big house on Queen Anne Hill in Seattle. All he had to do was shave his head and swear his allegiance to the group's charismatic leader. The leader was a trust fund baby, whose grandmother had invented the glue which was used on practically every mailing envelope in the world. In the group's Queen Anne home everything was free. There was always great music being played, the food was free, the lodging was free, the all night sex parties were free. The only thing the group required of its members was to take shifts wearing a robe and handing out flowers at the airport.

The man who was sharing the story in the meeting saw a huge business opportunity. He would take the "family" station wagon down to David L Jones Company, a floral wholesaler located in the Fairview warehouse district in Seattle. He would pick up boxes and boxes of flowers which were designated for airport handout. He would stash his robe in the car and change into street clothes. He went around Seattle selling flowers to stores and fruit stands. In fact he sold flowers to anyone who wanted to buy them. He acquired a decent stash of cash and one day left the station wagon running in front of the Braniff International unloading zone at Sea-Tac airport.

He walked inside the terminal and purchased a one way ticket to Reno. Six days later he came-to in the Washoe County lockup. He was pretty banged up and didn't know how he had landed in jail. He later found out he had spent five nights holed up in the

Sundowner Casino. He had partied hard and gambled hard and ended up getting busted for going through the buffet line three times and then trying to skip out on paying. The Sundowner used a little known Nevada law to have him arrested on check fraud. He had blown through the fifteen thousand dollars he stole from the Queen Anne cult. Then he resorted to writing rubber checks to cover his gambling debts. The police searched his top floor penthouse suite and discovered piles of cocaine, along with two strung out dancers from the Bunny Hop, a local go-go joint.

He ended up doing 90 days in the county jail before he could gain his release. A friend contacted him to let him know the cult leader had issued a death warrant on him. He found himself stranded in Nevada, penniless, under a death threat from the leader of a sex, drugs, and rock and roll cult.

I always look for the similarities instead of the differences when I hear the stories in AA meetings. I'm almost sure I wouldn't let myself get so screwed up I would end up on the run from a trust fund cult leader who gained his fortune from the simple idea of a billion people licking a billion envelopes.

Joe told me he understood my point regarding what had or had not yet happened to him. He said he appreciated my concepts regarding the First Step. He asked me to be his sponsor and I agreed to take on his case. I asked him if he was committed to staying sober and finding a permanent solution to his seemingly unsolvable dilemma. He said yes, he was.

Here's my question:

Isn't AA unusual in the way we laugh about what would make others cry?

Steve with a sponsee named Joe

***

AA Reply – January 2012

Dear Steve,

Your new sponsee is lucky to have you. Yes, it's ironic that one of our members could feel less than, for not feeling more less than. You are correct about hitting bottom being a personal experience for each member.
Keep up the good work Steve.

Sincerely,

AA

***

May 2012

Dear AA,

I recently purchased tickets to go see the Beach Boys. I was very excited to get to see the band live. I've been a big fan of theirs, going all the way back to the Sixties when I was a young kid. They were playing at the Wounded Eagle Casino, a local joint in my area. I went with a friend who is about ten years younger than me. She is also a big fan of the iconic band.

When the band came out on stage, we were a little surprised because so many of the members seemed too young to be real Beach Boys. We quickly realized this band contained no one from the original Beach Boys. The band was led by Brad Love, he is the great nephew of original band member Mike Love. There was one quasi original Beach Boy on the stage. He turned out to be a session player from the Pet Sounds album. He stood up there, wearing a white tee shirt and donning a stocking cap. He played with a Duncan yo-yo the whole time.

We were disappointed with the show. We were more than a little upset these guys tour under the name of the original band.

My friend said she had gone to see Foreigner and there was only one original member. The new lead singer was a twenty-three-year-old karaoke champion. She said they barely sounded like the original Foreigner. People in the crowd were booing and tossing water bottles at the band. She later demanded a refund for her ticket. The folks from TicketTron told her to beat it.

I think there should be a law requiring these bands to divulge their current lineup. They should have to disclose how many, if any, original members are still in the band. I would grant a waiver if an original member had died. The waiver would only apply if the member had died of accidental or natural causes under the age of fifty. If they were over fifty and died of an overdose, excessive brain damage caused by drugs and alcohol, or by suicide a different waiver would apply.

This would get a little dicey because some rock stars die in the bathtub at age twenty-seven and it goes down as an accident. Seems like you pick up the paper and it says, "Derrick Jones of the band REO Jourenywagon was found dead in his hotel bathroom, he was forty-three."

But come, on you know those guys always die in the bathroom. I mean look at Elvis, a forty-two-year-old guy goes to the bathroom and never comes out. And they call that an accident?

A lot of bands replace the drummers and the bass players. It's because, well you know face it, those guys just don't survive that long. It seems like bass players and drummers are easier to replace. This would not apply in the case of Keith Moon. But really, who expected that cat to live to age forty?

Keith Richards would be covered by my over fifty rule. We should call it the Keith Richards amendment. If that guy ever dies, I think everyone would understand. Really, this would apply to anyone in the Rolling Stones. Those guys have done more oil changes than a Jiffy Lube.

None of this would apply if Paul and Ringo wanted to recruit a new John and a new George and tour as the Beatles. I'd wait in line in the rain for twelve hours to get the tickets. Then wait in line in the rain for another twelve hours just to get into the concert. Even if I could get the tickets online and I had reserved seats I'd still wait in the rain for twelve hours just to enhance the experience. If I developed pneumonia and it got serious and I died at least they could say I died doing what I loved more than anything in the world. But I digress.

My point is, if I go see Journey, I know Steve Perry isn't going to be singing. But at least tell me who is. My legislation would clear all this up. But like most of my ideas I'm sure the legislature will never look at it. I've been clean and sober at hundreds of concerts over the past forty plus years. I've introduced many members to the joy of enjoying concerts sober. This isn't saying much for me. If I drank at a concert, I'd likely end up getting kicked out for throwing a phantom roundhouse at a security guard. At any rate I'm going to have to pay closer attention and do a little research before I buy tickets from now on.

I suppose you're wondering what, if anything, this letter has to do with recovery. I guess I'm thinking a person my age may live long enough to see most of my rock and roll idols die off. What will become of me, will I be like the hole in the donut?

Steve with a heart of rock and roll

***

AA Reply – May 2012

Dear Steve,

Concerts and bands have played a large and important role in your life. Seeing your idols age and die off is a sad fact of life. Just think of all the memories you have. You are not the hole in the donut, you've got a lot of living left to do.

Long live rock and roll.

Sincerely,

AA

***

February 2013

Dear AA,

On October 9, 1976 I attended an AA meeting at the old Aurora Fellowship Hall in the Fremont district in Seattle. It was the first time I climbed the twelve stairs which led up to the storied old Seattle meeting hall. When I entered the main meeting room, I heard the faint sound of a sports broadcast. I couldn't figure out where it was coming from.

Suddenly a disheveled old hobo jumped up out of his seat and started yelling and cheering. He was holding a transistor radio up to his head and he yelled, "Yeah, touchdown USC. I love the USC Trojans!"

The Trojans were in town playing the Washington State Cougars at the Kingdome. Once the meeting started the old guy would interrupt with occasional outbursts of cheering and celebrating. The man's name was Chuck Armor. He was an old skid road drunk who boasted he had drunk Sterno straight out of the can.

Chuck had been sober about 15 years at the time, yet he always looked like he had just rolled in from the sticker bushes under the

Aurora Bridge. Someday I will write a novel about the old meeting hall. Every trip there was an adventure in the understanding of humanity.

The hall was full of characters. There was a guy named Boxcar Bill. Apparently, he had spent some of his drinking days traveling and living in boxcars. He always started his share with "My name is Bill McGovern and I'm a Democrat."

There was a crazy old guy named Perry. He would pace around while he shared. During his talk he would occasionally hold his finger up to his mouth and say, "Shhhh, don't tell anyone, this is anonymous."

Chuck Armor would always say "I didn't become no alcoholic because my momma put me on the toilet seat backwards. I didn't become no alcoholic because my momma fed me peanuts and Cracker Jacks. If you think little Chuckie is sick now just pour little Chuckie a drink. Then you'll see how sick little Chuckie can get."

Some of the other characters were Carl, Toby, Wino Tom, Tom the Cop and Tony S., who wrote a self- help book when he was drunk. There was a guy named Marv, he was an actor. He had a part in a Rainier Beer commercial and for his work the brewery had provided him with an ample stash of beer. He came back in a few months with a new sobriety date. Marv would always reference his time by saying "I've been 'around' this program for a long time now."

Chuck's sponsor was a guy named Mag. Mag got sober in the late 40's and was one of the pioneers of Seattle AA. He spoke at every meeting. The only time that hall quieted all the way down was when Mag spoke. He was the pillar of the old Fremont meeting hall. He said something that has stayed with me through my entire recovery. He began every share with this line:

"My name is Mag and I'm an alcoholic. I'll never take another drink again as long as I live so help me God."

This he followed with a gentle pound of his fist on the table.

Everyone in the room would say, "Hallelujah brother."

Here's my question, how come it seems like Mag's message has been lost? I mentioned being certain about long term sobriety at a meeting and some people freaked out. Is it true that the good old days were better?

Steve, stranded in Fremont

***

AA Reply – February 2013

Dear Steve,

It sounds like you have many fond memories of the Aurora Fellowship Hall.

Regarding your question, maybe today will be the best of the good old days with exception only of those still to come.

Sincerely,

AA

***

March 2014

Dear AA,

I've been thinking about sobriety and my recovery from alcoholism a lot lately. I've been clean and sober for quite a while and feel blessed to have been granted the gift of long-term sobriety. It hasn't always been easy for me.

There was the New Year's Eve bus trip through Colorado when I was fifteen months sober. Everyone broke out the weed and the booze and there I was, stuck on a bus with no AA and no Big Book. I was stuck on the rolling party bus with just me, listening to my mind. The great servant which resides upon my shoulders told me I could have two sobriety dates. One would be for Washington, the other for Colorado.

Next up in the insanity que was the notion I could easily handle some non-habit-forming marijuana. After all it was a program about not drinking, and I promised myself if I had a few tokes I wouldn't drink on the bus.

Then I tried to convince myself I could party for one night and then just quit again the next day. After that came the notion I could finally come up with the magic formula. The formula which would produce the perfect high. I had partied on busses before and it was almost impossible to get in trouble. I remember thinking what could possibly go wrong?

On my last night of drinking I was overwhelmed with a feeling I would never drink again. I believed this was a genuine spiritual awakening. I was filled with grace and love and a certainty I would never drink again. Yet fifteen months later I found myself sitting on the bus listening to my insane mind try to convince me to pick up a drink. I thought if I went contrary to my previous spiritual awakening I would be going against the will of God. This was the point at which I first worked the Second Step. At that moment I reaffirmed what I had felt that night back in the field, where I was drinking Schlitz, smoking marijuana and listening to Crosby, Stills, Nash, and Young's Four Way Street on the eight track. I knew with certainty the quart bottle of Schlitz beer was going to be the last drink I ever took.

My sanity was restored somewhere near the Eisenhower Tunnel in Dillon, Colorado. When the bus got to Aspen, and we checked into our apartment, I called the AA number listed in the

Aspen white pages. A wonderful woman answered the call and invited me to come over to her house.

She didn't know me, yet she opened her home to me. We spent about four hours talking and rang in the New Year together. She asked me if I thought I could stay sober the rest of the week. I told her I was pretty darn solid, and I'd call her if anything came up. We hugged and parted ways. I never saw her again.

If I hadn't made that random call, she would have spent New Year's Eve alone. It was the classic example of how one member helps another by reaching out, thinking they were seeking help for themselves but in so doing provided help to another. I have thought about her over the years though I don't remember her name. I've wondered if she remembers mine. We had sat together drinking coffee under a midnight winter moon, two angels of Aspen, Colorado.

When tempted with the party life on the bus I was reminded of the feeling I had in the field that night. It was the knowing I would never drink again. It was the beginning of aligning my will with God's will. In a key moment on the bus God restored me to sanity.

At that vital moment I turned my will over to God. I believe deep in my soul my sobriety has a higher purpose. I believe my sobriety not only serves humanity but also serves those who are depending on me. Depending on me to be the best human being I can be.

There is the line in the Book, "...for with it goes annihilation of all things worthwhile in life." This refers to what alcohol does to the alcoholic and those who are affected by his/her drinking.

Each September, when I pick up my coin at my home group birthday meeting I always say, "I'll see you guys next year, I expect to be sober next year. In fact, I am certain I will be sober next year."

I never talk much about my faith or spirituality in meetings. I'm not religious and I am certain any religious person could kick my ass in a God debate. But that's okay because I've always been an intense over-thinker, yet I seem to have a real simple God game plan. I used to think I had to do a lot of foot work before I could present my case to God. It would be kind of like a credit report repair. I figured God would never accept me the way I was.

Then I was reminded of the grace and power I felt in the field behind the elementary school on the warm August night, Schlitz beer in hand. I was there with Bart Lumpkin, Tiny Dale, Sturd Nelson, Nick Marx, Hoot Lee, and Greg Guitar. The obsession to drink was removed and I've never had a drink since.

God took me, bad credit report and all. It's closing in on half a century now. I'm blessed and amazed by what an experience I have had.

You might be wondering why all my friends were guys. It's not to say some of us didn't have girlfriends, we did. It wasn't like we never had girls around because we did. Most nights though, we just sat around and talked about doing something. We would always smoke another joint and then we would talk about doing something again. We didn't know the THC was like glue on our shoes and our feet were stuck to the ground. We rarely did much, except smoke another joint.

Sometimes we would hang out in Hoot's basement and get high with his brother Rainbow. Rainbow had been away at college but decided to take a semester off to find himself. He had a friend named Fountain and they took a lot of LSD together. Rainbow had on one occasion taken too much acid and jumped through the living room window. He spent a few weeks relaxing at the Rubber Room Sanitarium after that incident. Rainbow and Fountain would sit and listen to albums by the band Yes. Yes, Yes. At first I said no, but eventually I said yes.

One night Rainbow put on the Grateful Dead's Mars Hotel album. We were smoking Columbian and I had an early buzz going and I discovered the Grateful Dead for the first time. I told Rainbow and Fountain I really liked the album so they decided to put on another Dead album. They put on Asomoxamoxa or whatever it was called. It was complete crap and I split with Sturd and Tiny to go grab a pizza. I went out the next day and bought the Mars Hotel album. It didn't sound quite as mystical in my bedroom as it had in Rainbow's hippie wonderland, but I digress.

I've become a dependable person people can count on. AA, you can always count on me, I'll be here until the day I die.

Steve with a touch of grey

***

AA Reply – March 2014

Dear Steve,

Your story is an inspiration to all who know you and those who will cross paths with you on their sober journey. It also very well speaks to the miracle of AA; of one alcoholic speaking to another about their common problem and how important that is and remains to be in our journeys of recovery.

Sincerely,

AA

*****

I received and replied to ten more letters over the next two years. Compared to past years they seemed to come in a flurry. Life for me was also coming in a flurry. I was experiencing a sense of urgency. Things with Donny, with whom I'd been living and sharing what I thought was a relationship as stable as the rock of Gibraltar for the previous eight years were beginning to crumble.

On one level I knew this to be the case and on another I refused to believe it thinking this sense of impending doom I was feeling could be chalked up to residual effects of my past inability to pick the right man to be involved with. Alcoholics in recovery often talk about their *pickers* being broken. This is why so many seem to become involved in relationships which don't stand the test of time. I was no exception and it was easy in retrospect to see how my *picker* was definitely broken when it came to Bobby from Brooklyn along with two before him and two after. But it was early on with Donny when I stopped feeling that way. I had thought my picker had finally been fixed after all my years of hard work in the Program.

Today I know the best course of action for me with regard to all that is to not focus on some mentally ethereal construct like a *picker* as being responsible for anything in my life. Today I find it much more constructive to simply be true to my own self. To the best of my ability. Be true to myself in all things and let the cards fall as they may.

I can go on and on about all this. Rather than doing that let me get back to the sense of urgency I was experiencing. For me, any heightened sense which has an anxiety component – as with urgency – is a dangerous thing in there is an addictive power to it. There's something akin to an adrenaline rush when I'm living daily with urgency. And like the adrenaline up, there follows a down. And that down can be difficult to escape from. I'd experienced these ups and downs in sobriety before and I was adamant I would ward them off in the future by taking action upon the onset of feeling that sense of urgency I previously described.

And I'm happy to say I did just that. The last six months Donny and I were together he traveled for business more regularly than normal. More often than not I was in our apartment alone. I could have brooded or faked my way through my loneliness by going to more meetings and smiling until my face cracked. And that would have helped as it has for me in the past with situations of this sort.

But I needed to do something different so I worked one on one at least three nights a week for two months with my sponsor Darla. Darla taught me a technique of meditation which she has used in her own life for many years. I was soon able to regularly practice on my own and I have done so ever since.

With me, it would be accurate to say I'm a slow learner but once I learn something I do it fairly well. The meditation I regularly engage in has changed my life. But at the same time it hasn't changed my life. I'll let those last two statements stand because I can say it in no better way. Today I am as happy as I have ever been and as content as I have ever been and at the same time I feel just as driven as I've always been to experience life and explore new things with new people. What's really changed if I had to put my finger on it would the *urgency* thing. When I feel that coming on, and I still do on occasion, I don't run from it nor do I grab ahold of it so to vanquish it in battle like an AA Wonder Woman. I accept its existence and then watch it float on by like a cloud in the sky disappearing over the horizon.

When Donny and I split up I kept the apartment and he moved to San Francisco. Things were hard for a time but I can't say I struggled because I just didn't. I felt pain and sadness. I hurt and I cried. But I didn't struggle. I felt safe and protected, as if I had been placed in a position of neutrality. I felt strong and no longer needy - for lack of a better term - to be in an intimate relationship. It would be accurate to say I was no longer *needy* but I was still *wanty*. Meaning I wanted to be in a relationship, to have a close companion, a partner in life but no longer felt any sense of urgency about acquiring it. I was happy with myself. I was happy living in the apartment I had shared with Donny for eight years. I was happy with my job at the Central Office. I was happy with my core three meetings which I still attended every week. I occasionally ventured uptown and to Brooklyn to visit new meetings along with those I hadn't been to in years.

Life was good. And through the miracle of AA it continued to get better. Of course, Steve's letters continued to arrive.

*****

LETTERS A Twelve Step Journey

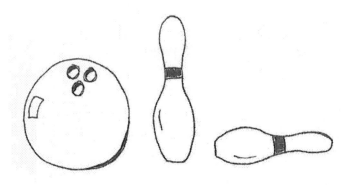

Chapter Eleven
Seriously Groovin'

June 2014

D*ear AA,*

There has always been confusion surrounding my sobriety date. My ascension to living the clean and sober life has been marked by two vital spiritual experiences. The first was the night I took my last drink and became overwhelmed with the certainty I would never take another drink. The second was the last time I smoked weed in the fall of 1976. I had not had a drink in over two years, was attending meetings, yet was extremely toxic from two years of non-stop weed smoking. The old timers in my local community said my AA birthday was the last time I had a drink. Old Fred and his gang did not want to hear any drug talk in the meetings.

In my early AA pitch I would say Richard Nixon was president the last time I drank. I used this Nixon line in order to add credibility to my talk. It was 1976 and by saying Nixon was in office when I got sober it established that I had some time sober already. I went back and looked at the timeline of my last drink. The date of my last drink was August 20, 1974. I looked in the encyclopedia Britannica and learned Nixon resigned on August 8, 1974. It turned out Gerald Ford was president when I took my last drink. This fact would change the entire theme of my AA talk.

I decided to take action in order to clean up this situation. I could not consider the previous two years of daily weed smoking as being completely sober. I had been smoking like I was a member of Bob Marley's horn section and I was serious about getting off on the right foot in recovery. Therefore I changed my sobriety date to September 5th of 1976, the day after I smoked weed for the last time. I stopped worrying about how much sober time I had and got down to the business of going to meetings and not using in between.

As the decades have rolled by my story has taken on an air of nostalgia. I have been clean and sober through seven different administrations. My sobriety has spanned the first and last Seahawk game at the Kingdome. In September of 1976 Warren Moon was the quarterback of the Washington Huskies. Back when I first got sober the Seattle Mariners were an expansion team. Disco, the mechanical bull, punk rock, new wave, grunge, MTV, Sean Cassidy, Cabbage Patch Kids, the Pet Rock, Jim and Tammy Fae Baker, New Coke, the DeLorean, and the movie, "Chairman of the Board" starring Carrot Top, have all come and gone.

In this time Rocky Balboa trained in the meat plant, beat Clubber Lang and Ivan Drago. Rocky is still making Rocky movies, but he is too old to fight anymore. Keith Richards was and still is playing for the Rolling Stones. The Betamax lost to VHS, VHS lost to the DVD, the DVD lost to Blue Ray, which lost to cable, which lost to streaming, which will lose to something else.

Blockbuster started, became huge, then went away and turned into a coffee shop. A coffee shop where aspiring writers peck away at novels and screenplays, in between their shifts at the local grocery store. The grocery store, which will lose to instant online *delivery by drones swarming out of a giant, faceless, and lifeless warehouse with no windows and no people inside.*

Oh yeah, and the Berlin Wall fell, and the Soviet Empire collapsed. Millions of people were allowed to pursue their dreams of personal freedom. But I digress.

Whew! I forgot this was a letter to AA, an organization which has never taken a political stand on anything in its history.

Steve, steeped in history

P.S. Do you find it odd that Betty Ford went to treatment at Betty Ford? How did that happen?

***

AA Reply – June 2014

Dear Steve,

You have been sober a long time and in so doing we are sure you have provided and continue to provide much hope and promise – along with a few laughs we are certain - for members in and outside your local AA community.

Sincerely,

AA

P. S. The enigma surrounding Betty Ford and the Betty Ford Treatment Center may forever remain a mystery.

***

November 2014

Dear AA,

We experienced a big loss in our local AA community. One of our longest standing members, Old Fred, recently passed away.

Old Fred had a huge following and was loved by countless members in our local community. He passed the message on to thousands of people over his forty-five years of sobriety. The outpouring of love was evident at his memorial service. There were over seven hundred people in attendance.

I've written in before about Old Fred, his legacy, and his chair at the 12 Step Club. For the past few years I've wondered if possession of his chair would get passed on to another member. This ties in with my desire to be a heavy hitter in the AA community. I want to sit in that chair and have the minions come and ask me questions like:

"How has AA changed in the gazillion years you've been sober? How did you stay around so long based on how young you were when you got sober? Have you ever been tempted by drugs and alcohol. Will you be my sponsor? Will you come speak at our convention in front of five thousand people? Abbey Road or Revolver?"

I've been thinking about my AA legacy and Old Fred's chair at the 12 Step Club. Imagine how surprised I was when I went to a meeting last week and I couldn't even remember which chair it was. I knew the wall he always sat against, but I couldn't remember which chair it was he sat in.

I stopped for a moment and thought about the whole AA legacy thing. I realized I was putting too much time and energy into worrying about it. I couldn't even identify the chair that I had coveted for all those years.

When I saw how many people showed up for Old Fred's celebration of life, I realized the best I could hope for at my memorial service would be a hundred people tops. And only if the weather was good. If it was raining or too cold outside all bets would be off. The other wild card would be whether or not I ever find a decent AA image enhancement coach. The way things stand now I might have to accept an over/under betting line of people at my memorial service at 52 1/2.

Old Fred did the work, he walked the talk, he reached out to thousands of people over his time. I've never been as dedicated to the cause as he was. I hope my experience and my sharing has reached a few people over my time. It's time to start being more like Old Fred. It won't be long and I'll need to get rides to meetings.

A ton of sand has passed through the hourglass since 1976. I knew Old Fred when he was barely middle-aged Fred. I'm finally learning the things I covet so much today might not be important in the end. My plan is to be true to my inner-most self. That will be my legacy in this life.

I've abandoned all hopes of ever levitating a Big Book. I've come to my senses and decided to try it on one of the AA pamphlets instead, they are way lighter.

Here's my question:

Things didn't turn out too badly, did they?

Steve looking forward

***

AA Reply – November 2014

Dear Steve,

It sounds as if Fred provided the hand of AA to many people over the years and that is as commendable a legacy as one may hope to build in their life. The balance of developing personal growth while being of service to others is no easy feat.

To your question, it sounds as if a trudging may have blossomed into a comfortable and invigorating walk along the road of happy destiny, Steve.

Sincerely,

AA

**

February 2015

Dear AA,

There is a lot of this social media stuff going on these days. There is the Facebook, Twitter, Snapchat, Instagram, Pinterest, and many others too. I have some friends who have become obsessed with social media. It seems like Facebook has become the most popular medium among them. I know a guy who recently posted on Facebook sixty-three times in one day. His friends commented on the posts and then everyone jumped in. They all start calling each other names. The whole Facebook thing is going totally crazy. This brings me to the point of my letter.

With all the posting and responding going on there appear to be signs of addictive behavior. My sponsee Junk Bond John sees a potential money-making opportunity through the haze of smartphones and social media. He wants me to help him write a business plan for his new idea. He thinks he has invented a new addiction. It is called Chronic Over-Posting Syndrome (COPS).

John is planning on getting the patent on the syndrome and the trademark on the name. He thinks since he invented the addiction, he could thus invent the cure for it too. John sees this as a potential multimillion-dollar idea. He has heard most of my story and he must have thought I would get excited about it. He has a rough draft for a book which the addicted chronic over-poster will be able to use as a handy guide to kick the habit. John wants to open a group of regional in-patient treatment centers. They will have Facebook and Twitter detox programs to get the people started. Then they will introduce their patients to a Ten-Step program. He chose Ten Steps because he plans to throw away unpopular Steps like Six and Seven. Junk Bond John's Steps will all be hip, slick, and cool.

He is currently working on a draft for a pamphlet which would be like the questionnaire they give to alcoholics. This is a sample of what he's come up with so far:

1. *Do you get excited when the little world notification icon on your Facebook page has the 9+ number on it?*
2. *Are you bummed when you click on the icon and discover several notifications are from stupid groups you belong to?*
3. *Are you bummed when your updates are birthday announcements from people you haven't seen since eighth grade?*
4. *Are you bummed when your update number is high, and you discover one person went through the pictures from your Grand Canyon trip and hit "like" on a bunch of them?*
5. *How long do you wait after a post to check your updates?*
6. *Do you feel better when cool people with lots of cool friends "like" or comment on your posts?*
7. *Are you let down when the person commenting on your post has less than 200 friends?*
8. *Do you post and then comment on your own posts?*

9. *Do you think your political commentary will ever change one person's mind?*
10. *Do you panic when the battery is low on your phone, thus impeding your ability to check your status updates?*

If you answered yes to three of these questions, we might suggest our simple seven day "Spin Dry" treatment program. You will be free to roam our 80-acre sprawling campus. You will be encouraged to reintroduce yourself to nature by hanging out at our duck pond. The seven-day plan may include some of our patent pending electric Jolt-O-Matic mild shock treatments. We attach a Flash Gordon helmet to your head and send a series of mild shocks through your brain. It sounds scary but we guarantee you will never use Twitter again when we're done with you. Just the sight of a hashtag will make you violently ill.

If you answered yes to more than three questions, then we recommend you complete our 30-day program. At first you'll be a little rummy from our patent pending Thorazine Paper Slipper Sedation seven day detox program. You will spend the remainder of your inpatient program learning how to read newspapers, magazines, and books. We will teach you how to communicate without the use of emojis and poorly abbreviated words. The thirty-day program includes some brutal stints with the old Jolt-O-Matic. It's a little rough but darn well worth it in the long run. When we get done with you, you will be using a rotary dial phone for the rest of your life. Soon you will discover there is a whole new world out there waiting for you.

Our compassionate intake counselors will help you determine which treatment program is right for you. They'll also do a financial makeup on you as well. If you can afford it, we'll send you in for the thirty-day whole enchilada. We're running a business here not a charity.

***

John spent a great deal of his life coming up with ideas and schemes which would benefit from the sale of low-grade high-risk venture capital bonds. His ideas are usually farfetched and crazy concepts for new businesses. John's grandfather made a fortune manufacturing life size plastic merry-go-round horses. John's Uncle Joe invented the squirt gun carnival horse race game. John made a small fortune many years ago when he managed to raise the money to start the world's first lawn dart company. Things went well for a few years in the lawn dart business. Disaster struck when a slightly intoxicated man accidently stuck his wife in the head with an errant lawn dart. The lawyers and the insurance companies got involved. John was wiped out, he lost everything.

John wouldn't quit talking about his COPS idea, so I agreed to work with him, mostly just to shut him up. I'm helping him design his pamphlet and his Ten-Step program. I suggested he might want to tone down the talk about the Jolt-O-Matic. He wants to hit the late-night TV circuit with an infomercial. John reminds me so much of a younger version of myself. In my early recovery I was always coming up with crazy money-making ideas.

John has an overactive mind. He's always thinking and over thinking everything. He's neurotic and nervous and requires a lot of attention from his sponsor, me. Where do I get these sponsees? Why are they attracted to me as a sponsor?

I know John's new idea will never come to fruition. He will spin his wheels for a few weeks and then lose interest. By next month he'll have an idea to design a golf course specifically for left-handed golfers.

I've learned the value of choosing my battles in life. John is a good person with a big heart, and he works diligently carrying the message to new members. He works a day job at a big box hardware store. I encouraged him to take regular work to create a steady cash flow. I told him the work would buy him time so he could come up with a big idea. Believe me, he comes up with a lot of big ideas. Working with men like Junk Bond John has produced many rewards for me. I feel as if I am slowly helping him steer his life in the direction of becoming a productive member of society. Now he is imparting his knowledge about recovery to other members.

I must admit he had me thinking about the social media addiction thing. I love the acronym "COPS". For a brief time I considered getting in on the ground floor of this exciting new venture. I was proud of John for coming up with such a creative idea. For about one minute I saw myself as the CEO of a giant corporation, flying in a Lear Jet, checking in on the nationwide network of treatment centers. I was able to get myself out of the daydream before the enterprise crumbled and the Lear Jet crashed into the side of a mountain. A crash I might say which I survive followed by me hiking out over treacherous mountain terrain in a pair of Adidas tennis shoes. I show up at the ranger station and my business partner, Oprah Winfrey is waiting for me. But I digress.

I love spending time with people like Junk Bond John. Isn't it rewarding to help people in their quest for lasting sobriety?

Steve, suffering from COPS

***

AA Reply – February 2015

Dear Steve,

Junk Bond John is fortunate to have you as a sponsor. Working with others along with taking regular personal inventories and improving our conscious contact with God as we understand him provides the best defense from picking up the first drink. This process also allows us to grow as human beings beyond our wildest imaginings. You are proof of this, Steve. Continue to live your dreams.

Sincerely,

AA

***

June 2015

Dear AA,

I was recently involved in a situation with a family member which brought me immense pain. As you know, I'm not adverse to telling long stories, but for the sake of time I'll boil this one down to the basics. My father recently passed after a long bout with dementia. It wasn't until he died, I learned he had systematically been coerced into removing me from his will. I say coerced because at the time he signed the various documents he was in an advanced state of decline. I know my dad, I know he wouldn't have willingly removed me from his will. So I'll cut to the chase here so I can get to my question.

I'm struggling with a resentment against the member of my family who coerced him into cutting me out of the will. This action has had a profound effect on my life. My life would have been much different if I had received the land and the cash gifts my father intended to leave me.

A friend suggested I send this family member a gift, a peace offering of sorts. I went online and browsed one of the large shopping sites. I was going to send a pair of pajamas but unfortunately, they only sold the flame retardant kind.

I toil away as a common laborer, wondering where I would be if I had received the piece of my dad's estate he so lovingly had planned leaving to me. This situation has presented me with a big challenge.

I've tried hard to look at this situation objectively. I have assessed all the wonderful things I have in this miraculous life. In fact I have many things on the positive side of my life's ledger. I'm healthy, have great relationships with my kids, I have many friends in the Program and of course I have my sobriety. This has created for me a kind of prosperity which can't be measured by money. I'm enjoying my independence and am pursuing my dream of writing in my humble five hundred square foot studio condo. I've also been able to eliminate the scoundrel family member from my life forever.

Nevertheless the resentment persists. I've been working on it, however it still nags away at me. I'm sure I can control the resentment while still pursuing a life with God. In fact I'm absolutely sure I can. Which brings me to my question:

Is there an official AA department I can talk to about this resentment? I feel mine is worthy of holding on to. I want to receive permission from the AA Resentment Board to hold on to this resentment. I have an entire Power Point presentation on the resentment ready. Just give me an email and I'll send it in. I can't wait for your response.

Steve, with a justified resentment

***

AA Reply – June 2015

Dear Steve,

The Grand Supreme AA Resentment Council is not currently in session, having recently begun its summer recess. They convene on the first Monday in October, much like the United States Supreme

Court. To make matters worse we are sorry to inform you their docket is already full for the upcoming session. Again, I'm sorry to report you are far from first in line with an appeal to retain a justified resentment.

In the meantime you may want to resolve the resentment the old-fashioned way. Find someone in AA to help you with it. You're going to have to go to Denny's or Starbucks and hammer out a deal.

You can do it, Steve. It seems you are already halfway home based on what you said in your letter. Remember you don't have to build a campfire, break out your guitar and sing *Blowing in the Wind* with this person - if by chance you play guitar and sing.

You can find a resolution for this situation. Resentments not only occupy valuable space in our Universes but they become focal points from which we perceive all around us .

God only gave us one life to live Steve. You have been sober a long time and have been remarkably successful. Do the work you need to do to be free of your resentment and continue on our shared road of Happy Destiny!

Sincerely,

AA

***

November 2015

Dear AA,

I've been clean and sober a long time now. Sponsoring a former stockbroker has led me to believe the sobriety journey is much like the Dow Jones Industrial Average. It has good days and it has bad days. There are setbacks and events which may cause one to want to give up and bail out. However, over the long haul the return is well into the positive range.

Just like someone investing their capital into the stock market, I have invested my soul long term into this thing called life's journey. And the payoff has been nothing short of amazing! My mere existence is a great miracle of the Universe.

I have come to a point where I realize this is God's true path for me and sobriety is my way of honoring God and his magnificence.

Anything involving a man-made alteration of this miracle is an abomination of God himself (or herself, or itself, or any other self, attached to said Heavenly deity).

So, there it is in a nutshell. Here's my question:

How can I adequately convey the message of perseverance and determination to these principles which form the foundation of my recovery?

Steve turning yet another corner

***

AA Reply – November 2015

Dear Steve,

You'll never know how many people you have reached in your recovery journey. Each day you move forward in your life others see this progress. And they cannot help but to be inspired.

Keep living the example Steve, one bullish day at a time!

Sincerely, AA

***

December 2015

Dear AA,

I stopped by the local bowling alley recently to play a few games of pinball. I read on their website they had the game "Revenge From Mars." It's a fun and challenging machine and I played several games. It has a progressive multi-ball feature and a radioactive rooster which grows to immense proportions. I hit the replay a couple of times and gained several extra balls on one game. I'm rambling about pinball and thus have committed something of a silver ball digression.

I noticed there was a kid's birthday party going on. The kids were bowling using the advantage of gutter bumpers. With these bumpers every ball thrown was guaranteed to knock down a pin or two or more. These kids were destined to never experience the feeling of throwing a gutter ball.

When I was a kid my older cousin took all of us bowling at the Bell Lanes in downtown Bellevue. I was five and I grabbed the six-pound ball and tossed an entire game which yielded a total of nine pins knocked down. There were no bumpers on those lanes. My older brother and my cousins laughed uncontrollably every time I threw the ball. Most of my shots went straight to the gutter. I vividly remember two of my attempts somehow managed to balance precariously on the crown of the lane. One ball rolled at an agonizingly slow pace on the crown and tailed off at the end and caught two pins just as it fell into the gutter. The collapse of those two pins represented the greatest athletic achievement up to that point in my life. Two frames later another ball stayed in the lane. This ball tailed to the left and connected with such force it managed to knock down seven pins. I was as excited as Rafer Johnson must have been two years earlier when he won the decathlon at the 1960 Summer Olympics in Rome.

By letting today's kids use bumpers they'll never know the experience of listening to your cousins and brother laugh uncontrollably as you roll gutter ball after gutter ball. They'll never experience the joy of the eruption of applause when you finally roll one down the lane and knock 'em down in big numbers.

I see a lot of this bumper bowling mentality in the world today. I see it in the rooms and the meeting halls. I remember a day when we came to meetings and sat on hard chairs, put a buck in the basket, and sat through meetings in smoke filled rooms. There was no time limit in those days. Sometimes people rambled on for fifteen minutes talking about their boss, or their bad day, or their ex-wife or whatever. Everyone smoked in the meetings, everyone. On Monday nights at the Aurora Fellowship Hall they used to bring a van full of teen moms over from the Home for Wayward Women. The moms came to the meetings with their babies. The moms chain-smoked through the entire meeting. The moms smoked, the old timers smoked, heck even the babies smoked.

In these smoke-filled rooms we listened to old men talk about living in the sticker bushes behind the Public Market and drinking Muscatel at nine o'clock in the morning. We heard tales of drunk housewives who wet their pants at the PTA meetings in the suburbs. There were tales of hobos riding the rails and sitting inside boxcars watching sad rain pour in some obscure railyard in some obscure nowhere in America. These people lived the tough life without bumpers.

Which brings me to my question:

Have we turned recovery into a Fantasyland where everyone rolls a strike just for showing up? Have we softened our approach to dealing with the disease? Is this the beginning of the end of the end?

Steve, bowling a nine all the time

***

AA Reply – December 2015

Dear Steve,

I understand your concern and will answer unequivocally no, this is not the beginning of the end. Or that of the end of the end. Life is filled with change, Steve. Cultures are constantly evolving and as a result attitudes and expectations alter .

The Steps of AA remain a constant, however. The Fellowship may change with time - it's certainly different here in New York today than it was in 1986 when I first came in off the streets. But the Program remains the same. Over the 76 years since their inception The Twelve Steps haven't been altered one iota. Not one word of the first 164 pages of our Big Book has changed in all that time - nor have the appendices in the back of the Book.

I would say if anything, this is the beginning of the beginning for AA and all it may offer humanity. Think about this, Steve...76 years ago only a handful of people in Akron, Ohio and a small few scattered about the country knew anything of the AA Program and the Twelve Steps of recovery. Hundreds of thousands if not millions still suffered from alcoholism with no hope in sight and a likely outcome of only institutionalization and/or tragic death before one's time.

And consider all those non-alcoholics who were directly and indirectly adversely affected by the disease as family members and loved ones of alcoholics. The numbers could easily be in the millions in just the United States alone.

Now consider today, only 76 years later. Consider the millions if not tens of millions worldwide who have altered their paths for the better through the application of the Steps into their lives. Also consider the additional millions who as non-alcoholics have become educated about the disease and the success of AA in helping their loved ones recover from alcoholism. In fact, I think it would be safe to say that at least in our nation of over 300 million people you'd be hard pressed to find anyone who hasn't at least heard of Alcoholics Anonymous and the Twelve Steps.

So with that in mind I offer the thought of embracing change in all areas of life, Steve. Even changes in the AA Fellowship and even when those changes seem like they may be watering down the coffee of having lived the hard knocks of life, so to speak.

Many Regards,

AA

***

January 2016

Dear AA,

I'm getting old. I just realized this. I heard Linda Ronstadt singing Neil Young's "Love Is a Rose" and I was reminded of seeing her in a concert at the Kingdome. She performed an acoustic set with John David Souther, but she struggled because the sound echoed in the cavernous stadium. Pete Townshend of the Who said of the Kingdome, "It was like playing in a giant fishbowl."

In case you guys don't know, the Kingdome was a giant concrete stadium which stood in Seattle for a few decades. It was originally part of a bond issue called "Forward Thrust." The voters decided in 1968 to build a King County Multi-Purpose Stadium. It ran into funding issues and was put on the back burner for a while. Weyerhaeuser Corporation said they would pay for the stadium if they could build it out of wood. Can you imagine all the damn trees those people owned in 1968?

Eventually they got their wish and built a domed stadium out of wood in Tacoma. Tacoma is a town down the road which has always wished it could be Seattle but has never quite measured up.

In the early 1970's we had a County Executive named John Spellman. He pushed for the construction of the King County Stadium. He was successful in his efforts and the construction began in 1974. Along with the stadium, the region had gained a promise from the National Football League of an expansion franchise. The first ownership group was led by former University of Washington and NFL football star Hugh McElhenny. The team would be called the Seattle Kings. To help promote the team McElhenny had a large plastic football erected across the street from the construction site. McElhenny's group ran into financial difficulty and for a moment it looked like the Seattle NFL franchise might be on the ropes. Then a new ownership group came forward led by Lloyd Nordstrom. The Kings went away, and some Pioneer Square bums moved into the big orange Seattle Kings football, eventually setting the thing on fire. McElhenny went back to selling bananas and the team was eventually named the Seattle Seahawks.

In 1976 the Seahawks played their inaugural season. I was excited to see the debut of the NFL in Seattle. When we were kids, we could listen to San Francisco Forty Niner games on the radio. We also received Kansas City Chiefs games on a local station. I remember sportscaster Jack Buck with his unique delivery, "Stenerud on to try the extra point. The snap, the hold, the kick, aaaaaaannnnnnd, its good." With the coming of the Seahawks we were going to have our team.

I was nearing the end of my drinking and drugging career toward the end of the summer of 1976. I went to my first Seahawk exhibition game late that August. I don't remember who they played that day. I do remember I was really stoned on marijuana cigarettes and hashish. There was nothing special about this day.

I was always high, every day, all of 1976. It didn't matter if there was a Seahawk game or not. I had long given up on the idea this would be cool, or that would be cool if I were high. I was just always high. So if I witnessed a lunar eclipse, I was already high when the earth cast its shadow on the moon. I may have thought the experience was enhanced by dope, but it wasn't.

I was suffering from extreme paranoia at this point. I drove down to the old produce warehouse on Occidental Avenue and parked. Then I went out on the back-loading dock and smoked a couple of bowls of Blonde Lebanese hash. This stuff wasn't that good. I doubted that it even came from Lebanon at all. In fact the closest that crap ever got to Lebanon was probably Lebanon, Oregon. I grabbed a Tab and a bag of peanuts and walked the four blocks down to the Kingdome. I don't remember too much about the game. I do remember being sure everyone in the Kingdome knew I was high. I was convinced the Seahawks were talking about me in the huddle. I was miserable, afraid of everything, I wanted to die.

That was one of the final days of my old life. It was a few days later when I smoked the last of that hash and I made the decision to give up all mood and mind altering chemicals and drugs. I had quit drinking alcohol two years before on a warm August night in a field behind the elementary school. Thus began my journey of living a clean and sober life. I made a commitment that no matter what happened, I would never go back to drugs and alcohol.

Lately I've been getting worried about growing old. I'm afraid a time will come and no one I know will even remember the Kingdome. I have visions of me, old and in a home, telling the young nurses and caregivers about the Pink Floyd concert in 1988. I'll become that old guy who says, "I saw Paul McCartney and Wings at the Kingdome on June 10, 1976." Then I'll tell them about the Rolling Stones with J. Geils in 1981, the Who with The Clash in 1982, the Eagles in 1976, and McCartney again in 1990. And I'll tell them about all the Seahawk games. The Broncos game when we won on a last-minute field goal, only to have the play erased by the infamous twelfth man on the field, offensive guard Dave Kraayeveld. We had lined up to kick the field goal again and Efren Herrera shanked it wide right and we lost. Seahawk coach Jack Patera said, "Efren missed the kick because he got a bad case of enchiladas." Later that day Seattle sports legend Royal Brougham died.

I'll tell the kids about the Mariners vs the Yankees in 1995. About Edgar Martinez hitting the double and Griffey getting waved in and scoring the winning run. About all the players running out of the dugout and celebrating in a big pile by home plate. I'll tell them it was the team that saved baseball in Seattle. I'll tell them how we came two wins away from going to the World Series. At this point one of them will look at a new employee and say, "Old Steve has a vivid imagination. He thinks the Mariners almost went to the World Series. He thinks he went to concerts and games in some big concrete building in Seattle." She'll go on to say, "We just let him rant and tell his stories. We're not sure who the who is, or this Pink Floyd, or if he saw some eagles flying around and he sees beetles in his visions. We just nod our heads and say, "Wow Steve, what a life you lived."

But I digress.

Here's my question:

In the words of Mick Jagger, it is a drag getting old, isn't it? When I'm really old do you think we'll still have AA?

Steve, in a Kingdome state of mind.

***

AA Reply – January 2016

Dear Steve,

You will continue to see the sun rise and set. And the night sky shine its heavenly stars down upon you. You will see leaves on the wind, a twig carried in a river fed by the gentle melt of Cascade snows under an August sun. You will hear the playful bark of a dog melding with a child's laughter. You will smell newly cut grass and a neighbor's barbeque down the street. You will feel the cool breath of Fall, the invigorating bite of Winter, the warmth of Spring and the heat of Summer. You will see moons, full and crescent, blue and eclipsed. You will see leaves on the wind.

AA will be here as long as you are here, Steve.

Many Regards,

AA

P.S Mick Jaggar was only 23 years old when he wrote that line. What did he know?

***

January 2016

Dear AA,

I recently recalled a day last summer. I was driving through my neighborhood and noticed some kids had set up a table and they were selling lemonade. They had made a big sign on butcher paper advertising their product. As I got closer, I saw the familiar message on the sign, "Lemonade, 50 cents." Fifty cents?

It was a warm summer day and I pulled up slowly and rolled down my window. I said "Hey kids, the wage and price freeze was lifted by President Nixon in 1971. This fifty cents thing needs to come to an end. Raise your darn price for gosh sakes."

All the kids saw was a crazy old guy yelling at them. They ducked behind the table and waited for me to pass. As I drove away all they heard was me shouting, "Anyone who is going to shell out fifty cents for some lemonade will gladly pay a buck."

This brings me to my point. Obviously, the kids should raise their price. That point needs no debate, what with the cost of the cups and the raw product. The other point here is whether I was within the bounds of functional behavior by making the suggestion. Which brings me to my real point and my question.

How do we know who or whom to take advice and input from? Is unsolicited advice ever justified? I'm not all that excited about getting unsolicited advice from other grown-ups. I've found a few people I trust and those are the people I share my personal information with.

Steve, thirsty for some lemonade

***

AA Reply – January 2016

Dear Steve,

I was once told the only good advice is the advice that is asked for. I thought for years that to be a clever way to essentially say people are not open to advice, or constructive criticism for that matter unless they first become willing to receive it. And that willingness usually follows a self-admission of needing a constructive critique, advice or help in some way. This because the advice seeker has realized they cannot do whatever it is they want to do on their own. They need the help. They want the help. Help from a power greater than themselves quite possibly.

It seems interesting that without even trying to, one may unravel a concept and find themselves looking at the Steps. In this case Steps One and Two.

You have reached a point in your recovery where the doctrine of the Program may be examined on a deeper level.

You are uncovering the lotus flower, the Zen Heart of AA, Steve.

*****

Chapter Twelve
Paradox Unraveled

It was late in January of 2016. I was sitting in my apartment. Darla's dog Ruben slept comfortably next to me. He was staying with me again while Darla and her husband were out of town. I got up and walked to the kitchen to pour a cup of coffee. I was thinking I had definitely veered off the straight and narrow path of AA replies to Steve's letter with my last. I had thought long and hard about sending it and in the end based my decision on a remembrance of Beryl's voice saying, "Summer Anne honey, in my life it is intent which guides everything I do. I must always then, examine my intent."

In this case I had done just that and determined my intent was to answer Steve's letters from here on out in a more personal way because I too - as Steve had said in his letter - I too was getting older. And while I was content with my life, I was wary. I've found in my life contentedness is much akin to resting upon one's laurels.

Contentedness can lead to stagnation for the alcoholic, for this alcoholic. I need to be moving forward, always moving forward.

And what was behind my intent? I could say it just felt like the right the thing to do and that was good enough but it wouldn't be saying all there was to say. I also wanted to reciprocate by letting Steve know he had impacted my life in a great way. But was I assuming too much. Did I think my input when put forth on a personal level was something which he would appreciate? Was this a classic case of me doing something which though it seemed on the surface benign to be in reality more of an act lacking in humility? Could I be overthinking the whole thing? I had been pacing for a while. I'd never even poured my coffee. I looked over at Ruben. He was awake and it was time for a walk. I put on his leash and out the door we went with both of us ready for doggy time. The mental and physical focus required to prevent myself from being dragged through the park was a welcome respite.

*****

February 2016

Dear AA,

In the Sixth Step the book suggests we read the first Five Steps. It asks us, "... if we have omitted anything, for we are building an arch though which we shall walk a free man at a last."

It goes on to ask us , "Are the stones properly in place? Have we have skimped on the cement put into the foundation? Have we tried to make mortar without sand?"

When I work with people in recovery, I try to emphasize the idea of building a solid foundation. I tell my sponsees it is important to build our recovery on firm bedrock. Any structure built with no foundation or on sand is bound to sink when subject to the pressures of the elements. *This is a new life we are building through the work we do on these Steps so we cannot skimp.*

The Sixth Step doesn't get a lot of ink in the Big Book. I regularly go back and read the brief paragraph on page 76. It assumes we have done thorough work on the Fourth and Fifth Steps. I remind the people I work with we are building a new life. This is a new life which doesn't include the need to alter our reality by using alcohol. I try to emphasize to my sponsees the recovery success rate goes up exponentially for members who do the hard work required.

Step Six has always seemed daunting to me. It says, "Were entirely ready to have God remove all the defects of character." I have sat with the Book and read that Step back to myself over and over. It requires us to make a commitment to be willing to ask God to remove our defects entirely. It is a lot like the commitment I made to giving up drinking and drugs entirely, forever.

One night at a meeting I shared my angst involving this Step. Old Fred pointed out the Step suggests we are willing to let go of the character defects we identified in the Fourth and Fifth Steps. Old Fred had a way of taking the dark wind out of my sails. For me, the willingness to let the defects go entirely is akin to quitting liquor entirely. There must be no reservation of any kind or any lurking notion we will be immune to alcohol. The same is true with the defects of character. I maintain this resolve with the work I do in the maintenance steps, Ten, Eleven, and Twelve.

Here's my question:

Do you think the Sixth Step should get more publicity? I'm willing to carry the Sixth Step flag for all of AA if that's what you think it would take. I'll carry it for a few years, then pass it on to someone else.

Steve, entirely ready

***

AA Reply – February 2016

Dear Steve,

The Sixth Step, as you point out, is an important building block for the foundation we build in the first Nine Steps. In fact, I would say it is critical. Building that solid foundation through committing to the Sixth Step is important because at some point in our recovery our resolve will be tested. In fact it will be tested more than a few times.

The old phrase, *keep it simple*, may have been suggested to Bill W. by Dr. Bob when it was time to discuss the Sixth Step in the Book. And that may be why Bill chose to say only what he did about it. It is simple, straightforward, and true. Bill may have felt writing more on the subject could have a watering down effect.

Carry that Sixth Step flag Steve and when ready to pass it on, I'll be here with an open hand. From one Sixth Step enthusiast to another,

Keep up the good work Steve!

Sincerely,

AA

***

March 2016

Dear AA,

Ken Davies and April McKernan

It was the last day of school before the Easter break of 1973. I was a fifteen-year-old tenth grader at a high school in my hometown of Bellevue, Washington.

Don Melvin pulled up in front of my house at 6:30 am to pick me up. We both had a zero period 7:00 am class together. Don had a fifth of Gilbeys and I had a fifth of 151 Rum. He had two empty cups and a bottle of Coca Cola. He poured himself a Gin and Coke and made me a toxic concoction of 151 and Coke.

We took off toward school, listening to top forty radio on KJR AM 950, the two of us sipping on our cocktails. The rum and coke in an old plastic cup, with no ice, mixed with no science was quite harsh. I listened to Steelers Wheel and forced as much of the drink down as I could. On the way we stopped at 7-11 and bought a couple of Coke Slurpees. I poured my rum and coke into the Slurpee and the quality of my drink increased dramatically.

I was feeling happy when we pulled into the back-parking lot at the high school. We sat in the car and finished up our drinks. The radio played, "Some people call me the space cowboy, some call me the gangster of love." The Joker, by Steve Miller was on when Don shut off the engine. Two slightly drunk jokers took off for first period. We walked across the campus to a history course taught by Mr. Lackman.

We made several trips back out to Don's rig that morning. We traded off our bottles, so I had a gin and coke between third and fourth periods. I was fairly hammered by the time I went to the lunchroom for fish sticks and chocolate milkshakes. Following lunch, Don and I went to visit a hermit who lived in our neighborhood. He was the same guy who had purchased the barrel of Blitz for my kegger party the year before. We took this guy to Prairie Market and he bought me a bottle of Boones Farm Apple and a fifth of MD 20/20.

It was the last day of school and I was going on the Doug Fox Travel Spring Break Ski Holiday in the Grand Tetons of Wyoming. I went home and packed my ski gear and some clothes and got ready to go to the White Front store parking lot where the busses were lining up to load all the kids and gear for the trip to Alta, Wyoming. Alta was the home of the Grand Targhee ski resort. I was still buzzed from the gin and rum and was excited about going away for a week to ski. I had my stash all set. I had the remains of a fifth of rum, the Boones Farm, and the Mad Dog all packed away in my luggage.

My friend Gary Gordon and I boarded the bus with the rest of the kids and chaperones. We pulled out of the White Front lot about 7:00 that night. I had stowed away the booze and felt confident about my stash. Our bus was full of some of the rowdiest kids in the Bellevue School District. They were from three high schools. Bellevue, Newport and Interlake and all of us were traveling together. One kid went on to infamy as he got busted for burning down the Newport High School library. There were other dropouts, dopers, drunks, and everyone, everyone smoked cigarettes. This group combined with the world's lamest chaperones made for a toxic combination. We were rolling charter party bus number one.

When we stopped in Yakima at the bus station I went inside and bought a pack of cigarettes. It was one of those old vending machines where you deposited sixty-five cents and pulled a metal lever which released the pack of death sticks. The smokes landed in a bin at the bottom of the machine. I was so drunk I didn't even notice I had pulled the Winston knob. It wouldn't have made any difference which one I had pulled. I didn't know the difference between one brand and another. The truth was I didn't even smoke cigarettes, I never had smoked, I never did smoke. I was fifteen and drunk and standing in the Yakima, Washington Greyhound terminal. It seemed natural to buy some smokes. I pushed the little button on the side of the machine and a pack of matches also fell magically down into the bin below.

Gary Gordon was surprised at my purchase. He and I were chums who hung out quite a bit around school. Neither he nor I had ever seen the other smoke a ciggo. We got back on the bus and both of us immediately lit up a Winston. Our transformation was complete, we were chain smoking with the rest of the hoodlums. I puffed on my Winston, the pride of R.J. Reynolds of North Carolina, the official cigarette of Betty Rubble and Wilma Flintstone. I took a pull off my bottle of rum as the bus pulled away from Yakima bound for the Tri Cities and then to Pendleton, Oregon, the Blue Mountains and journeying on through the hinterlands of Idaho to eventually reach the angel like snow of Tetonia in the wild land of Wyoming.

Sometime near sunrise a kid nudged me awake. He was the son of a famous local radio personality and he was yelling at me, "Hey Interlake, wake up. You said you wanted to watch the sunrise."

I had no memory of ever informing Ike O'Shay of my intention to watch the sunrise. He was still up or had briefly slept and liked the idea of having some company on the now quiet bus. The sun rose above the horizon and shone down on a landscape of rolling almost barren hills we had never seen before. I thanked Ike for shaking me out my drunken haze. We rolled through the Blue's scrub pine and tumbleweed towns stranded in a frozen museum of time.

It was the first time I experienced the beauty of America rolling by, outside the window. I had been on road trips before with the folks when I was little. Mostly I squirmed in my seat and couldn't wait until we got to wherever it was we were going. I fell back to sleep or passed out at some point and when I awoke, we were in downtown Boise.

Boise, Idaho in the spring of 1973. The driver walked off the bus and went into a hotel across the street from the Greyhound terminal. We received a fresh driver and soon we were on our way to the metropolis of Driggs. Bob was our new driver and he took to the microphone a few times announcing we were approaching, passing through, and had left the town of Alcohol Falls, Idaho.

LETTERS – A Twelve Step Journey

We went through Pocatello and Blackfoot without as much fanfare from Bob. Neither town was anything to write home about, so I didn't bother writing home. It was cloudy when we went through Driggs and we couldn't see the mountains. Soon we were climbing steadily up into the Tetons. After a series of switchbacks we saw a sign which marked the Wyoming state line. The ski resort was located a mere eight miles inside the state of Wyoming. The base elevation of the resort was 7,408 feet above sea level. The top of the Bannock chairlift was parked 9,862 feet above the closest ocean.

At the end of the first day of skiing I boarded the bus to head to Driggs for supplies. Gary Gordon went to the grocery store and bought some essentials. On his list were Cap'n Crunch, milk, chicken noodle soup, and Ritz crackers. We figured this would be close to all we would need in order to survive a week in the Tetons. I went into the fishing tackle store to pick up the rest of our survival supplies.

A kid who had been on this trip before had told me to go to the fishing tackle store for the buy. This kid told me the guy would ask me for my ID. He then said I should tell the man I left my wallet back at the mountain, but I had cash to pay for the beer. This sounded to me like a sound plan so I walked up to the counter and told the proprietor I was interested in buying ten cases of Coors beer. He looked across the counter at me and said, "The legal drinking age in Idaho is nineteen. Do you have any ID with you?"

I gave him the, "I left my wallet at the mountain but I have cash," line. He looked at me and said, "It's going to cost you eight dollars a case son." I showed him four twenty-dollar bills and he broke into a big smile. He asked me, "Do you want a hand truck?"

It was at this moment I felt like I had scored the motherlode of beer. The only time I had ever had that feeling before was when we had hoisted a full keg of beer out of the back of Andy Thomas's car the year before at the kegger party.

I paid counter man for the beer, wheeled the stack out to the bus and loaded it into the luggage area. I closed the compartment and got back on the bus. Gary Gordon saw me and asked me if I bought the one case of beer I had gone in the store to buy. I told him he was in for a big surprise when we got back to the mountain. When we returned I brought the boys from our room down and we each hoisted two cases of beer onto our respective shoulders. We carried them up the stairs and into our room. We carried them like a gang of longshoremen slinging groceries on board the S.S President Adams.

The result of the purchase was a continuation of the weeklong drinking spree which had started in the car with Don. I had almost sobered up between the sunrise with Ike O'Shay and the moment I walked into the fishing tackle store in Driggs. Now that I had the beer safely stowed in the hotel room, I set out to get completely polluted. I was successful in this endeavor. I managed to drink massive quantities unabated for the next six days. In between this drunken spree I enjoyed some of the best skiing I had ever experienced.

One day we took a side trip to the Jackson Hole resort. The mountain was shrouded in fog and it was raining. The skiing was generally lousy. We took a shuttle back to town and spent the afternoon walking around Jackson Hole. It was in Jackson I first saw a real American pickup truck with a real American rifle mounted on a real American rifle rack. I had never seen anything like this in my hometown of Bellevue, Washington. Bellevue was a clean town with a noon whistle, a wishing well, and perfectly manicured rhododendrons in its town square. Jackson, Wyoming was a western town with cowboys in cowboy hats, wooden sidewalks, and rifle racks. It was a real awakening for a kid raised in a lily white, lily bright town located on the outskirts of Seattle.

One night in the middle of the dreary haze of my drunken adventure I met a girl named Jan. She was from Renton, Washington and attended Oliver Hazen High School. I was soggy drunk on my fifth straight day of mass consumption. We danced in the lodge to a two-man band brought in to entertain us high school kids. Jan noticed I was a little down, down like a dark cloud was hanging over my party bus. We went back to her room and we sat on the couch in the living room. She asked me if there was something wrong. I told her I was a mess and had been drinking nonstop for close to six days. I told her I was an alcoholic and I had a premonition I was going to die. She freaked out and started to cry. She said she felt bad for me and asked if I wanted her to help me. The room was crowded, and she suggested we go to the laundry room where we could talk in private. She said she had an answer to my alcoholic problem.

We went down a flight of stairs and entered the laundry room. When we were safe inside, I told her I was an alcoholic and I would have to quit drinking soon if I expected to live long. I told her when I stopped drinking it would be for good, forever. I told her I would never be able to control my drinking. She was crying and said she didn't want me to hurt myself anymore. We were standing close to each other. She hugged me and told me I would need the help of Jesus in order to stay sober.

In that moment in the laundry room at seven thousand feet up in the Tetons I had my first moment of clarity. When Jan told me she cared about me, when she told me she didn't want me to hurt myself, when she told me I would need Jesus to stay sober, she was being honest. We were truly connected at that moment. Nothing ever happened physically between us, yet we had a shining moment shared together in a motel laundry room situated under the vast Wyoming star swept sky.

I drank like Bukowski the rest of the trip and we ended up with a pyramid of empty Coors cans which measured twenty-four at the base. If you do the math of half the base times the height you come up with a total of 288 cans. One day I drank an entire case of beer all by myself. I got involved in a poker game and woke up with a pocket full of quarters. I have no memory of winning or playing cards at all. When I got back to Bellevue, I went to my grandma's house and slept in her back bedroom for sixteen hours. On my first day back at school my friend Cary noted I had gained about twenty pounds in one week of skiing in the Tetons.

This experience during the Doug Fox Travel Spring Break 1973 Ski Holiday firmly solidified my membership in the society of alcoholics. My laundry room drama with Jan from Hazen High was the first break in my alcoholic dam. The laundry room discussion is firmly entrenched in my memory. It was there in that laundry room I admitted for the first time I was an alcoholic. I knew it then and I know it now. I told her of my resolve for permanent, lasting, lifetime sobriety. I'm just as convinced this is true today as I was then.

Looking back now I realize the laundry room meeting was the beginning of my spiritual journey. Jan, oh Jan, wherever you are now I'm sure you've been someone's angel for a long time. You were my angel that night in the Tetons.

Steve in waist deep powder

***

AA Reply – April 2016

Dear Steve,

That's a beautiful story. And you have a way with words. Reading your letter reminded me of a trip I took with my sponsor to Asheville, North Carolina ten years ago. We drove back roads as much as possible and stopped at roadside diners. We saw a slice of America I didn't know existed except in old movies.

I didn't realize how interested I was in American history, geography and our shared cultures in general.

I can go on and on and I'm writing a reply to you from AA and not telling my own story, right? Of course that's right.

I'm having a hard time with this response and I just now realized why. It's because there is no question to reply to. That's not all because you always say enough to warrant a reply without a question. It's just that this time I'm struggling because there is something you don't know, something we never told you.

This is not something which was hidden. It just never seemed germane to mention until now.

Here's the thing, Steve. I can't speak for AA anymore but I can speak for myself. Even though I do work for AA – yes, I'm a *special worker* at the Central Office and in fact have made a career of it for the last 25 years – I am an alcoholic and a member of AA first.

*****

In that reply - which I wrote the following day from my home office - I went on and on explaining to Steve how his letters had played a role in my life and Beryl's. I told him who Beryl was and what she had meant to me. I told him about Uncle Rick and how he had found me and saved my life, fuck a duck and all.

I told him everything I've chronicled here and then some. I thought it only fair since he had unwittingly shared so much about his life with me, with us, Beryl and me.

I gave him my contact information including my direct line at the office and said he should look me up if ever in New York. When I finished my reply, all twenty pages of it, I immediately left my apartment walking it the three blocks to the neighborhood post office, and I mailed it.

The following Monday I was surprised to find among the mail distributed atop my desk a letter from Steve. I was confused. How could he have received my letter and responded so quickly. It wasn't possible. I quickly realized this wasn't the case. He'd simply mailed two letters to AA a few days apart and I was now receiving the second of them.

Though Steve continued to write letters, the following - the letter I had found atop my desk on that Monday morning along with my reply - was to be the last letter he wrote to AA and the last I wrote for AA.

*****

April 2016

Dear AA,

I'm starting to wake up further to the concept of a higher power. I've always been in awe of the Universe, aware of its unlimited size and power. The fact that it is infinite and thus has no beginning and no end is almost too much for the human mind to grasp.

I went to Eastern Washington and observed a Lunar Eclipse. We were away from the city lights on a cloudless night and it was quite a show the Sun, Earth and Moon put on.

I realized I was a human being residing on a planet inside a solar system, in a galaxy, in a Universe, which stretched out in every direction for all eternity. I saw life for the miracle it truly is. Heaven and Earth, the stars, and galaxies all cohesive in a perfect order, directed by a divine power.

My son Andrew, whose soul left his earthly body, resides among the particles and sparks of energy included in this unflawed Universe. I saw him that night, he was in a perfect place. He was safe from the perils that haunted his mortal life here on Earth.

I knew I was destined to reunite with him someday in heaven. The lesson for me was to enjoy as much of the perfection of the Universe while I was still here on terra firma. Andrew became my guiding light, my spirit angel.

The gap between knowing and understanding everything, and the idea the Universe can't be explained, is where I found faith. The gap between knowing and not knowing. The gap between certainty and the uncertainty of not understanding infinity. This is how I explain my spirituality. The fear of walking forward is outweighed by the concept that I walk forward, with God, toward perfection.

I saw the miracle of life for what it exactly was. I am here and he is there because I still have work to do.

Old Fred would often share in meetings about how if man had risen from a single cell in a pool of primordial ooze he must be the apex of evolution and therefore the only God his universe can know. I guess what Old Fred meant is that there is a God and it's not me.

I can handle that. I can picture the primordial ooze, like a bubbling swamp of mud, surrounded by weird sulfur clouds, a single tiny cell wiggling back and forth, waiting for its chance to walk upright on the Earth's surface.

Here's my question:
Isn't this a little heavy for the average drunk to comprehend?

Steve, stuck with a simple concept that God is the Universe, in all its beauty and perfection and infinity.

***

AA Reply – April 2016

Dear Steve,

To your specific question: Not drinking is more than a little heavy for the average drunk to understand. Yet we end up understanding it on one level or another to the point at which we don't drink anymore.

The beauty of the Program is it fosters an understanding of that which seems beyond understanding. You are living proof of this. You have unraveled paradox and are illuminated by the Zen Heart and Mind of AA, Steve.

I am saddened beyond words to hear of the loss of your son. Nor can I express my gratitude in learning more about you while continuing to witness your ongoing success in this life. And that is a piece of my paradox unraveled.

I would love to discuss this more in person someday.

Sincerely,

Summer Anne DiFranco

*****

Two weeks later, returning to work following lunch I listened to a voicemail saying, "Hello Summer, this is Steve, I'll be traveling to New York soon. I'd love to talk so give me a call anytime."

*****

LETTERS – A Twelve Step Journey

Chapter Thirteen
The Crescent

August 2018

For the last ten years I had been something of a workaholic. I regularly put in over forty hours a week at the Central Office.

Ron H. retired in 2009 and I became Office Manager overseeing everything from correspondence and archiving to the donation accounts and IT department. The Trustees who years before were very close to ousting me permanently from the organization had unanimously voted me in to the position.

I had been to some degree burying myself in work. My sponsor Darla had suggested I slow down.

"Take some long lunches. Go play tourist. Show Steve around the city," she'd said. She was right. I needed to slow down with work and create more balance in my life. It wasn't long ago when I had resisted Darla's advice, thinking it to be a little on the patronizing side and probably based on her control issues she'd yet to work through.

Here's the good news about that. Whenever I resisted Darla's suggestions for my well-being it would take about five seconds for me to realize she was right. AA has taught me much and bettered my life in more ways than I can count but I often think above all is the ability to self-evaluate. But only under the close watch of a great sponsor like Darla in my case I might add!

So it's funny for me to often realize I - with over thirty years of living life as a member of AA - I sometimes feel as if I need a sponsor more than I did during my first five years. The Zen Heart of AA strikes again. And the Zen Mind tells me this is normal and healthy. And I wish not for the first time all people had a sponsor, a guide, a mentor, a sensei, one who had come before, to help navigate our way through life. I can go on and on about this.

Darla had met Steve at the first meeting he attended with me on his trip to New York in late July of 2016. He'd surprised me by saying he was coming to New York to visit family and explore the city. This was something he'd been wanting to do for years. We'd talked a few times on the phone since I'd reached out to him following his last letter to AA a couple months prior.

To say I was excited to finally meet this person who had strangely played such a wonderful role in my life of recovery would be an understatement. Steve and I met at the Central Office, he having been in town for a few days staying with family in Connecticut. There was an awkward moment as we started a handshake which morphed into a hug with me stepping on his open toed sandaled foot. I apologized and suggested I should have consulted his hugging guide sent in a letter thirty years before. We both laughed leaving awkwardness behind. I gave him a quick tour of the office, even showing him the locked file drawer with his letters. This brought up many questions of which I was only too happy to answer but we were both famished and decided to go straight to lunch at a café down the street.

We talked, ate, shared laughter and talked some more. I had to excuse myself to call the office and let them know I wouldn't be back for the day as two hours had passed before I knew it. I still had much to say to explain the impact his letters had played in my life and that of Beryl's. But we both had things to do so we parted ways, with a less awkward hug this time, having made plans to meet again over the weekend.

On Saturday we met for an early dinner followed by the big Saturday Night Alive But For The Grace of God speaker meeting. I had arranged for Steve to be the speaker and he had the crowd of 500 falling out of their chairs with laughter. He was just as much a character in person as in his letters. We had decided together it was perfectly fine for him to mention his 40 years of letter writing to the Central Office if he chose to. Neither one of us had thought this needed to be kept secret any longer. Of course for Steve, he never knew any of it was a secret much less that any of his letters would ever elicit anything other than the occasional chuckle from one or two of the army of hundreds who must be weekly going through AA letters with questions mailed from thousands of members all over the world.

I didn't think at the time – Steve confirmed this later – that he was entirely convinced of his letters being the only letters of that type Beryl or I had ever received at the Central Office. This was the source of much laughter between us over the next two years.

We had slowly begun to know each other, both of us being busy with our lives on two sides of the continent. Steve visited for a week in March of 2017, once again seeing family but finding time to go on a few walking tours of the city with me which we both thoroughly enjoyed. I was discovering playing tourist in my own city was allowing me to find out about things I had never known existed. We'd exchanged letters - actual written letters versus emails. We both to this day find something much more satisfying when reading a friend's words off of paper held in the hand as opposed to from a computer screen via an email. I guess we are both old fashioned that way. We laugh about that as well and how we are maybe simply becoming old in general.

LETTERS – A Twelve Step Journey

Steve and I went on an incredible day hike on the Pacific Crest Trail at the tail end of last summer, 2017. Steve had visited me in New York twice by then so it was my turn to go see him in Seattle.

It was the first time I had been out of town on September 11 in 16 years. The strange thing is I hadn't even thought about the date when making my flight and hotel reservations the month before. A few days later I realized I had done it. I wouldn't be there to honor and remember Uncle Rick and all those who lost their lives and I stopped myself right there. I remembered something.

Something Uncle Rick had said to me once many years ago. Just a few months after he'd scooped me off the street and brought me home. He and Beryl and I were watching a WWII documentary on TV and I asked him about his father who as a Marine in the South Pacific lost his life fighting the Japanese on Guadalcanal. Uncle Rick didn't remember him having been a newborn in 1942 when his father had shipped off. But he had a letter his dad had written to him just weeks before his death. It said if he didn't come back alive he wanted his son to know honoring life by living is far more important than honoring the dead by dying. He said the dead don't need honor, it's the living who do.

I was in Seattle for five days. Steve was a great tour guide showing me everything from the Pike Place Market where he once sold fruits and vegetables to the old produce warehouse district where his grandfather had toiled a century before building a successful company which prospered for fifty years. We toured an Alaskan crab boat moored in Ballard awaiting the sail north and the start of a new season of fishing. The captain knew Steve. Steve's company had once outfitted the boat along with others in the fleet with stores for the season. Everywhere we went people knew Steve. The coffee shops, restaurants and of course the AA meetings. Even the people operating the locks in Ballard knew Steve. The locks allow for boat passage between the fresh water of Lake Union and Lake Washington into or back from the salt water of Puget Sound and the Pacific Ocean beyond. I'd loved touring the locks. I stood behind the fish ladder viewing windows watching salmon rushing by, heading toward lakes and rivers and streams and home.

Two days before I was to fly back to New York Steve took me on an urban hike in Seattle. We'd met on Capitol Hill, not far from my hotel. We walked down to the Space Needle and then up Queen Anne Hill to a small city park with a fabulous view of Elliot Bay, the Puget Sound and downtown Seattle. Mt. Rainier and the Cascade Mountains ran north and south magnificently in the background. Far to the west the peaks of the Olympic Mountains sparkled like jewels under a late afternoon sun.

Mt. Rainier and the Cascades were so majestic and seemingly so near to Seattle I had remarked to Steve how much I would enjoy experiencing it up close. He smiled saying he knew exactly where we could go and asked if I was up for another hike the following day. I had said yes, absolutely. He said it would be a long, all day event. I told him my calendar was wide open for the day and I had brought my heavier hiking boots and day hike gear just in case.

The next morning he picked me up at 5:00 am outside my hotel in Seattle. In less than two hours we were parked at a trailhead five or ten unpaved miles north of the little town of Roslyn. The town looked strangely familiar yet I'd never been there before much less had I even visited Seattle or anywhere in the State of Washington for that matter. I mentioned this to Steve and he said the town, along with its bar and general store had been used as a set for the filming of a TV show I watched years ago, Northern Exposure. Uncle Rick had loved that show and with Beryl the three of us would meet for dinner at their place once a week to dine and watch an episode together during the early 1990's.

We hiked for four hours and reached the Pacific Crest Trail. Another hour and we arrived at Spectacle Lake just in time for lunch. I've never before seen such a beautiful alpine lake. And I've seen a few having hiked the Appalachian Trail and the French Alps with Rosalie just two years before during my annual trip to visit her and Marnie.

LETTERS – A Twelve Step Journey

Nestled in the palm of the North Cascades the little lake was a perfect picture of what you might see on a postcard from the Swiss Alps. We wound our way down to the lake skirting car sized boulders left from the thaw of mile high glaciers 20,000 years before. Dipping into the lake's edge was a large outcropping of basalt polished smooth by the elements over the eons. A perfect place to relax, cool down and have lunch. The lake was still, beautiful, and inviting under the late summer sun.

We shed our packs and outerwear and both of us dove right in. It was a cloudless day, at least 80 degrees and both Steve and I were over heated from the trek up the trail. We thought a swim in the lake would be perfect to cool off but that water was as cold as I'd ever felt. The two of us gasped after diving in yelping and hooting while treading water for about ten seconds before swimming back to shore and climbing out.

We ate lunch while drying off. I went on a short walk by myself along a trail which slowly rose, leading to a pass along a ridgeline in the near distance. About halfway up I found a flat bench size rock in the shade of the spruce and cedar trees along the trail. I sat looking down at the lake. I had a perfect view. The lake was as still as glass and the reflection it held of the sky above was so clear it was hard to tell where one started and the other ended. I thought of Beryl and Uncle Rick and I thought about honoring life by living. I looked around admiring the surrounding peaks and I smiled with another thought. I knew this place.

I walked back along the path I'd taken and found Steve sitting cross legged where I'd left him on the shore of the lake under the golden sun and the bluest sky I had ever seen. I asked him if by chance this was the lake he'd hiked to when he had tried so hard to meditate in the mountains thirty years earlier; where in his attempts he had thought up a fantasy of starting a business with Oprah only to have it all get crushed in a landslide of classic alcoholic thinking.

He nodded chuckling, shaking his head at the memory, saying this time he may have actually been meditating. He explained while I was on my walk he had been considering the Zen Heart and Zen Mind of AA and not a single money making venture had crossed his mind. I laughed at that. Both of us smiling and now dry under the September sun we threw on our packs and began the hike back down.

Steve dropped me at my hotel at 8 pm that night and by 9 o'clock I was fast asleep. I woke up the next morning early and refreshed. Steve met me for breakfast at my hotel and we said our goodbyes with promises to visit again at some point in the future. I flew home to New York and was back at work a day later. I had a bounce in my step. People at the office and at meetings noticed. Over the phone during our regular Sunday conversations Rosalie in France noticed.

I told everyone who commented exactly what I was feeling. Hiking with a friend in the Cascade Mountains was good for the soul.

*****

August 2018

I was sitting in the waiting area in Penn Station in New York City. Summer and I were going on an adventure together. We were booked for the 2:15 pm departure on the Crescent to New Orleans.

I'd be lying if I said I wasn't a little anxious about the trip. I'd be lying if I said the old Steve hadn't lived out a few daydreams about what will happen if I travel with Summer Anne. For instance, one of these was of her becoming my muse inspiring me to write a great novel. She is Scarlet O'Hara in all her glory coming down the stairs in her Tara mansion. I sell the story to Ron Howard and he cuts me in for a percentage of the box office. Summer is sitting with me at the table when they call my name at the Oscars. I thank her in front of the world for being my inspiration.

I was jarred out of my fantasy by a familiar voice. I looked up and Summer was standing there with her suitcase on wheels. She said, "Steve, were you daydreaming again?"

I replied, "Oh yes, we were at the Oscars, sitting with Ron Howard when they called my name for best screenplay."

She answered by explaining this was a Steve daydream so while accepting my award I had to make a misunderstood political statement or some such thing which would lead to my blacklisting in Hollywood. Of course following this I wouldn't be able to find work and would end up living in a small shack on a friend's property in Marin County spending the rest of my days writing poetry, posting it on a blog which had only fourteen followers.

We laughed together at that.

This was the beginning of a great road trip. We are travel partners and were heading off to the South and to who knew what. Maybe we'd feed croissants to the pigeons on our balcony in a French hotel like in a Rod McKuen dream.

We boarded the train and took our seats in the shared cabin. I looked at Summer and she looked back, smiling. I gazed out the window as the train began to move. The rails ran in lines, parallel, heading off to a sunset on the Gulf of Mexico.

*****

The End

Made in the USA
Middletown, DE
27 September 2021